Praise

"Court Stevens deftly weaves together all the strands of this novel into a complex, heart-wrenching whole. This is a writer that understands people down to the bones. Her characters are fallible and hopeful, flawed and loving, and so real they have stayed with me. *Tell Me Something Good* wraps wise meditations about love and justice around a propulsive tale of suspense; I can't wait to share this one with my book club."

—Joshilyn Jackson, *New York Times* bestselling author

"*Tell Me Something Good* is better than good. It's fantastic! Court Stevens has crafted a beautifully written tale full of heart and rich characters who live on long after the last page. If you like a just-one-more-page mystery that will keep you up late into the night, this one's for you. I absolutely loved it!"

—Lisa Patton, bestselling author of
Whistlin' Dixie in a Nor'easter and *Rush*

"I sat down to read a few pages and got up hours later having finished the whole thing, feeling like I'd just binged the most thrilling new drama on TV. Wow!"

—Mary Laura Philpott, author of
Bomb Shelter: Love, Time, and Other Explosives

"In her adult debut, *Tell Me Something Good*, Court Stevens delivers an unputdownable tale of murder, lies, and the extraordinary lengths we go to for the people we love. A haunting masterpiece."

—Rea Frey, #1 bestselling author of *Don't Forget Me*

Tell Me Something Good

Tell Me Something Good

COURT STEVENS

HARPER **MUSE**

Tell Me Something Good

Published by Harper Muse, an imprint of HarperCollins Focus LLC.

This book is a work of fiction. The characters, incidents, and dialogue are drawn from the author's imagination and are not to be construed as real. Any resemblance to actual events or persons, living or dead, is entirely coincidental.

Any internet addresses (websites, blogs, etc.) in this book are offered as a resource. They are not intended in any way to be or imply an endorsement by HarperCollins Focus LLC, nor does HarperCollins Focus LLC vouch for the content of these sites for the life of this book.

Library of Congress Cataloging-in-Publication Data

Names: Stevens, Court, author.
Title: Tell me something good / Court Stevens.
Description: Nashville: Harper Muse, 2025. | Summary: "The heart, hope, and pacing of Fredrik Backman's Beartown meets the Southern atmospheric storytelling of Flannery O'Connor in Court Stevens's adult debut novel centered around a decades-old murder that turns a small Southern town upside down"—Provided by publisher.
Identifiers: LCCN 2024048205 (print) | LCCN 2024048206 (ebook) | ISBN 9780840707413 (paperback) | ISBN 9780840707550 (epub) | ISBN 9780840707697
Subjects: LCGFT: Thrillers (Fiction) | Novels.
Classification: LCC PS3619.T4789 T45 2025 (print) | LCC PS3619.T4789 (ebook) | DDC 813/.6—dc23/eng/20241223
LC record available at https://lccn.loc.gov/2024048205
LC ebook record available at https://lccn.loc.gov/2024048206

Printed in the United States of America

25 26 27 28 29 LBC 5 4 3 2 1

A Note from the Author

I WAS A FRESHMAN IN college when a shooting at Heath High School forever changed the way I thought about gun violence in public spaces. *Tell Me Something Good* is not an active shooter narrative but it does begin with a threat of public violence. The story camera stays on the character attempting to stop a weapons auction that would arm the potential shooter. Public violence of any type should be sensitive and heartbreaking to all, but for those of you for whom this hits too close to home, please protect your mental health.

Prologue

HERE IS A NAME FROM a potential future: Corey William Turrent.

In one arrangement of time, Corey will take an assault rifle from his father's gun case. He will hide the weapon under his jacket. He will walk the three sweltering blocks from his home in Buckman, New Jersey, to Roseville Elementary. Once he's through the lobby doors, he will open fire.

If this future comes to fruition, Corey William Turrent will kill seventeen students and four teachers.

The thing that hangs between this atrocity and a safe and lovely day for Roseville Elementary is what occurs at the Lodges Royale in Bent Tree, Kentucky, many years before.

Here is also where I introduce you to Anna Ryder, and we find out which future is ours.

CHAPTER 1

ANNA RYDER'S NEED FOR A new job starts in a doctor's office.

Cancer sucks. Everyone knows that. And because the body tells on itself, Anna and her mother, Starr, feel the diagnosis coming before it stampedes into her colon. In the week before the appointment, they downplay the threat. They won't borrow trouble until the doctor uses the C word. The weight loss might be something simple: a vitamin deficiency, a thyroid problem. Whatever it is, it's fixable.

That is the lie you tell yourself when you love someone.

When they are alone, their fears run them into the ground. Each imagines what will happen if the worst comes for Starr. Neither of them can breathe. The mother because the cancer is metastasizing in her lungs. The daughter because there is no one she loves more.

✳   ✳   ✳

The women know they will continue to laugh, no matter the diagnosis, because Starr's doctor looks like he walked off a Hallmark movie set. Pretty instead of handsome. Fit. Salt-and-pepper hair. Five o'clock shadow.

No wedding ring. That's the first problem.

The second is his metaphors. When he delivers the diagnosis, he makes the mistake of describing cancer as a boxing opponent. His pep talk ends with, "Together with the treatments, we'll give cancer the old one-two. Right, Starr?"

Starr lowers the register of her voice and answers, "Right, Coach." Then she slips off the exam table, punches the air, and dances around chanting popular lines from *Rocky*.

Anna has never seen more than a meme of *Rocky*, but she knows every word to "Eye of the Tiger," which she begins to sing. Off-key. The women crescendo on the chorus. And despite their poking fun, the doctor leans against the exam room door, clutches his iPad to his chest, and laughs right along with them.

"What do you think, Doc?" Anna asks, gesturing to her still-dancing, still-gorgeous mother.

His answer: "Keep that sense of humor. It'll carry you through this thing."

Starr wheels toward him, winks, and says, "If laughter doesn't, flirting will."

"*Hallmark,*" Anna mouths as the doctor returns the wink.

Starr raises her eyebrows, pleased with his response. "If that's your bedside manner, break a HIPAA rule and call me later." She makes a phone with her thumb and pinky finger and wags it beside her ear.

Anna groans on cue, accepting her part in the shtick. At least this guy is a doctor. No belt buckle the size of his face. No mullet. And presumably, he doesn't owe a man named the Copter forty thousand dollars. That puts him several important steps above Starr's last romantic hoorah.

"You two ladies are a hoot," he says before he leaves.

He will go home that evening and ask his girlfriend to marry him. Something about Starr reminds him of what's important. She has that effect on people.

The minute the door closes, Starr collapses against the exam table, out of breath, out of energy . . . out of everything. Anna drops a kiss on her mother's head and helps her onto the table. "That was kind of you."

"Well," Starr says, her breath still airy from exertion. "Imagine handing out death sentences"—the cough starts deep in her throat—"every day. Sounds worse than cancer, dontcha think?" She is bent double by the end of the sentence.

Anna strokes her mother's back until her body quiets and then unties the gown. Redressing exhausts Starr, even with Anna's help. Anna is careful around the bruises, always gentle, and when she finishes, her mother's sweatshirt looks like it's still on a hanger. The treatment will take more of her. There isn't much left.

The nurse returns and explains Starr's treatment options. At the end of the speech, she tacks on, "Hopefully the procedures and meds will be offset by your insurance. Nearly free, if you ask me." She pats Starr's shoulder like it's all a done deal.

Starr and Anna paste kindness across their faces rather than burst this nurse's bubble. After all, she's doing her job, and "offset by your insurance" and "nearly free" is likely the whole kit and caboodle for most people.

People who aren't from Luxor.

Anna and Starr have the misfortune of being from a town so poor that even the mayor doesn't flush his toilet after every use. There isn't just a different set of rules for people who grew up in Luxor, Illinois; there are different games.

Years later, when that same nurse falls in love with a man from Luxor, she'll remember Starr and Anna and how helpless they seemed. She'll regret her choice of words. Her obliviousness. Her privilege. And she'll understand that the *nearly free* she offered Starr was similar to "free" circus tickets for those who visit traveling big tops. The ones that take over mall parking lots. Nearly free is actually very expensive.

So, as the nurse rattles off upcoming appointment dates and treatment schedules, Anna maths Starr's survival.

126 miles round trip
divided by an old, unreliable truck
times $4 a gallon
times a minimum of 25 appointments
plus "nearly free" co-payments that start after a $10,000 deductible
plus vitamins not covered by insurance
equals
bad news

CHAPTER 2

IN THE TRUCK, MOTHER AND daughter tap the radio volume at the same time and grin happily at their usual kismet. They do not discuss the diagnosis or the expenses ahead. They stare out the windshield as they pass the last of the city buildings. The music thrums and eggs them on. Their route home is a two-lane state highway with steep shoulders. You have to drive it like you mean it.

Starr reminds Anna exactly where the police cruisers often lie in wait, as she always does. And Anna says, "Yes, Mother, I've driven before," which pulls a huff from Starr. They agree on many things. Anna's style behind the wheel isn't among them. Anna needs the power of controlling the vehicle. Difficult emotions are better digested above sixty miles an hour on a curvy country road. Starr needs her darling daughter to slow the eff down so she can die of cancer rather than by putting the truck through a tree.

Fall colors their world orange and yellow and red. The leaves whoosh across the blacktop in tiny whirlwinds. The view offers a distraction from their thoughts. Fields and churches. Ponds added to front yards. Grain bins. A landscape so beautiful and simple it begs you to lower the window and take a huge drink of country air.

Starr says dreamily, "Baby, I can't imagine a world without fall or dogs."

"Why would you even try?"

"You should rescue another dog," Starr says.

"I'll think about it." Anna is actually thinking, *Dog food is expensive.*

Simon and Garfunkel sing them all the way back to Bent Tree and then across the long rainbow-shaped cage bridge to Luxor. They need a good rain. The shore of the Ohio is longer than it should be. From high on the bridge, Anna can't see the fish carcasses on the rocks, but they're there.

Without any hint of a turn signal, Anna whips into the Luxor High School parking lot and drives behind the school to the football field. Starr starts to protest and stops herself. If she had said what was on her heart, it would have been, "Darling, I have to pee." At which point Anna might have turned the truck toward their farmhouse, because holding your bladder is a brutal thing. She stays silent instead. Anna doesn't do anything accidentally. If they're here, Starr understands she has a reason.

At the small, dilapidated stadium, Anna wraps her arm around her mother's waist and leads her along the concrete walkway cracked by time and weeds, past the unmanned ticket booth, and up the bleachers. Neither woman likes football. They attended games when Anna was in high school out of boredom and then out of obligation when Anna went to work for the school system.

Anna is fairly sure her mother has to pee, but her gut says to sit on the bleachers at the football field, and she is a gut-follower. So there they sit, with clasped hands, humming "Scarborough Fair" under their breath, waiting on something unknown to happen.

The sun hovers near the horizon line, in that annoying place that turns your vision into tiny blinking balls of yellow light. The women squint at the practice below, their ears full of whistles, helmet slaps, and crunching collisions. Is there anything as vulgar as freshman boys cussing at each other?

Through all the noise, Anna thinks about her mother. That silly, wonderful *Rocky* dance. How in many ways it is the very essence of Starr.

For Anna, Starr is . . .

Better than a hero in a postapocalyptic movie.

A giantess of love.

A one-stop parenthood shop.

And her very best friend.

(Despite her need to offer driving advice. No one is perfect, after all.)

Meanwhile, Starr thinks first about the way her doctor looked in his khaki pants and questions if she might live long enough to slip them off his hips. Probably not. But she will live plenty long enough to fantasize.

Then they both think about cancer for far too long.

"Mom," Anna says after the boys jog to the locker room.

"When I'm gone, do not sell the farm." Starr's voice is harsh and scared for the first time that day.

Anna squeezes her mother's hand in that slightly annoyed, slightly reassuring way that daughters do when they've been warned many times about something they have zero intention of doing. *Don't drink and drive. Don't get teenage pregnant. Don't marry a Northerner.* The *Do not sell the farm* lecture is old and worn. But for the first time in their relationship, it's a viable option. Anna has been trying to think of a way to bring up the topic. "Mom, we'll do what we have to do—"

"No."

Anna scoffs at the stubbornness. "You're being ridiculous."

"Promise me," Starr says. Anna understands the plea. Starr is an intensely private woman. They aren't one of those "Welcome, y'all" families. The metal gate stretched across the end of their driveway has five Private Property signs.

"I won't," Anna says, but then she does promise, because if she only has eight months left with her mother—and that was what the doctor said, eight months if she forgoes treatments—she isn't going to spend them fighting.

Starr pats her daughter's knee and then squeezes it gently. "After I'm gone, the rule's the same: the house and barns are private."

"You're not going anywhere. Except to treatments," Anna says.

That draws a smile from Starr and a polite change of subject. "Baby girl, why are we here?"

The sun is down by then and twilight grays the field. Anna points to the perimeter fence where hundreds of Styrofoam cups press through the chain link. They spell out the words *RELAY FOR LIFE* in large four-foot letters, although most of one *F* is gone.

"Next year we're going to walk in the Relay for Life. You and me. We're going to do more than give cancer the old one-two. We're going to kick cancer in the balls with a metal-toed boot. You understand?"

Starr lays her head in Anna's lap. The gesture isn't a yes or a no; it's a thank-you for a love that looks into the future and grasps for hope.

The two women stay clutching each other until Starr lifts her face off Anna's tear-soaked thighs and says, "My silly goose, it's time for hot dogs and *NCIS!*"

"Okay, my crazy duck," Anna replies.

At which point they hurry home and Starr finally gets to pee.

Though she doesn't flush. No need to waste water when there is so much money they need to save.

CHAPTER 3

ANNA IS FOREVER THE SILLY goose and her mother the crazy duck.

She loves other people, but no one the way she loves Starr. Especially after she ended things with Jack. Jack is the ex-fiancé, ex love of her life, ex non-asshole of assholes, which is quite a complicated thing to be. How can a man be the best and the worst at the same time? And what does it say about her that she never let him explain himself?

Thanks to Mr. Heartbreaker, Anna is over thirty and hasn't gone on a date in over three years. And yes, she sleeps in her childhood bedroom; and yes, there have been job offers and partners from other towns, but none have been magnetic enough to pull her heart away from Jack or her life away from Starr.

Now Starr's the one being pulled away.

Without the treatments, there is little to no hope. Selling the farm makes sense. That will be more than enough money to put them in a small Luxor apartment and cover gas and needs. Anna understands the sentiment of loving land like a person, but not the actuality. Their property is breathtaking, but at the end of the day it's merely dirt and seeds.

"Dirt and seeds are hope and love," her mother always says.

But what good are hope and love without her mother?

To be fair, the farm is a Ryder legacy. In 1943, Luxor, Illinois, was a booming river and train town. Starr's grandfather built the family home on fifteen-foot steel risers. Wise man. His home, like the Lodges in Kentucky, avoids all the seasonal flooding that comes with living in a flood zone. The baby-blue clapboard farmhouse rises from the middle of their fifty acres like a squatty watchtower, and the Ohio River runs a quarter mile behind where the land turns to brush. When the wind blows, they are close enough to smell the cigarette smoke of the men working the barges.

In a non-flood year, the fields surrounding the house yield one of the best crops in the county. Starr lives on the crop money, so over time, even their small yard became part of the field. Two ruts lead from the old iron gate to a parking place under the house. They carry on all the way back to the barn, buildings, and creek. Everything else is cornstalks, beans, or wheat.

If you live on a river and farm, you spend more time praying about rain than you do breathing. You need it to come. You need it to stop. The spring before Anna was set to leave for college, Luxor had what the meteorologist called a five-hundred-year flood.

Everything within six miles that wasn't on risers was damaged. Many of the homes. All the crops. Anna and Starr were trapped in their house for four days. By the time the bottom steps of the deck dried and Anna put her foot back on the muddy earth, she knew she wasn't leaving Luxor or Starr. She turned down every scholarship and got one of the only jobs in town.

Her paycheck kept them from losing the farm.

When Starr has a glass or two of wine, she says Anna kept them from losing far more, but she never explains what.

Starr is a woman with secrets.

And while Anna sometimes considers it a betrayal, and sometimes fights about the secrets with Starr (and never wins), and sometimes grows restless with sacrificing so much for a cause she can't name or understand, she does it anyway. And somehow finds a way to do it with love.

※　※　※

Starr has a reason they cannot sell that has nothing to do with "the Ryder legacy" she spouts off about when asked. Many years before, something hideous was hidden in the barn at the end of the ruts. Starr knows she will have to tell Anna about it soon, but she's not ready.

The trouble with the truth is this: we can't always control when it comes.

CHAPTER 4

THE DAY AFTER HER MOTHER'S diagnosis, Anna explains Starr's condition to her boss at the high school. He is the only person she tells. How lonely is that. She wouldn't have told him except she asked for a raise and thought an explanation might help her cause.

He laughs at her request so hard he snorts. Dan isn't an attractive man and he has a rather large nose, so the snort sounds like a goose. "Look around," he honks. "You're smarter than that question."

"I know." And Anna did know. Luxor High had cut programs right and left. They even sold their buses after the school district confirmed it couldn't afford to fuel them for the third year in a row.

Anna sighs deeply at Dan's rebuke and decides she'll ask the school's janitor if she can hide out in the library after hours and pick up some type of online work.

Starr won't allow the internet at the farmhouse, and both women have pay-as-you-go phones. Even during the years they can afford better service, connectivity of any kind makes Starr suspicious. Anna regrets the day she opened Google Earth on a school computer and showed Starr the satellite images of their house and land. "Why in the name of Peter, Paul, and Mary is the government allowed to do that?" Starr had asked. "I might have been making love on the deck and they'd have a picture of my hind end for all the world to see."

Across from Anna, Dan clears his throat of all honking and fiddles nervously with the top button of his dress shirt. "Actually, Anna . . ."

The blood drains from Anna's forehead to her chin. She slouches lower in her chair.

Dan continues, "I realize this is extraordinarily bad timing, but the superintendent called last night and . . . well, they're cutting the in-school suspension program."

"What about the students?" Anna manages to ask when she wants to rage and stomp and scream, "What about my mother's cancer?"

Dan raises his hands, helpless. "What about the ones who need a bus? We don't have two pennies to our name. You know I'm sorry and I need you, but I don't have a choice."

As Anna is the only employee of Luxor High willing to break up a knife fight and the only person on his staff, other than him, who has lasted longer than three years, he is right about needing her.

"When?" Her brain whirls with fear, tears already welling in her bright gray eyes.

"Today," he says uncomfortably. "End of pay period. I'm sorry. I'll write you a great recommendation."

She stands to her full height, which is considerably higher than his, shakes his hand, and forces a nicety he doesn't deserve. "Thanks, Dan."

"Anna."

"Yeah?" she says, hoping he might offer a job suggestion.

"Don't forget to collect your take-out containers from the staff fridge."

Anna marches straight to the kitchen, removes her containers as well as Dan's, and leaves Luxor High without looking back.

She wastes no time. She drives from the high school to the Methodist church. Bless them, they pay for strong Wi-Fi. All the cars in the lot are occupied with people on their devices. She tugs a red knitted hat over her ears, makes a résumé, and eats Dan's cold leftovers.

After four hours of searching, one thing is clear: there are no jobs in Luxor.

Day One

CHAPTER 5

FOUR GUNSHOTS SPLIT THE MORNING air. A man's blood seeps into the backwater marsh. The man, still warm and nearing the veil, is dragged onto a tarp and rolled like a carpet.

Who is he?

A seasonal lodge worker in the wrong place at the wrong time who made the mistake of confronting his boss. The moment he said, "I overheard something about a crate of missiles you plan to sell and I'm not okay with it," his ticket was up.

You don't threaten the livelihood of the Lodges' owners.

The dead man knew nothing of the auction taking place during the upcoming hunting event.

Or the three thousand straw sale assault weapons.

Or which of his bosses runs the illegal operation.

He'd just been a man who needed a job.

CHAPTER 6

IT'S EARLY MORNING, BEFORE THE alarm. Gunshots echo across the Ohio River. Anna doesn't count the rounds. Four? Five maybe? Her bedroom window faces east, and when her curtains are pinned back, she has a perfect view of the Kentucky marshes and the Luxor Bridge without even moving her head.

She questions which hunting season it is and checks the date. Duck or goose.

Those gunshots, usually an annoyance, signal a strange slice of hope. The Lodges hires seasonal workers every fall. Luxor doesn't have jobs, but Bent Tree might.

Oh, Ryder, she thinks, *that is a very bad idea*, and she pulls the covers over her eyes the way she did as a child.

Sometimes a bad idea is the only idea.

When you need a job, you need a job. Even if the employer is tied to your ex-fiancé and your mother's ex-boyfriend and you've been told your entire life, "You can work anywhere you want except the Lodges."

Down the hall, her mother coughs. The rattle of her lungs is louder than all the gunshots in Bent Tree put together.

Anna breaks down and types *The Lodges, Bent Tree, Kentucky* into Google and reads the "We're Hiring" banner.

"Of course," she says to herself, laughing at the horrible irony.

CHAPTER 7

FOSTER PORTAGE HAS SECRETS.

Many are secrets she shares with her husband. Many are not.

That is the way life works. Some words and conversations roll through your mind like they must be composted prior to speaking. Others you spit out of your mouth like a cannon.

Foster can't afford to stay in cannon mode, which was once her natural state of being. Not since she agreed to be Gary Portage's wife and inherited the task of dealing with her mother-in-law, Marth (not Martha, heaven forbid you make that mistake), and Lavinia Collins. Those women are a vibe. Rich. Powerful. Opinionated. They wear high heels in the mudflats and drink champagne for breakfast. Foster pretends she is cut from the same silk.

Gary lied to them about Foster's past, which doesn't bother her in the least. In her husband's narrative, Foster belongs to one mother and father, rather than the forty-three homes she occupied from age three to seventeen in the swamp that was Miami. No one at the Lodges knows she was in the military prior to becoming an influencer, and no one knows about her former ties to Bent Tree.

The money is nice, but the upkeep of being Mrs. Gary Portage has its downside.

Currently she lies in a tiny room receiving a Brazilian wax from a woman named Cindi Leechman. These "services" always make her cry, but she never screams. She closes her eyes while sweet Cindi talks about her obsession with the baby monkey videos on Facebook. She even pauses mid-wax to show one and it takes everything Foster has not to say, "Bitch, get on with it."

Does Foster need to go to this extreme? Unfortunately, yes. Rich women have many means of sussing out frauds. Primarily beauty rituals: saunas, massages, mud baths. Therefore, Foster has been lavished with milk sprays and bee venom and rare scented oils. She is so oily she can get a second job as a bowling alley lane.

Foster knows she will end up naked in the same sauna with her mother-in-law and Lavinia Collins before the Royale ends, and they know luxury better than anyone. If poverty has a smell, wealth has a texture. Foster can't afford to have one hair out of place.

This is Starr Ryder's fault, and at the moment Foster wants to kill her.

CHAPTER 8

THE MORNING OF THE GUNSHOTS,

   . . . the morning Foster is being waxed,

   . . . the morning the murder takes place,

   . . . the morning she finds Starr crying in her closet, where Anna isn't supposed to hear her, Anna accepts her collision course with Jack Higgins.

Jack breeds, trains, and boards hunting dogs for the Lodges. Such a position means he not only works there, he lives on the property year-round. His parents and grandparents go back generations with the Lodges' owners. Anna's level of pain and resentment for this man is best captured by understanding their proximity: the former love of Anna's life lives and works four miles away by road, less than one mile as the crow flies, and she hasn't laid eyes on him in years.

Except online. Once on a dating website, which she checked using her mother's profile. Thereby confirming that he had moved on from their engagement. And also on his Facebook business page, where he sells hunting dogs. Spaniels and retrievers. She was checking on the dogs, she told herself, and then hurriedly x-ed out of the page when her mother caught her spying.

Online, Jack had looked the same, except more chiseled in the face and stockier than the stick he used to be. His kind eyes were still the fixture of his face.

Seeing him gutted her.

Love can make you feel so powerless even if you're the one with the power.

Back then, at the end of them, Jack had begged Anna to listen to reason and she blocked his number. He then attempted to explain his situation and Anna yelled through the gate that she would call the cops if he showed up on their property again. She cut him out of her life with one sharp slice. But you can't cut someone out of your heart so easily.

Who has the power now? she wonders.

Much like the day she canceled all her college scholarships, what has to be done, has to be done, whether she wants it or not. There is a job open at the Lodges and Jack has the clout and connections to get a woman from Luxor a job.

But how to go about asking? Unblock his number and call? Drive over there? Unless he has radically changed since they were together, she knows what makes Jack tick. Connection. Being a hero. Choosing kindness. She will go in person, tell him about Starr, and he will help. Even if he despises her.

Helping is who Jack is.

CHAPTER 9

BENT TREE, KENTUCKY, HOME OF the Lodges, is a drive-through town in a drive-through county in a drive-through state without a single drive-through restaurant. Still, they hold three claims to fame.

First, the convergence of the Ohio and Mississippi Rivers: Luxor, Illinois, on one side; Bent Tree, Kentucky, on the other. A river convergence doesn't sound like a tourist attraction, but Anna once heard of a visiting high school track team that drove an extra hour to pee off the bridge into the exact place the waters mixed. And their coach did the same thing twenty years before.

Then there are the Choir Girls. To date, eleven podcasts have covered the unsolved crime. Gruesome stuff, but honestly, the people of Bent Tree don't think about it much. Maybe that's because not many of them are deep thinkers. Maybe it's because there isn't a dang thing they can change about the crime now. But it's probably because every last one of those murdered girls was from somewhere other than Bent Tree. If those had been *their* girls, they wouldn't have rested until there was revenge. In this case, they've been resting on their "oh wells" for thirty years.

Lastly, hunters know the area like parades know Macy's. The hunting is exquisite. The Lodges has been named a top-five destination by everyone from *Guns and Ammo* to *USA Today*. And every year the Lodges hosts a world-famous hunting experience called the Royale. Despite the jokes and stereotypes, hunters are not poor, snaggletoothed men with *Momma Forever* tattoos who drive rusted-out pickups loaded with Bud Lights. These days, hunters are women and men, Republicans and Democrats, gays and straights, Christians and atheists, and among them are the rich and the superrich. The 1 percenters. The people who buy five-hundred-dollar coolers the size of a Happy Meal.

Also the ones capable of purchasing weapons illegally.

Once a year this armed variety converges on the Lodges like someone rang a bell calling all the camouflaged souls to gather at the river.

The 99 percenters trickle into Bent Tree on everything from four-wheelers to Land Rovers to river barges. They camp. They rent. They motel, as there are no proper or reputable hotel chains in over seventy miles. They partake of the local BeeGee Restaurant's pond-raised catfish. Spend money at Bent Tree's gas pumps and dollar stores. They know they're lucky to have a ticket to the Royale.

By contrast, the 1 percenters land on a private airstrip and Jack Higgins hauls their duffels and hard cases to one of the three hunting clubs on the Lodges' property. Together, the clubs own a hundred thousand acres of the best waterfowl marshland in the world. Each club is filled with various accoutrements for the modern-day hunter and employs a stack of experts: civil engineers, chefs, bourbon distillers, Humvee drivers, and so on.

Jack Higgins is the dog expert, and he's as good as they come.

Except when it comes to Anna Ryder.

Audio File #1

I found out about you today.

I've spent most of my life being wordy. And right now I'm speechless.

This would be easier if I knew your name.

For the sake of this recording, I'm going to name you Beck. *Beck* means "someone who lives by the water." It was my great-grandmother's maiden name, and when I saw it written on the family tree in my mother's Bible, I said to myself, "If I ever have a kid, I'll name them Beck."

So . . . Beck, I'm sorry you don't know me. You've never heard me say I love you or I'm proud of you. And I'm sorry for whatever you've been told about me. It's likely not good. I'm starting this audio journal today hoping that someday we'll meet and I'll be able to show you how much I've always loved you. And God forbid, if something happens to me before we meet, you'll have some sense of me through these recordings.

I'm currently driving through Bent Tree, Kentucky. This is the place you came from. Since I don't know where you are, or what home feels like to you, I can only try to explain what it's like here.

The land almost feels like a person. Like the first friend you ever had. There's loyalty and love in the soil. When I was your age, I ran little plastic cars through the dirt and swam in the creek. I dug holes and planted seeds. I made forts in the woods and ran barefoot through the tall grass. I stepped on bumblebees and caught lightning bugs in jars. I fed the ducks bread and the dogs table scraps. I stepped in cow poop and drank from a water hose. We stare at the sky in the morning because the geese fly this way on their own little highway and at night because the whole universe is up there waving like a firework. I've heard cicadas so loud they sound like a helicopter landing, and I've watched a tornado move across the big field and throw a tree through the air like a pebble.

Oh, and there's so much water here, Beck. Creeks and rivers and ponds. They swell up and shrink down like the rafts we tube on in the summer. One minute all that water is out of control and the next it runs on down to Mississippi and leaves us dry as cracked pottery.

There's a feeling I wish you knew. Tackle box in one hand, fishing rod in the other. A dog loping by your side. You put the worm on the hook and wait for that first fish to nibble. Fireworks go off in your belly as you reel in your catch.

I guess what I'm trying to say is: my home is beautiful.

I hope wherever you are, your home is as beautiful as mine.

I hope wherever you are, you know you are loved, because that's more beautiful than any place can ever be.

CHAPTER 10

ANNA TOASTS THE BREAD HEELS for Starr and leaves them on her mother's bedside table with a cup of water and pain pills. Then she heats half a cup of quick oats and calculates how mad her mother would be if she pawned one of their rifles. The cabinets are empty. She'll hit the church food pantry on the way home, but she doesn't have any solution for gasoline other than selling something.

Unless she calls Waylon.

Starr has another doctor's appointment coming up and Anna's truck is down to three gallons of gas. The vehicle is already dustier than a windowless house in Kansas since she hasn't used the heat or air in a month, hoping that sacrifice might provide a little extra fuel economy. She needs at least twenty dollars to get to the appointment. If she's going to ask Jack for a job, she might as well pile on the fun and ask Waylon for money.

The raw belief among the Ryder women is Waylon Collins can fix most situations if they are willing to ask. Which isn't true, but it feels true, and a felt truth is sometimes more powerful than the real thing. Especially if you are sick or desperate, and Starr and Anna are both.

Starr would never ever ask Waylon. Period. Too much pride. Too much anger. And too much love, Anna thinks.

This isn't the first time the Ryder women are in a bad way financially, but it's the first time Anna is without a job. Anna types Waylon's name into her phone and reads her last message to him from three years ago.

ANNA: Hey, need some gas money. Any chance you can help?

WAYLON: Sure.

That time he met her at the gas mart, filled up the truck, and handed over a red container with five more gallons. "Text me if that's not enough," he said and climbed into his big old Ford and drove away. The time before that, they met at the grocery. Before that, at Luxor High, on a day one of her tennis shoes fell apart and he brought her a new pair.

In Anna's youth, Waylon was always around. He was the first person other than Starr or Anna to have a key to their property's iron gate. He was always helpful, showing up with groceries and a *People* magazine. Starr loved *People* magazine and never bought one. For Anna, Waylon splurged on sparklers and chocolate and Ring Pops. There was even one Christmas Eve, when Anna was small, that Waylon brought over a firepit and a bucket of Kentucky Fried Chicken. "Ho, ho, ho. Winter picnic," he said through the hole in their screen door.

That was such a happy Christmas. The three of them lounged on deck chairs late into the night—Anna curled on Waylon's lap, fire swirling smoke into her dark hair, a light snow falling, while Waylon and her mother sang Hank Williams Sr. songs. When Anna woke in her bed, it was Waylon who had carried her there and Waylon who had left a goldfish bowl on her desk. Her first pet. Winky.

Waylon and Starr would have married if love was the only thing two people needed.

Love can be so big and so very, very small. And sometimes it can be both at the same time. That's how it was for Waylon and Starr. Too big for one, too small for another, and never the same size at the same time.

Waylon is Waylon Collins of Bent Tree. He looks like his name sounds, as though he missed his best chance to be a country music star, big bushy beard and all. Ruddy. Every last bit of him is ruddy. The Collins family owns the smallest hunting club on the Lodges Incorporated property and the largest ego. Little Lodge is the nick-name bestowed to their measly parcel of five thousand acres and their measly three-story state-of-the-art, twenty-five-thousand-square-foot facility. Between the main building and its outbuildings, Little Lodge sleeps one hundred people, not including staff. The property taxes alone are more than the average yearly income of someone from Luxor.

When Waylon professed his desire to marry Starr, his older brother, Topher, lifted his steak knife into the air and twisted it for effect. "You won't be doing that." A significant argument followed. First words, then fists. Neither brother won, and they only stopped the brawl when their mother, Lavinia, fired her pistol into the air and said, "Enough. You." She flicked an index finger at Waylon. "Starr Ryder is off-limits. It's settled." Next she glared at her oldest son. "And, you. Don't act like all this mess didn't start with you. Don't be useless or I'll cut you both off."

Waylon considered disregarding his family's mandate, right up until Topher said, "You know I can tie you to the Mayfield Creek scene, so it sounds like you're one anonymous tip away from a very small cell. So what'll it be, little brother: Starr or freedom?"

Waylon sighed with defeat. They had him over a barrel. He wasn't scared of prison. Still isn't. That he could do. But if he goes away, there is no one to look after Starr and Anna. Even if from afar. So it wasn't a lack of love that tore Waylon and Starr apart; it was a failure of imagination.

Waylon lied to Starr about his predicament. He told her he loved her but had zero intention of marrying her. She and Anna would always be an important obligation and a business partnership, and sure, they had fun when they were "playing house," but he needed to keep friendship at the forefront instead of intimacy.

After which, a previously silent Starr asked to see Waylon's gun.

Waylon removed the pistol from its holster and checked to make sure the safety was on before handing it over to Starr.

"This is safe?" she asked.

"Absolutely," he assured her.

Starr broke his nose with the butt of the pistol. They both heard the cartilage snap. Tears had sprung to Waylon's eyes faster than the blood rolled into his mouth. "What'd you do that for?" he asked, the swelling already slurring the words.

Starr wanted to say something clever, something Waylon would remember when he looked in the mirror and spotted that crooked nose. All she came up with was, "Because you're an asshole," and then she set the gun on the coffee table and went to take a bath.

That night Waylon and his pistol disappeared over the Luxor Bridge.

Back to Bent Tree. To Little Lodge.

Seven miles by road. Seven hundred yards by water.

He could have moved to Tibet and been closer to Starr.

* * *

Starr still misses Waylon. There's no doubt in Anna's mind. Her mother bit her head off when Anna asked if Starr planned to tell Waylon about her diagnosis.

"No," Starr snapped. "And you're not going to either." There was so much passion, right at the surface, that Anna had grinned and Starr had said, "Oh, shut up."

The last time Anna brought up Waylon, she and Starr had been home alone on a Friday night eating knockoff Lucky Charms. Anna made the mistake of saying, "You remember that Christmas Waylon came over with Kentucky Fried Chicken? Whew, I'd love some chicken right now."

What followed was a thirty-minute lecture on why the Ryder women didn't need Bent Tree men. "Stupid Waylon had his chance. Stupid Collins family. Not now. Not ever. Not even for the best chicken in the world." Starr could no more hold back her bitterness than a levee can handle thirty inches of rain in an hour.

But Anna could. To beat cancer, Anna can hold back damn near anything.

Anna types out the text to Waylon.

I need your help.

CHAPTER 11

IT'S EARLY MORNING. FIVE GUNSHOTS sound from somewhere across the field.

Jack Higgins sniffs the air for gunpowder and smells nothing but the death of falling leaves. The Lodges property is massive enough that the shots might be ten miles away. He smiles. Bring on the Royale. Bring on the money. He and the dogs are ready to hunt.

Fear is location-specific. Which is not something people from Bent Tree usually learn because they rarely leave. But if you're not from somewhere rural, gunshots have a different connotation. Any *bang-bang* in the city and your adrenaline spikes. You lock the door. You pray.

At the Lodges, gunshots are like crickets; you don't hear them every day, but nearly. They are the sound of industry, and industry is money, and money makes you smile.

Jack doesn't suspect anything sinister that morning as *bang-bang-bang-bang-bang* ricochets in the air.

He has no idea that less than a mile away from where he stands, a man is questioning the best way to sink the body of a nosy guide in the pond he dredged out the year before.

Jack goes on about his day not knowing his life is about to change.

* * *

It is now late afternoon on the same day. Anna has not found the courage to confront Jack, so he's undisturbed emotionally and has moved through the workday with rote precision. A cool wind shakes and scatters leaves across the Lodges' manicured lawn. The day has been full of errands and sunshine and not nearly enough food. Jack is famished. Maybe after he finishes unloading the deliveries, he'll hit the cafeteria for a pizza.

The packages aren't heavy, merely awkward, but he's stubborn. He deems making three trips from where he parked his truck in the roundabout to the west den of Little Lodge unnecessary. Technically, staff aren't allowed to use the front door, not even this week, but he's delivering for Lavinia Collins.

Still, he wants to be quick. Jack tries the packages in his arms, then on one shoulder, and eventually settles them atop his head. The weight distribution is better. No wonder those women in *National Geographic* carry pots of water like this.

Jack hums with a happiness he hasn't felt recently.

Leader, his favorite dog, is about to have pups. The Royale is this week. And to top it all off, he met a woman online who also trains hunting dogs. She is from Germany and won't tell him her real name yet, but he's oddly hopeful. He imagines her: blonde hair in a high ponytail, freckled nose, copper-colored puppy in her lap. Her checkered flannel shirt gapes as the animal nuzzles into her chest.

Jack is deeply afraid of being alone. But hey, who isn't?

Everyone he knows already has their person, and some of them have already been through one person and started on a second or third. All he's managed is sex, screwups, and four dogs. He wants far more.

Jack isn't particularly mystical or superstitious. Except when he is. Which means he isn't the kind of guy who stops at a palm reader's booth, but he does believe dating is a magical cosmic matching contest. This belief came courtesy of his mother and father, who were married for forty years, as well as both sets of his grandparents, who made it beyond their golden wedding anniversaries.

In the Higgins family, couples are a perfect one-to-one ratio. No divorces. Pure soulmates. And then there's Jack. He met the wrong person first and complicated his life. Then he met his true person and lost her. Even if by some miracle he ever got Anna back, and chose to be completely honest, he'd likely lose her again. Most of him has given up. The rest of him keeps scrolling through dating websites.

Here are the lessons he has learned from online dating.

When a woman says, "I'm not good with love," she means it. You can't love someone enough to make them good at loving you. You end up an untrue version of yourself and they end up humiliating you on social media, and in a small town, *that* ticks off your mother. Image isn't everything, but Facebook is 90 percent of your identity to your neighbors.

Jack is starting to believe he's bad at love because he wants it too much.

This German hunting-dog woman will be different, he tells himself.

This evening he'll send her a few lines of a Pablo Neruda poem or a quote from Saint Augustine and the photo Anna took of him sitting on the dock, shirtless and laughing. His head is kicked back and his smile is genuine. There's a dog on his lap, and it even looks like he has abs. He'll write, *I was thinking of you and this is the smile that matches best.* That photo isn't on his dating profile. He has saved it, like a secret weapon, until there is a solid connection. He isn't particularly vain, but he knows he has stud quality in that one.

❈   ❈   ❈

Jack's favorite week as an employee is the Royale. "The empty week," he and the rest of the staff call it. The only week of the year that the Lodges closes to reservations. Even the owners discourage each other from allowing special guests to arrive early. Preparing for the event is a massive job.

It's his least favorite week as a best friend. Murray, his boss and oldest friend, is a different person when his father is in town. Jack has planned an elaborate set of surprises for Murray that he hopes will lift Murray's spirits and carry him through the Royale. The first is a Halloween costume for Murray's spaniel. Jack plans to swing by Murray's office after he delivers stuff for Lavinia and deck out Pippa as a tarantula.

He chuckles at the idea of Pippa scurrying around with eight legs, swallows a deep breath of fall, and lifts his hands several inches away from the sides of the lowest cardboard box. Lavinia's packages shift slightly and wobble above his head. He re-centers his weight. The boxes settle. He takes another step and then another, and the boxes appear perfectly balanced. Slowly, triumphantly, he lowers his arms to his sides. "Somebody put me on the cover of *National Geographic*," he calls to the wind.

There is a crunch behind him. Footfalls on the concrete. Too heavy for the dogs. He doesn't risk turning and upsetting the packages. He hopes it isn't Lavinia. She always catches him goofing off.

"Jack!" a voice says.

Anna's voice.

The voice that disrupts gravity.

CHAPTER 12

JACK'S BOXES FALL.

The jute binding breaks on impact, and the smallest package tumbles over the other two and smashes into the concrete path. Glass breaks. The tan cardboard darkens to mud brown as whatever liquid inside escapes. Bourbon, most likely.

Jack exhales and the breath erupts like a growl.

During the Royale, Lavinia Collins borrows alcohol from a friend in a local bourbon club. She displays the expensive stuff on her top shelf, and when the Royale ends, Jack discreetly returns the bottles to their owners. No one the wiser. If Jack is right on his bourbon prediction, he has a very, very expensive problem on his hands.

And a more exorbitant expense on his heart.

Anna arrives at his side.

Bending over the leaking box, she examines the tied jute. "This knot wasn't going to hold. Why didn't you make a couple of trips?"

Ignoring her, Jack slips the knife off his belt and cuts through the now-soggy packing tape to read the label on the bourbon. He points at the broken bottle of Pappy and says, "This is your fault, Ryder."

"Seriously?" Anna says and pretends to balance imaginary boxes on her head. She lowers her voice. "Are you sure about that . . . *National Geographic?*" She punctuates *National Geographic* in a bad imitation of his husky voice.

"You're so funny."

She starts the old return, "Funniest person—"

And he finishes, "You know."

The rhythm of a single sentence.

The way they anticipate and respond to each other. Still. After all this time. It's pure magic. For a single instant, Jack forgets his loneliness.

They let themselves look at each other then. A five-second permission slip that is five seconds too long. They intake their changes. Haircuts and weight and age. They have changed as much as they've stayed the same.

Anna speaks first and all of the haughtiness is gone. "I'm sorry I startled you."

Jack says the first thing that comes to mind. "Sorry sounds good on you, Anna Ryder."

Anna shakes her head the way only a woman can.

The judgment stings. Women don't tell you that you are outright stupid; they shake their heads.

Jack picks up the largest pieces of glass from the bottle of Pappy. The remnants are too splintered to superglue. He'll likely steam off the label and slap it on another bottle, probably Weller, since that's the best he can afford, before Lavinia and the bourbon club are the wiser.

Anna rests one of the fallen boxes against her hip. "I shouldn't have been a jerk. That was stupid and unfair."

Because she is more apologetic than he has ever heard her be, he takes a risk with his next words. "Uh . . . not your first go at jerkdom, Ryder, considering that the last time we spoke you threatened to call the police on me for trespassing."

"You knew I wouldn't call," she says, red blooming across her cheeks.

Jack hadn't been sure at all. Annoyance hits him. It pinches his face and his words. "No," he says, "I *knew* you tossed your engagement ring in the lake."

"I stand by that decision."

Then the real question comes. "Anna, why are you here?"

"I need a job, and I'm hoping that you'll—"

He scoffs. "Wow. Just wow."

Anna isn't in Bent Tree to have an adult conversation about what broke them, or to finally hear the truth; she's here because she needs something. A tiny part of him inflates. When a self-sufficient woman lets herself ask for help, it means something. But so do the years and hopes she tossed down the drain when she left.

"Does your mother know you're here?" Jack pictures Starr reaching across the river and throttling Jack and then Anna with her bare hands.

"No. I don't run everything I do past Starr," she says, which is mostly a lie. "Also, back then, that day you came to the house, I wanted you to leave. I couldn't handle seeing you. I . . . But I wouldn't have called the police." She speaks with tenderness. Waits a beat, grins, and adds, "Mom was another story. She wanted your head . . ."

She says this teasingly to make him smile, and it works.

Jack feels no pleasure in what has to be said next. "And now, I need you to leave." He does not mean this. He only says it to see if she'll stay anyway. He's not playing a game so much as performing a test.

She says, "You owe me—"

He cuts her off. "What? A chance to explain?" Jack chucks the largest piece of glass into the field and watches the raw edge scalp a head of corn. "Five years ago that's all I wanted too." He stops and looks at her. She is thin. Too thin. There are dark circles under her eyes. Lightning-shaped streaks of red cut the white around her gray irises. It takes all of his willpower to say, "Please go home. Don't show up during the biggest prep week of the year and screw up my life."

"Me asking for a job is about you? Oh, that's rich. This isn't where I want to be either."

"Don't gaslight me, Anna."

"I taught you that word," she snaps.

"Well, let me present you with a vocabulary trophy for your accomplishments."

"No, thank you. I'll take a job instead."

"Gosh"—he pastes a sardonic grin on his face and does his best to hold it—"the dogs and I don't have any openings. I work here. I'm not in charge. Besides, you have a job."

"You're a legacy around here and Murray listens to you. Plus, I was fired."

He cocks his head to the side, unbelieving. Unless you counted Jack, Anna never failed at anything.

"Financial cutbacks," she says.

Jack flinches and then counters, "You got full rides to fifteen different schools. You're one of the most brilliant and creative people I've ever met. Get out of Luxor. There are jobs everywhere for people like you."

"I can't leave."

"Won't."

Anna folds in half. The length of her. Head against her shins. When she straightens, there are tears on her cheeks. "Listen, I know this is awkward. I left my house at eight thirty this morning and I've been sitting in the truck all day trying to get up the nerve to ask you for help. I'm sweating like a pig, I'm starving, and I'm embarrassed. You're the last person I want to ask, and that should tell you something. Since it obviously doesn't . . . here's the truth: Starr's sick." Her voice catches. "She's dying, Jack. And if I don't find work, I can't even afford the gas to take her to treatments."

There is only one response, and he states it with complete empathy. "Okay, I'll get you a job."

*   *   *

The property is huge. The wealth and scale, utterly embarrassing. And the Royale is busy. He barely sees anyone during the event except paying hunters. As long as Anna's job is away from the kennels, he can avoid her. *Think about the German woman; focus on her.*

Jack need not worry about the German woman, as she is currently on a date with a woman named Valentine. In three months' time, they will marry and prefer adopting dogs over children for the rest of their lives.

He definitely should worry about Anna.

Audio File #345

Beck, I'm having a rough day.

On a rough day, my brain is mean. There's a spin cycle in my temporal lobe that tumbles my mistakes on endless repeat. A county fair is the best way to explain it. Have you ever been to a county fair? I don't know if you're old enough or tall enough yet or even live somewhere near one. But if you are, maybe you've been on a ride called the Centrifuge? It's an enclosed spaceship that spins you into a g-force. You go so fast that your body is sucked against the wall and your skin slides around. My friends used to dare each other to slip out of their fastening and flip upside down.

Honestly, Beck, it's terrible. The entire time you're worried that someone might throw up on you or you might throw up on someone. There is a trick to it, though. If you keep your eyes focused on the center column and don't move your neck, the spinning isn't as bad.

That's my brain. It whirls and whirls. Some days I keep my eyes in the right place, and others ... I end up throwing up.

The thing that spins me the hardest is you.

I can't believe we've never met. I can't believe I'm missing your life. It makes me so sad that sometimes I wish I were dead.

I hope you never ever feel this way, but if you do, please know I love you so so so so so so so much. And no, I'm not always this sappy. Sorry. These aren't supposed to be sad.

CHAPTER 13

THERE IS ONE SURE WAY to land a job at the Lodges.

Murray Orlov. Murray, not his given name, is a five-six, crooked-nosed, flame-haired forty-year-old with abs like a wall and a smile like the devil himself. A man to love. A man to hate. In that order.

He has one great trait: he likes dogs.

He has one terrible vice: he is obsessed with the approval of the people he loves.

He has one huge secret about his father. A secret he has hidden for so long that he can't remember which part is true and which part came from one of his nightmares.

Because of his position and his abs, everyone at the Lodges wants to sleep or drink with Murray. Or at least be invited to do so.

After you drink with Murray several times, he vacuums you toward him by saying, in that way that makes you feel like he has never told anyone before you, "My father hates me."

That single line of vulnerability gains him miles of power and adoration. It is said for that precise purpose. Calculated and brilliant. Another winning strategy Murray uses because he understands that most people don't like winners and they hate a rich winner even more.

Underdogs are loved, so he finds a way to show everyone his losses. Life gave him too much lemonade, so he makes lemons when it suits him.

He'll continue, "I mean, he truly hates me. He dumped me here to get rid of me."

It's like catching fish with a forty-foot net in a thirty-foot pond.

Gleb Orlov didn't hate his son initially; he just doesn't like children, and Murray came into life as a child. Sticky and needy and loud. Gleb likes things tidy and neat. By the time other truths were added, Murray was put on a plane from Florida to Kentucky to live with his cousin Noah and work in the Orlov family's cover business. He was only five at the time of his dismissal.

From the air, Kentucky was rivers and baseball diamonds and swimming pools. Like Florida without an ocean. Minutes before they landed on the private airstrip in Bent Tree, Murray spotted the property snaking along the Ohio that the pilot said was their destination. The scale, even from the air, overwhelmed the child the same way it makes every millionaire who visits rethink their stock portfolios. Nothing prepares anyone for the Lodges.

Noah met him on the airstrip. The man was older than his father by a decade. When he climbed aboard and spoke to the pilot, Murray cowered in his seat. Noah was so big. And he had a ponytail. Murray didn't know any men with ponytails. When Noah turned his big eyes on Murray and said, "Where's your stuff?" Murray almost wet his pants.

"Papa said no stuff."

"No stuff, eh?"

It was like Gleb to send his son with no clothes or instructions about favorite foods or what might send the kid into fits and starts.

Nope, the only thing that arrived was a pilot in a hurry to return to Gleb and one tiny boy wearing a pair of too-tight swim trunks.

The old man and child stepped together into the Kentucky humidity. Steam rose off the blacktop of the runway, the smell of pigs and chicken shit in the air.

Noah said, "Your father is an idiot."

Murray said, "Papa said you'd say that."

"Yeah, well, I've been saying it his whole life 'cause it's true. Now, let's go solve your 'no stuff' problem."

Gleb remained an idiot to Noah.

An idiot the child loved and would do anything for.

* * *

The idiot visited the Lodges once a year.

The Royale.

During that week, Gleb accepted the barnacle that was Murray while he hunted and drank with Noah and got the necessary updates on his hunting club. Murray's childhood wasn't a consideration for Gleb, except that he liked to bring the boy art from around the world. Their reunions began with gifts that no child wanted and ended with Murray begging his papa to take him home, hoping he might finally be what his father wanted. "Maybe next year," Gleb would say as he boarded the jet to leave.

Each year.

And each year Noah stood beside the crying child and told the truth. "You live here. Stop hoping. Hope will break you."

Noah was right. Hope broke Murray Orlov.

If only the beauty industry learned how to bottle parental rejection; it has to be the most effective antiaging agent on the planet.

Murray, now a competent businessman who runs one of the most successful hunting clubs in the world, keeps his five-year-old self perfectly intact for all matters related to Gleb and father figures.

When Murray was a teenager, Noah, who indeed handled *stuff* and many other things, told Murray, "My father was a prick and his father was a prick and then it's prick, prick, prick, skip Jesus, all the way back to Adam. Get that idiot out of your mind and move on. You hear me, kid? Move on. Find a woman. Or get a dog. I don't care which. I do care if I have to keep cleaning up your life because you can't handle your daddy issues."

*　*　*

Murray didn't find a woman for years, but he went looking for a dog.

That's how he met his first friend. A little kid in the Lodges' kennels system named Jack Higgins, who practically worshipped the ground Murray walked on. Jack, at five, was a superb listener for the fourteen-year-old Murray. The strange and unlikely pair became almost inseparable. First, because Jack was a pest who wouldn't leave Murray alone. And then because Murray made a discovery: adoration was a magic substitute for Gleb; and if Murray cultivated his friendship with Jack correctly, it would hide all the ways he was unloved by his father.

Adoration became Murray's lifelong addiction.

CHAPTER 14

MURRAY SITS AT HIS DESK, which is in a large office adjacent to the lower lobby of Orlov Lodge. His to-do list and inbox are only manageable because he's been on the clock since 7:00 a.m. the day before. He doesn't like to work all night and all day, but "them were the breaks" of leadership according to Noah.

Noah should arrive soon. The old dodger outworks Murray most days, but he's finally starting to slow. Even a year ago he wouldn't have taken a day off in the two months leading up to the Royale, much less the two days before it started. Noah told Murray yesterday that he'd see him at four thirty.

Murray had said, "A.m.?"

And Noah had said, "P.m.," and that was that.

It is 5:05 p.m.

Murray is trying not to be a jerk about a seventy-something-year-old man ditching him. Truth be told, he's piling up passive-aggressive phrases and practicing them on his dog, Pippa. "Good thing one of us worked, eh?" And "Should I tell Gleb you're slowing down?" It's actually fine. Murray's all-nighter caught them up.

They do need to go over Noah's list for tomorrow's last-minute tasks. First on the list: freezer duty. Between the chef's orders for the Royale and the space they'll need for meat from the hunts, the freezers have to be spick-and-span. There are fifty-three chests on the property, so that task will take a couple of hours.

Everything needs to be perfect for Gleb.

As such, Murray spent the night and most of today rechecking facilities, shipments, and water tables in the lowlands. He has a slight plumbing issue at Little Lodge that Noah can fix if they're lucky. That is, if Noah's up to the task. He's been on another planet lately. Staring off into space when they are supposed to be chatting. Going home at lunch to nap. Stuff like that. He's worried the old man is sick.

Murray's office phone rings. Probably his latest girlfriend checking on him or Noah saying he's running late. He doesn't pick up because he never picks up, not even for his father. That's how Noah taught him. "Make them leave a message. Messages are proof," his cousin likes to say.

Murray opens the voice mailbox and listens.

"Hello, Mr. Orlov. I'm calling from Mercy Baptist in Paducah. Noah Bright has you listed as a next of kin. Can you return my call as soon as possible?" The nurse reels off a number and extension.

If Noah has gotten himself sick or injured before the Royale, Murray might kill him.

Murray dials the extension and asks for the nurse. "This is Murray Orlov. You rang about Noah Bright."

There is an uncomfortable pause. And then a sweet voice says, "Well, yes. There was a terrible incident with a donkey. I regret to tell you that Mr. Bright suffered extensive injuries and is deceased."

The phone slips from Murray's hand and lands on the desk. He stares at the receiver and listens to the nurse bellow his name through the speaker before he scoops up the phone and says, "What did you say?"

"Mr. Bright is deceased. I'm so sorry. We need someone to release the body to a funeral home of your choice."

Murray, still in shock, repeats the obvious. "Noah's dead." He pictures Noah telling him, "When I die, pitch me a ditch and plant some corn."

On the other end of the line, the nurse responds with trained compassion. "Sir, I'm so very sorry for your loss. I do need to tell you that from what emergency services reported, you might want to check on that donkey before he hurts someone else." Then she explains the next steps and Murray ends the call in a state of panic. After launching an Indonesian statue—a gift from his father—into the office wall, he puts his face in his dog's office pillow and screams.

The start of a headache pinches the skin around Murray's eyes. The tears are there but don't fall. There's no time to grieve. Not now. His mind leapfrogs to the disastrous week ahead. Without Noah, he'll what? Work the Royale by himself? Stand with the hired staff rather than participate in the hunts with his father?

And why? Because the man who raised him to be whip-smart and anticipate everything had a fatal incident . . . with a donkey. A donkey Murray should now check on? How is he supposed to make arrangements for Noah, pull off another perfect Royale, and find a donkey?

Plus, he's now down two employees.

Noah. And a man one of the Collins brothers fired for no-showing. Topher had called a little after 6:00 a.m. and said, "Hire another guide. Preferably one who likes to work."

That guy, Murray doesn't know his name, will be difficult to re-place. Although certainly easier than Noah. The timing is the real doozy. Everyone qualified is already on payroll. Unless Murray can steal someone from another hunting club out of state, he's in trouble.

If Noah were alive, he'd know what to do. Noah had also been relegated to the Lodges by his own father, Murray's great-grandfather, and had a lifetime of connections in the elite hunting business. Strangely enough, what Great-Granddaddy Orlov meant as a punishment became Noah's delight and the family's cash cow. Under Noah's guidance, the Lodges became a five-star establish-ment. He often made them more money legally than the Orlovs made illegally, and that took talent.

It was Noah who convinced Lavinia and Martin Collins and Gary Portage Sr. to incorporate the lodges. "We need to tailor every mo-ment to a hunter's delight. Ensure guests receive the same experience regardless of which lodge they book."

Noah was right.

At Noah's sixty-fifth birthday, Gleb said to Murray, "I've spoken to Noah and the other owners, and we agree that you will take Noah's place. For now."

Murray had squeezed his fists inside the suit coat pockets. "What do you mean, *Noah's place?*" He had hoped Gleb might deed him his portion of the property. Put him properly in charge as an owner. Not as a family figurehead.

"I mean *Noah's place*, Merkoul. If you are perfect, I will be proud. That is the only bar."

Murray stands and catches a glimpse of himself in the mirror. He needs a shower and shave before he drives to the hospital. Maybe he'll text his girlfriend about Noah and see if she'll meet him at the house after he returns from the hospital. First, he wants to find Jack and ask him to take the Ranger over to Noah's and shoot that damn donkey.

A scream interrupts his plan.

* * *

Murray doesn't move. No one should be inside his lodge other than the cleaners. This is the one week of the year they don't rent to anyone so they can perform a full restock and fall clean. The other owners and their guests aren't due to arrive yet.

The scream repeats, and as it does, Murray has a vague memory of Noah saying, "Heads-up. Mrs. Portage Jr. is coming in early to meet with a local chef."

Murray vaults over his desk and takes the hall at a run.

CHAPTER 15

THE NAME—MRS. PORTAGE—BEFITS an elderly lady who is perhaps an elementary school principal or a strict dormitory mother. In reality, Foster Portage is younger than Murray by nearly a decade and gorgeous. And according to Noah, she hates everything. The hunting, the lodging, the choices of alcohol, everything.

When she's on-site, she is the bane of Murray's mental health. Foster is the only guest who has ever complained. "Flaccid bacon," she said on the message that Murray erased from the office phone before anyone was the wiser. "Should I post a review on my podcast or can I expect changes?"

Murray took care of Foster Portage's complaint diplomatically. He ordered a lovely basket of chocolates and apologized on behalf of his master chef for any pork that was less than stellar. Foster's husband, Gary, is the son of one of the owners. Portage Lodge is the second-largest facility, and Gary has been hunting the Royale since he was big enough to hold a rifle. In truth, Murray feels a strike to his pride when he thinks of the Portages because Gleb loves Gary. So much, in fact, he sent Gary and Foster a Land Rover for a wedding gift. The most expensive thing Gleb has given Murray is a nervous breakdown.

When Murray arrives in the lobby, he stops comically short and almost tumbles over one of the overstuffed leather ottomans. The late-afternoon sun filters through the blinds like a dying lightbulb. The only lamps in the room are more metal wildlife decorations than light fixtures, but even with the copious shadows, he sees tiny Mrs. Portage on the shoulders of a tall woman.

They stand with their backs to him in the corner by one of the dozen sleek gun safes. Murray intends to demand an explanation when Mrs. Portage calls instructions to her human ladder. "Closer. Closer. I've almost got him. Up on your tiptoes—I need another inch."

Two glowing eyes catch the light. Murray watches slack-jawed, thinking of insurance claims he doesn't know how to file without Noah, as Mrs. Portage reaches for a baby raccoon perched on top of the metal cabinet.

"I've got you," she tells the creature and squeezes the nape of his neck.

The woman serving as the base of the pyramid cheers. A second later, she squats and Mrs. Portage climbs off her shoulders. Next to each other, they appear to be the same age. Foster wears her in-laws' wealth like skin, right down to her sculpted arms, which are perfectly tanned because Gary likes to play golf at Pebble Beach this time of the year. The taller woman has her eyes hidden behind a fringe of black hair and looks like she bought all her clothes secondhand. Both are easy on the eyes and hard on his supply of valium, given their current proximity to the baby raccoon.

This is such an embarrassment. To have an owner's family member and a wild animal in the lobby is an omen for a very bad week of hospitality. The raccoon fusses and then Mrs. Portage nuzzles its head against her neck. He can't help but think that's the most maternal thing he's ever seen her do. Her sharpness softens the way his own does when he's with Pippa.

Across the room, someone coughs.

Jack Higgins's eye catches Murray's. The look contains something between awe and fear, the same as when Murray had Jack sneak Noah's liquor out to the kennel when they were much younger. Jack moves toward Foster Portage and speaks in a calm, professional voice. "Mrs. Portage, if you'll hand him to me, I'll take the little fellow outside. We apologize this happened and will make every effort to—"

"Absolutely not. I'll need a collar and leash." Foster sniffs the fur of the creature. "And some shampoo. Thank you, Jack," she says, making it clear this is not a suggestion but a demand.

"Uh," Murray says, beginning his objections.

This syllable announces Murray's arrival to the women. Jack raises his eyebrows to Murray and Murray waves his arm at the door and glares as if to say, *What are you waiting for? Get the woman what she wants.* Jack hustles away, still smiling. Murray will send him for the donkey after they've handled the damn raccoon.

The woman he doesn't know stands sideways, tickling the baby animal's cheeks. "What shall we call you, little one?"

Foster says, "Gary."

"Gary it is," she says.

Does she know Mr. Portage's name is also Gary? Murray can't get a good look at her face to know if her laugh is one of irony or ignorance.

Mrs. Portage whips her head toward her companion. "And what shall I call you?"

"Anna."

The women exchange a hearty handshake. As they do, Murray runs through the register of his current staff. He counts two Annas. One in housekeeping, another in accounts payable. He doesn't think either one is as tall or as pretty as this woman, but she looks familiar. Maybe Noah hired her last week for the kitchen and he's seen her serving in the cafeteria. Her eyes are the color of gravel, and while they're laughing now, Murray notes their intensity. If you could bottle a tornado, it wouldn't generate even half the energy contained in her face. He is immediately enthralled.

Mrs. Portage continues her introduction. "Well, I'm Foster," she says to Anna with a wry smile, "and since I've had my crotch wrapped around your neck, and that's likely a marriage commitment in some countries, how about we agree to be friends?"

Anna blushes and looks at her feet. "Well, that's quite an invitation. Let's say I'm in."

Pleased with the response, Foster turns then to Murray, who is frozen behind the leather couch, and says, "Mr. Orlov, we've had our differences, but I must say that you have the best staff in the world."

Anna's cheeks brighten to an even deeper shade of red. Yes, she's certainly familiar. Murray is now positive that she isn't either of the Annas already on his staff or someone he's seen on the property. That means, in his mind, she is available. Perhaps he'll make her available if she isn't.

Murray makes his play. "I'm so glad you agree, Mrs. Portage, as I've hired Anna here to replace Mr. Bright."

CHAPTER 16

FOSTER FEELS HERSELF TUMBLING THROUGH time and into a childhood hole that has taken decades to dig her way out of.

Anna. Can this be her Anna?

She takes a deep breath and tries not to stare. She can't help herself. Maybe.

The hair is much darker. Features sharper than expected. And her height? This woman is what? Five ten or eleven? Imposing and present despite her waiflike form. She has always pictured Anna as someone sprite-sized, like she is. This Anna is no sprite. She's also breathtaking.

If this is Anna, her Anna, Foster isn't sure how to play her next hand.

CHAPTER 17

DECADES BEFORE ANNA AND FOSTER rescue a raccoon, on the very day the Choir Girls die, a man named Winchester James wakes at 3:03 a.m. The world is dark and lovely. He has his mind on Canada geese, not murder. Birds. Birds. Birds. They are nearly the only thing he thinks about, which says more about his love life than he cares to admit. Pathetic or not, the waterfowl business is his greatest obsession. The first time his grandfather touched the butt of a rifle against his shoulder, Chester connected with the most successful part of himself. How lucky is that? Now he is twenty-five and employed by one of the best hunting destinations in the world. He's living his best life. Or the best life he can dream of knowing what he knows.

Chester yawns. His long arms stretch high above his head, the song from his dreams still playing in his mind. Other than hunters, who else is awake? Doughnut makers? Trash collectors? His mother, for sure, unless she took an Ambien. She told him she'd get up and pray he did well in the competition.

Chester hates getting up early. Once he's up, he's happy. But those few minutes between the alarm sounding and tossing back the covers require a battle of wills. At least he has learned to sleep in his gear to save time. That means he's clad in camouflage and has his grandfather's antique goose call in his pocket.

Until the day Chester's grandmother died, she swore to anyone in hearing distance, "God intended for my husband to be a twin, but he musta got distracted by Vietnam. It took two generations but he finally slapped some saints on the back and said, 'Better late than never'—hee-hee—"and that's how my sweet Chester came into the world. Spittin' image. Spittin' spirit too."

She had cackled her way through this story so frequently and with such convincing joy that Chester could match her exact pitch. He sometimes finds himself wondering if Meme Carmichael was right.

Though he's never said that aloud.

He hardly says anything aloud. His hunting and fishing do most of his talking. Chester is one of the best guides, if not *the* best guide, in the South. Just like his grandfather before him. Both are known for an eagle eye, a steady hand, and an uncanny penchant for predicting the exact migration of waterfowl. He has a skill you can't learn, and the millionaires who stay at the Lodges pay him to use it.

In fact, it was one of them who sponsored him for the day's hunt. They'd been in the blind last year and Chester had been perfect in his role and the man said, "You should compete instead of me. I've never seen anyone as talented as you." Chester had shrugged, too proud to say anything. The man had been around enough poor men that he understood why Chester was staring at the marsh instead of meeting his eyes. He said, "Name your favorite competition, son, right now, or I'll never hire you again."

Boxed in, Chester said, "Stuff That Bird."

"Ah, the Lottenmeir and Little Lodge event?" There was a hint of judgment from the hunter, but it went no further. "Consider your entry fee paid," he told his young guide.

Chester had called his mother after the hunt and shared the good news. "You write that man a proper thank-you note, Winchester."

"Yes, ma'am."

"And don't you go hobnobbing at that silly Royale party. You're from Bent Tree and don't you forget it."

She had good reason to warn him. The Lodges' guests left an impression on the people of Bent Tree. One week fueled the gossip mill year-round. He once heard his mother describe the Royale to one of her out-of-state girlfriends. "Louise, imagine if hunters were in charge of their own Mardi Gras. Lots of sin and debauchery."

It is a fairly good comparison.

Chester works the Royale and the other hunts, but he loves Stuff That Bird. Participating in that competition means you aren't wealthy enough to purchase a ticket to the Royale, but you are talented enough to split the shaft of a feather at two hundred yards. Thousands of "poor" hunters pay the ten-thousand-dollar fee to enter the Stuff That Bird lottery. Only one hundred are chosen for the private hunt.

Ten thousand dollars and the luck of the draw buy you the opportunity to compete for seven days of exclusive hunting at Marsh Lake, a grand jewel of a property near Bent Tree. It's private land so the only way you can hunt it is to win Stuff That Bird. The Royale winner only gets twenty-five thousand dollars. Not a soul who wins the twenty-five from the Royale keeps it; why would they? That amount wouldn't buy a car they'd let carry them between dinner and dessert. But the winners of Stuff That Bird always show up to hunt Marsh Lake.

Always.

Chester knows because he is their guide.

When he finds out he is one of the lucky lottery winners for Stuff That Bird, he visits the cemetery to share the news with his grandfather. He can almost hear the slosh of his grandfather's tobacco before he spits and says, "Chester, your gut will tell you where to go. Trust your gut."

Chester's gut spoke clearly that morning. *Put your boat in over by the owl tree off Mayfield Creek.*

He wouldn't have access to a blind, but there is a nice beach and then marshland a hundred feet off the creek. He plans to start there and work his way west to the Ohio riverfront.

Chester shivers as he checks his trailer connection. When he's sure he has his boat secured, he cranks the heat in the Jeep and enjoys the ride to the put-in near Mayfield Creek. Maybe a hundred yards after he launches, an irregularity on the beach draws his attention. He squints. Unable to identify what he's seeing, he trolls closer.

His jaw falls and tears well instantly at the horrific scene.

The nine women on the rocky beach wear only bedsheets. A single word, written in blood, stains the otherwise pristine fabric. *Sing.* Their bodies are bound to driftwood posts with decking rope and are arranged in a pyramid formation to resemble a choir. Their painted lips pout at the narrow stream of water.

Chester beaches the boat and runs in their direction, screaming for someone to help.

They've been dead for hours by the time Chester reaches them.

They are so cold.

✳   ✳   ✳

That isn't all the details. There's the ungodly smell, for instance. But that's enough of the wretched picture to understand the audacity of this particular evil. I'll spare you what the killer did not spare Chester James.

Before you give up on Chester, he's got five words in this story that'll make you smile in your deepest heart. Even when there is a great deal of death, life always outnumbers its counterpart. Because life is little things and death is a singular event.

CHAPTER 18

GARY THE RACCOON HAS NO idea what he's gotten himself into.

He squirms and fidgets, but the woman's arms are an iron cage. Foster uses her thigh-length Fair Isle cardigan like a blanket, tucking the scared animal to her chest. His heartbeat slows as he adapts to the idea that she doesn't plan to hurt him.

Across the room, Murray Orlov flexes and relaxes the muscles in his arms. A nervous tic. Foster relishes her power and then intentionally lights into him. "Why in the world would you replace Mr. Bright?"

Murray stands stock-still, eyes as wide as those of the animals mounted on the wall.

If Foster's life coach were here, she would offer commentary on the tone Foster takes with Murray. *"Foster, would you answer yourself if you asked like that? Imagine what would happen if you didn't snap off everyone's head."*

Foster doesn't snap off everyone's head. It's mostly men. And not even all men. Just men who wear shorts year-round. Men who pout their lips and kiss the air twice. Men who humble-brag about bank accounts or lifting free weights. Men who can't sit on a plane with their knees less than two feet apart. Men who cheat on their wives. Men who love big guns they can't shoot.

So maybe it is all men.

And maybe she hasn't invented this brash tongue as much as she likes to think. Maybe she can't help herself. Honey might draw more flies, but until honey starts breaking glass ceilings, Foster keeps her inner alligator ready to snap off a head or two.

A trait that serves her podcast well. She gets more information out of an interviewee than Barbara Walters.

"Murray," Foster says, breaking with the usual formality she maintains for the Royale. "What's wrong with Noah?" She hopes this might disarm him. It doesn't.

She snaps her fingers directly in front of Murray's crooked nose, trying to bring his eyes back from the middle distance. "Yoo-hoo. What did you say about Noah being replaced?" She turns apologetically and says, "No offense, Anna."

Anna dismisses this with a wave and sinks into the leather couch corner. One boot falls over her knee and begins to bounce like she is equally curious. Later, Foster will register Anna's response to this whole encounter differently, but for the moment, she stays laser-focused on the facts.

"Noah Bright is dead," Murray says.

"Dead. How dead?" Foster asks.

Murray raises one eyebrow and offers a literal answer. "Completely."

Foster's shoulders fall and she rolls her eyes. Why are men so stupid? Which is of course the exact mirror of what Murray is likely thinking about her. She clarifies. "When? *When* did Noah die?"

"Yesterday? Maybe this morning? I'm not sure."

"How?" she asks him, which is one question too many.

"None of your business," Murray says, sweat beading on his brow. His khaki shorts hang almost to his knees, and when he puts his hands in his pockets, they slip lower on his hips. He looks years younger when he's vulnerable. From what Gary said, Noah is one of the men who raised Murray.

"Whoa," Foster says, to remind Murray he's speaking to Gary Portage's wife. She almost adds, *Can I quote you for the podcast?* because it is such fun to trot out that threat, but the *whoa* does the trick.

Murray straightens, hitches up his shorts, and wipes the skin around his mouth. He returns to his professional self. "I apologize, Mrs. Portage. I found out about Noah minutes ago and . . . well, it's hard news. I hope you'll not let this get in the way of another wonderful visit with your in-laws." He sounds like a greeting card.

Foster wants more information, but she makes amends instead. "You're fine, Mr. Orlov. All's well. And I only meant, how did you come to hire Anna? Not how did Noah die. My in-laws will ask about a change of this nature so close to the Royale." After a breath, she adds, "Gary said you loved Noah. I am sorry for your loss."

To everyone's surprise, even his own, Murray Orlov replies, "I did. I really did." Then he speaks to Anna. "I believe you and I need to have a conversation. If you'll come with me to the office, we'll square things away."

Anna stands as though in a daze. "I'll come right back?" she asks Foster instead of Murray.

Foster nods and pets the raccoon, who now has his eyes closed.

Murray addresses Foster. "Moving forward, if Anna or I can do anything to make the Royale memorable for you this year, please let us know."

Foster lifts the limp raccoon off her lap. "Oh, we're off to a very memorable start."

CHAPTER 19

WHEN THE LOBBY EMPTIES, FOSTER mutters every four-letter word available, and when she leaves, she makes up more.

She is certain this is her Anna.

That's problem number one.

Problem number two is Noah's death. Given the timing and proximity to the Royale, to the auction, his death is suspicious. An accident? Old age? Murder? People close to the Orlov family usually die for a reason.

Foster pictures Murray's bewildered expression, searching for any sign of emotional manipulation as he announced Noah's death. There was none.

The auction is two days away and the Royale guests will begin arriving in the next day. Gleb Orlov is already en route to Bent Tree. That doesn't leave Foster much time to figure out if Noah Bright was killed for what he was about to do or if someone knew about the two of them.

And it certainly doesn't give her much time to handle Anna Ryder.

CHAPTER 20

ANNA WALKS THE LONG, DARK hallway with Murray in the lead.

Back when they were dating, if Jack wasn't with Anna, he was with Murray and the guys.

Still, she knows very little about Murray.

Jack kept her separate from his best friend whenever he could. When Anna used to press Jack on the topic—typically when she was on her period and feeling all her emotional nerve endings—he claimed his boss and coworkers had Bent Tree ideas about Luxor women and Jack didn't trust them to be civil. Jonesy, one of the guides, dated a woman from Luxor and someone keyed "Lux-whore" into the hood of her car.

Her nerves flip-flop as they approach his office. If Jack and Murray are still best friends, this man is predisposed to hate her when he figures out who she is. But he could already know. Maybe he overheard Jack and her fighting through his window and put two and two together. This is starting to feel less like a job opportunity and more like a trap.

Anna's first look at Murray's office tells her a great deal.

First, the space runs in direct opposition to the ambience and aesthetic of the Lodges. The property brims with statements of wealth. In the landscaping, the stonework, the sheer number of buildings. Busy is the kindest statement Murray's office makes. Files, dog hair, and accumulated junk. Hunting magazines, international-looking trinkets, guns, pens, stray bullets, a computer, an iPad, a new bag of dog bones. All on the desk.

The floors are dirtier. The carpet dingier. The walls busier still. Every square inch is consumed by a mounted dead animal, and they all appear to be very pissed about their fixed place in the afterworld. None of the display plaques have Murray's name as the hunter of record. The name *Gleb Orlov* has been laser cut into every last one.

A small brown dog dozes on a tiny leather bed under the window. Or at least Anna hopes the dog is sleeping. It might be stuffed as well.

She uses Murray's silence to collect her thoughts and focus her energy toward the task at hand: proving to Murray she can handle whatever he asks, regardless of her prior relationship to Jack.

"I'm sorry about Noah," she says, hoping an expression of sympathy keeps them on the right path.

It appears to have the opposite effect. Murray walks to the other side of his desk and rakes half of his stuff off the edge of the mahogany surface. Items clatter to the floor and land on open Styrofoam food containers.

The dog barks at the commotion.

She's alive. And a beauty. The spaniel has a gorgeous brown coat with floppy long-haired ears and sweet, sad eyes. Jack raises Boykin spaniels, and from the looks of this one, she could be one of Leader's pups.

Murray gently snaps his fingers. "Sleep, Pippa, I'm fine." The dog lowers her chin.

Murray rests his fists on the desk, leans toward Anna, and smiles warmly. Too warmly, if Anna's being honest. "I'm having a very bad day," he admits. "But if you can handle me in this state, plus a loose raccoon and Mrs. Portage, I'm trusting my instincts. You're my new Noah. Wherever you currently work, call them and quit. I'll make it worth your while."

So he most likely doesn't know who she is.

"I'm the new Noah," Anna repeats.

Anna is familiar with Noah from Jack. She recalls a stoutly built older man with cowboy boots and a long white ponytail. The type of man who passes as fifty for forty straight years because he drank enough to look old when he was young and worked hard enough to look young when he was old. Capable. That's her memory of Noah.

Anna is also capable.

She feels fluttery and hopeful. The best she's felt in days.

She takes a calculated risk and maintains eye contact with Murray. Men often misinterpret her intensity as flirting, but since Anna doesn't have much time on her employment decision, she needs to read Murray quickly.

On the surface, his eyes are bright green and alert. They glow under the redness of his hair but are dim in comparison to his smile. Murray has a smile large enough for more than one planet. How many people have slept with him for that smile? She doubts she can count them on her hands and toes.

Evaluations pass both ways.

In seconds, the employer and his new employee accrue facts and assumptions.

Such as they are likely within ten years of each other's ages. Neither wears a wedding ring. Both are in clothes that don't quite fit. Murray's too tight, the way he likes them. Anna's too loose. She hasn't been eating much, and what she has managed, she has shed from walking. Anna's at least three inches taller than Murray, which means the first thing he asks her to do is take a seat.

The leather chair—everything is leather—is smooth as silk. Its cushion is deep and forces Anna to slouch. That's likely by design. Short men use all sorts of tricks.

Starr's voice echoes in her head. "Honey, if you want a job or a husband, teach yourself to slouch. Men are scared of tall women. Idiots." She'd responded to her mother's life lesson the way many, many daughters have: "If men are idiots, why do we want them?" And Starr had answered, "Because, unfortunately, we're idiots too. The only smart people in this world are the lesbians."

Since Starr was never in need of a man, Anna considered the advice to be gospel. Therefore, she had slouched in her job interview at the high school and slouched when they came to evaluate her classroom and slouched when she went to a bar for drinks with a man.

But the Lodges wasn't Luxor High, and Anna calls on a different version of herself to sell her capabilities. Sitting ramrod straight, she towers over the desk with authority. Murray's eyes move up to hers and he says, "Where do you work now, Anna?"

She lies. "From home. I'm in sales."

"Even better. You're your own boss. I don't feel as bad about stealing you." Murray opens a filing cabinet and removes a set of paperwork, which he places in front of Anna. "A nondisclosure," he says and indicates for her to pick a pen. "Everything we do on property is private. You talk about this operation, any part of it, to anyone and you're fired."

"Complete privacy. Got it. What else?"

"Oh, it's fairly simple. I need you to be perfect for the next week," Murray says.

"Perfect at what?"

"At whatever I ask you to be."

He said *be*. Not do. Perfect at whatever I ask you to *be*.

"Is that what Noah was?"

Murray runs his hand through his hair and the part falls in an un-flattering direction. "No, but Noah practically invented the Royale. You don't have time for training so you will act like you've been here for years and our guests will believe you have been."

"And what compensation should I expect for my *perfection?*" she asks, trying to sound like she is teasing.

Murray's smile borders on flirtatious. "You make it through the Royale and I'll cut you a check for twenty thousand dollars. You make it through the Royale *and I still love you*, there will be more where that came from."

Anna's insides leap with hope. Twenty thousand dollars. That's more than her annual salary at the high school. She searches for the catch.

Jack's stories about Murray were often framed by his childhood ideation, which amounted to a deep and abiding brotherhood. But there was regret too. Like Murray wasn't the person who brought out Jack's best. Jack often preemptively apologized before they went to an event Murray might attend. "Remember," he'd say, "Murray and I grew up together. He knows all my ghosts. So if he says something crazy, ignore it. We all grow up."

A raucous childhood didn't mean Murray was a bad employer. *And even if it does*, she thinks, *how bad can he be?*

Only bad enough to change her life.

Big decisions are often small decisions at first. They are like children, growing when our backs are turned.

*   *   *

Anna makes up her mind. Whatever ghosts might pop up, she doesn't care. She'll let Murray pay her twenty thousand dollars for a week of privacy and perfection. Gas for the truck, food for the kitchen, electricity for the house, and her mother's health. Simply put: everything she needs and came here for.

"That work for you?"

"I guarantee you'll love me," she says.

Murray gives her a pleased nod. "All right then. Your job is hospitality at the highest level. Noah handles . . . handled," he corrects with a dismayed huff, "everything from staff to facilities to guests. Whatever I needed from him. He was my solution finder. My guy. He trained me. Made me. Empowered me. Over the next week you will empty garbage and drink champagne and you will smile like this is the best job that has ever existed. I'll sync Noah's to-do list to your phone as soon as you tell me your number. Got it?"

Anna gives him her number and signs the contract.

As she dates the document, she remembers something her mother taught her: devils don't always have pointy tails and they often have offers that make hell sound like Disney World.

"Okay, so what do you need first?" She hopes she sounds more confident than she feels.

"How are you with donkeys?" Murray asks at the same moment Jack walks through the office door and says, "I got Mrs. Portage and the raccoon settled."

Anna laughs, her eyes on Jack, and answers, "Oh, donkeys are my specialty."

CHAPTER 21

NEWS OF NOAH'S DEATH TRAVELS quickly.

The Lodges' unofficial text thread pings and pings as staffers send crying-face emojis to each other when a worker admits she found their boss's body at his cabin. Some of the staffers care about Noah; others use the opportunity to prod the young housekeeper to say something about her relationship with Murray Orlov. "How is Murray doing?" they ask. The woman doesn't answer. She knows better.

She has been texting Murray since the moment she discovered the body. He hasn't answered. And it's pissing her off. She is excellent at many things. An observation many have made about her over the years. She's as capable as Noah Bright ever was. But not quite as patient.

When Murray doesn't answer the sixteenth consecutive text, she texts his father, her true boss, the news. Thirty minutes after she texts Gleb Orlov, Murray texts back.

My phone was on silent. Are you okay? What do you need?
I'm losing my mind about Noah.

The housekeeper types out a confessionary text. Something like . . . I got frustrated when you didn't answer and texted your dad. But she erases it. Later she'll tell Murray her phone was on silent.

✳   ✳   ✳

Topher Collins overhears two of the kitchen ladies talking about a donkey and an ambulance. He's freshly showered and there's no evidence of blood except a single drop on the aglet of his shoelaces. The gun he used to shoot the nosy guide has a new, full cartridge and is on his hip.

"I'm sorry, what did you say about someone being dead?" he asks.

The women show him the texts. Topher doesn't call his mother with the news. He wants every second available to gain control and prove Lavinia is right to hand the auction and the Lodges' management over to him alone. To do so means he needs to locate Gleb's crates. The missiles.

Noah has been secretive around this year's auction details. Almost suspicious. Even regarding Lavinia's usual purchases. Although those are stashed in the designated storage buildings they agreed to in their last meeting. Topher laid eyes on them this morning after he dropped the guide in the lake.

The missiles are a different story. They arrived on a different barge, supposedly a secret delivery. But no one docks at Warrior Landing without Topher's knowledge. So he's aware of the crates and the inventory—that Gleb has a side hustle with higher stakes—but Topher has no idea where Noah stored them after they arrived.

Noah's office is next to Murray's, so Topher waits until Murray exits the rear parking lot and then he lets himself in through the back door and swipes his key card at Noah's door. Topher doesn't trust Murray Orlov to clean his boots, much less to handle a weapons auction, and he fears that Gleb will have no choice but to invite his son into the operation now. After all, who will broker his secret deals on the property? Not Gleb. He doesn't dirty his hands at this level.

As soon as Topher locates the missiles, he'll call his mother and then the two of them will reach out to Gleb and lobby against Murray being added to the auction staff. Murray is the heir apparent, and yet because of his propensity to come unglued, he's always been left out. With Noah dead, Topher might be able to gain control of both sides of the operation. But he'll need to pull off this Royale and auction without a single hitch.

He starts his search for the missiles in Noah's office. The furniture has layers of dust and the papers on the walls and desk curl from the moisture. The only thing purchased this century is the desktop computer and the wall-to-wall photos of dogs. Ironically, the hunter is an animal lover. And a vegetarian. He claims he has a food allergy, but Topher doesn't believe in those. Doesn't believe in men who don't eat meat.

Topher wedges his bulky body into Noah's wheeled chair. In another life, this Collins brother would have been a great pro wrestler. Topher even keeps the same mullet as his childhood hero, Hulk Hogan.

Clues and pieces about the missiles come together from the plethora of Post-it Notes and scribbles on the flat desk calendar.

Noah blocked out two hours to move Gleb's crates late last week and he had no one scheduled to help him. That means they were small enough for Noah to move on his own. So the inventory likely fits on a dolly. Topher then watches the security footage around the delivery window and concludes Noah never leaves the property.

That's good. They're here.

The only other thing he finds that might be something is a pale pink note attached to the underside of the desk calendar that reads:

M crates?
Lodges or Luxor?
Waylon's ex?

Topher flicks the corner of the Post-it with nervous energy. Is that M for missile? The note could have been there for years, he realizes. Either way, seeing his brother's name is jarring. Lavinia intentionally leaves Waylon out of all things related to the auction. Waylon isn't straight as an arrow, but he's a lot straighter than Topher. He has always been friendly with Noah, though.

Topher lets his brain dance around a new idea. Is there a chance Gleb and Noah cut Waylon in after Topher and Lavinia cut him out? Gleb is the one person who has the power to remove the threats that hold Waylon in his place.

Topher needs to have a chat with Waylon. See if he can suss out whether his brother is working with Gleb. Above all, he needs to locate the missiles.

* * *

Waylon is boating their mother, Lavinia, to a leisurely brunch in Paducah. They cruise the Ohio and chat about the coming hunts. A time-honored ritual. At the Gold Rush Cafe, his mother orders her usual chicken and waffles and says, "I'm planning for my retirement."

Then, when he shifts uncomfortably in his seat, she asks, "What? Did you think I planned to do this forever?"

Waylon sips his coffee, keeps his face fixed. Yes, he thought she would die at her desk or in a duck blind.

"Topher will be the inheritor of my Lodge shares and property," she continues.

The inheritor. Waylon shoves his plate away, his hunger gone. The anger swells like she has hit him with a baseball bat.

"So when Topher asks you to follow instructions, you'll know he can put you out on your ass. Darling, we both know you're prone to a conscience and a bit of mutiny. We can't have that. We *won't* have that." Then she tucks into her waffles and says, "Ah, gluten."

*   *   *

Later, Waylon drops Lavinia at her car. He hasn't even glanced at his phone, so the news about Noah and Anna's request for help haven't reached him yet. He is solely focused on the taillights of his mother's BMW. They disappear down the lane. She has a massage booked, which gives Waylon more than an hour to search her house.

The home office in the house where he was raised is decked out in rich cherrywood with bright blue accents. His father had a University of Kentucky obsession. Followed by a golf obsession. Long after his death, the office remains his shrine.

Waylon needs evidence about the upcoming auction.

Noah let it slip that there are stolen missiles up for grabs this year. That merchandise is far outside the usual stock his mother and Gleb Orlov sell. Every year the pair purchases and auctions thousands of weapons to the highest bidders. Bidders who have a reason to use a straw sale instead of a legal purchase. Which means there aren't QuickBooks entries or purchase agreements. Nothing obvious.

But Noah is aging, and he seems . . . jaded. Maybe he's jaded enough to have made a mistake. The acquisition of the missiles must have left a footprint of some kind. A hired team or compensation for a rogue military group. The details and purchases were likely on Gleb's side of the arrangement, but if there's anything linking his mother and brother, he needs it at his disposal.

Murray's call interrupts his search for the copy of *1984* that holds all of Lavinia's passwords. "Yeah, go ahead," Waylon says, sliding his finger over the spines of the books on his father's shelves.

"Stop answering like you're a trucker. This is a place of business."

"Stop talking like you're a prick," Waylon responds. "This is my personal phone."

"Noah's dead."

"No way. How did he die?" Waylon expects an aneurism or a heart attack. Noah smoked like ninety of his eighty years.

"Donkey injury," Murray says.

Waylon shouldn't laugh. But he does. And hard.

"Shut up," Murray says.

"Sorry. I know you were close. It's sucky timing. The donkey part got me."

"We weren't close." Murray's lie doesn't land. "Listen, I can't get Lavinia or Topher on the phone, so will you tell them about Noah and let them know I hired a woman named Anna Ryder to get us through the Royale? She's the new Noah. Also, Foster Portage is already on property. So basically it's safer to act like the Royale has already started."

Waylon hangs up, his mind on hyperspeed.

The computer chair groans as Waylon kicks back and laces his hands behind his head. Murray hired Anna? How did that come about? Does Jack know? Does Starr? Better yet, what will happen when Lavinia and Topher find out Starr's daughter is working the Royale? Waylon does not want to be in the room for that conversation. Lavinia will eat Murray for breakfast, and when she is finished and still hungry, she'll come for Waylon next.

Waylon calls Lavinia. "Noah's dead."

Lavinia curses and honks her horn like it's a response to Waylon.

"Murray called to tell us. He had some kind of accident with a donkey."

"Hmm. Has Gleb been informed?"

"No idea. I doubt Murray will call him unless he has to," Waylon says, and Lavinia agrees. The kid has been on the outs since the day Gleb dumped him on Noah, and he's stayed that way, despite being surprisingly good at managing the staff. As far as Waylon knows, no one has ever read Murray in on the auction. They let him pretend to run the Royale while Noah pulls the real strings.

This is an interesting development. Maybe even an opportunity for Waylon. He waits a breath and moves his knight. "You need me to move any crates, Mom? Topher said there's new merchandise this year."

After the Choir Girls, Waylon learned his mother and Gleb's operation backward and forward. On more than one occasion he has considered turning them all in. But Waylon has never come up with a play that lets him turn in Gleb, Noah, Lavinia, and Topher that doesn't end up with Starr or Anna being killed and Waylon going to prison.

Noah's death presents a potential chink in the armor. This year the auction will be vulnerable for the first time. And with Anna in

Murray's immediate sphere, maybe he can use that to their advantage. That would mean telling Anna everything.

Sometimes you can feel things coming to a head.

For Waylon, this is the moment he glimpses the future. He knows, beyond a shadow of a doubt, it's time to have a conversation with Anna that he and Starr should have had years ago. Truth telling requires a courage that most people never develop. But it's time. Past time. The three of them will decide together what to do.

No matter what, this is his last Royale.

Beck, my first friend was my grandfather. He was a simple man. Ate the same foods nearly every day. Used the
same phrases too. When I opened the door to his cabin,
he leaned forward in his ancient recliner and said, "Git on
in here."

He spit tobacco, which you are never allowed to do. I
only bring it up because he always smelled like dirt and
mint. To this day I can't smell either without missing him.
He carried a pocketknife that he sharpened nearly every
morning with a stroke or two across the flint. And he could
carve a stick into a whistle or a limb into a bird. He had this
Bible that was so large that he built a special shelf to hold
it. He told me once that he liked Saint Augustine better
than God. He said it was because Augustine talked about
farting and God never did. A big oversight, if you asked
him.

His best friend was a man named Noah Bright. They
grew up around here. Wild as bucks, from what I can tell.
They taught me to fish and hunt. To fillet and field dress. I
wasn't much for it, to be honest. I liked the dogs. I was good
with them. Patient. Noah loved them too. Loved animals of
every kind. He had his own stool in Granddad's kennels,
and most days, as the sun set, he'd be there "shooting the
bull," as he liked to say. I'd sneak out of the house and back
to the dogs, and Noah, Murray, and I would sit together

while Noah told stories about my granddad when he was a boy.

I'm telling you all this to explain my relationship with Noah. After Granddad died, Noah stuck around for me. Staying present. Checking on me in his own way. I check on him too. I mean, he's old and stubborn, and I feel sort of responsible for him.

I'm worried about him. I left his house the other day and he asked me to do him a "good turn." That's a favor, Beck. I said, "Sure, Noah, anything." And he said, "When something happens to me, burn my house to the ground. Ain't nobody needs to be in my ark. You hear me?"

I laughed but he didn't. "I mean it, kid. And while you're at it, burn the rest of this property to ash."

Old people are crazy. Noah's getting crazier by the day. I do hope he's still alive when I meet you. I'd love to bring you up to his house and show you the table we made. We carved it together from an old stump. Did the whole thing by hand. Oh, and you'll get a kick out of this. We did the carving in the living room, so we used a shop vacuum to clean up the shavings, and wouldn't you know, I opened it up to empty the thing and three little mice were in there. They'd been in there while I was vacuuming. Probably thought they were in a tornado.

Guess every creature takes a little g-force trip on the Centrifuge, eh?

All that to say, Beck, I will not be burning anything down. You will always have this place. Always have me. Always have mice in vacuums and pocketknives and stories.

CHAPTER 22

JACK RESPONDS TO HIS BOSS'S declaration of Anna's employment like they aren't on the clock. "You've got to be kidding me," he says too loudly. Across the room, Anna sinks into the chair and turns her head away.

Jack hauls himself up and guides Murray to the hallway with a firm hand under the elbow. The lights are off and the shadows are huge. Anna remains in the office, behind the closed door. Jack tries to lower his voice and temper his emotions, but he's still roaring loudly. "She can't be Noah."

Murray doesn't argue. He says, "Jack. Go to Noah's. Find that donkey. Put a bullet between its eyes before it gets dark."

"I understand what to do about the donkey," he said. "It's the part where you hired Anna to be Noah that I'm struggling with."

"Noah's dead."

The knowledge stings and shocks. But as it settles, it draws the tiniest smile. Jack imagines Noah and his grandfather sitting in heaven's lawn chairs counting cars that travel down the gold lane. His grand-dad would be cracking pecans; Noah would be whistling. The smile fades and reality hits. Noah's dead.

Jack says, "I'm so sorry."

"I'm fine," Murray says.

But Jack clasps Murray's arm, pulls the solid man tight against his chest. Murray holds them there. No words. Just two men whose fists dig into each other's backs. Jack has always understood that men need comfort when they claim they're fine. Murray especially. And Jack is wired for love. The only little boy in Sunday school class who always put his arm around his friends and hugged their necks. The only teenager who kissed his parents' cheeks when he left the house. The only guy who cried harder than his date when he proposed.

Jack waits until Murray breaks the embrace and then turns away in case Murray needs to wipe his eyes. Murray says, "Thanks and sorry to spring the change on you, but that woman is your boss for the week."

"No," Jack says. And not just for his own sake, but for Anna's too. He was fine—well, not fine but willing to get her a job that would be insignificant. A place to blend in with the hundreds of other people attending the Royale and the dozens of other workers. Like as a cook or a maid. But he is wildly uncomfortable with her working for Murray, which places her in the direct path of Gleb. The man is a monster.

"Yes, she is," Murray counters.

Jack immediately thinks of something his grandfather used to say. *"If you're walking with an Orlov and you spot a hole in the woods, check for a body. If you see one, it's your lucky day. If you don't, say your prayers."*

Jack received his grandfather's advice like an urban legend. He'd even told Murray and they'd laughed together, until Murray became still. A tennis ball gripped tightly in his hand, he had whispered, "Your granddad's talking about my father."

Jack hadn't laughed, but he'd also thought his grandfather was exaggerating. That was before he watched Gleb twist his best friend in knots. And before Starr told him flat out the man was a murderer—and hinted that she had some kind of proof—and Jack needed to keep Anna away from the Lodges. When Jack pressed Starr for more, she'd said, "Promise me you'll keep this between us. Anna doesn't know I have a history with Gleb and I'd like to keep it that way. I want Gleb to forget all about us. If he sees Anna running around with you, eventually he'll figure out she's mine and he won't think twice about hurting me through her."

Jack felt weird about it, but he promised.

"She can't be," Jack says decisively to Murray. He will give Anna money for Starr's treatments. All he has, if necessary. He will take double shifts. Extra hunts. But she can't take Noah's place. He's the head of the auction.

"She is," Murray says. "Period. A to B, Jack. Onward and upward. At least she's gorgeous."

And while he more than agrees with Murray's assessment of Anna, he hates his boss's tongue practically lolling out of his mouth when he says her name. *Watch it*, he wants to say. He barely stuffs down the threat.

"What's your problem with it?" Murray asks.

Jack points sharply toward the office door and tries another tactic. "That's *Anna* in there."

"Yeah, I know." And then the name hits him like bricks. "Wait. Your Anna. *The* Anna."

"*The* Anna," Jack repeats, his teeth gritted.

Murray begins to laugh. "She looks different."

"She grew out her hair and her bangs. And she doesn't wear makeup anymore." He likes both changes but has to admit she looks like a different person if you don't know her well. He expects Murray to pop his head into the office and say, "Sorry, there's been a mistake"; instead, he smacks Jack two times across the chest and says, "Well, this should be fun. I always hated that you hid her from me."

* * *

There is no short history on who Jack and Murray and Anna are to each other.

* * *

There isn't a specific age when you become a man.

If you're doing it properly, you become a man over and over, each version better than the last.

Jack's father liked to brag that Jack started the journey younger than most.

At fourteen, Jack drove the tractor alone and was offered a beer in the deer stand by the old men's club. He ran the kennels when his parents were away on private Canadian hunts and stayed home alone with a pile of frozen meals. Gary Portage even leased Jack one hundred acres of corn to manage that planting season. He was that kind of fourteen-year-old.

A young man.

Eager. Earnest. Sunny-side up.

Everyone liked Jack Higgins.

Any why wouldn't they? He played life like a game of chess. Always predicting, always forecasting. Winning the game meant he stayed three steps ahead of other people's needs. He met expectations before they were presented. This anticipation was his superpower. And his kryptonite.

Jack needed to be a hero.

And Murray was the first person he ever truly wanted to save.

Jack's singular focus and platonic obsession. Although, if he was being truly honest, there was and is a charged magnetism between the men. It isn't sexual for Jack, but it's as intense as any relationship he's ever had. Sometimes he catches Murray looking at him like he wants to eat him and Jack never looks away. He merely smiles with the pleasure of knowing there's more below the surface than there is above, which means there's always more to find out.

Jack's mother warned him about Murray. "Honey bear, you can't rescue the world and you certainly can't rescue Murray Orlov."

"Mom," he said, embarrassed. "I'm not trying to rescue the world, and I know Murray's a complete douchebag."

"Do you?" Her head was cocked sideways, her lips curled with skepticism. She knew her boy. Honest and smart and kind. And dumb enough to lie to himself.

✳   ✳   ✳

You can see logic from where you sit. Jack is better than Murray.

But when has that ever mattered?

If you place a gregarious, bombastic, lonely, bored, and hurting man in front of an empath, you get a chemical reaction.

Combinations that potent are like pipes in winter; in the case of Jack and Murray, the pipes burst all over both of them before Jack even knows he's wet.

*　*　*

Let's momentarily move backward in time.

Murray, fourteen. Jack, five. They were in the kennels. Jack was on a stool at the feet of his grandfather, and Murray was sulking because Noah wouldn't let him out of his sight. They learned to play checkers. They petted the same dogs. They peed on the same trees. They both loved the old men who spanked them for stealing chewing tobacco.

Years of this familiarity passed. Daytime jaunts in the woods. The kennels at night. The spaniels lounging at their feet. A whiff of cigar smoke in the air.

Noah stopped coming after Jack's grandfather died, but Jack and Murray kept showing up. They aged toward each other, Jack up and Murray down, because that's what happens when you live in such isolation. Jack went from riding on Murray's shoulders around the Lodges or in the pool to running next to him along the trail.

School. Dating. Sex. Hunting. Jack's good-hearted obsessions. Murray's dark side. They discussed them all. Jack would be going on and on about ideas for solving climate change and racial injustice and what the world would be like if they listened to Saint Augustine and Murray would interrupt with some version of goading Jack's manhood.

Jack resisted Murray's ideas about women until he turned twenty-one. That night, for the first time in their long, strange friendship, Murray and Jack left the kennels and went to a bar.

Under alcohol and Murray's spell, Jack became a man again.

And again.

And again.

And not a better man.

He dated every woman Murray wanted him to. Sometimes the same woman for months. Sometimes he traded them like weekly contacts. Always the same type: Murray's type for him. They'd be at a bar and Murray would say, "That one. Try for that one."

And Jack would try for that one.

Women were not prepared for a twenty-one-year-old in jeans and dusty boots from Bent Tree, Kentucky, to quote Saint Augustine, make direct eye contact, and tell them that his one hope in the world was to be a great father. They felt his hope and his sadness and his heroics, which meant they unbuttoned their clothes at the bar.

Murray took home the girl's best friend.

The next day, after work, when the women were long gone, Murray and Jack would sit in the kennels talking about the night before. Murray always seemed happier and more at peace in the kennels. He'd sip a beer and tap cigarette ashes into yesterday's empty can while Jack stole Murray's tennis ball and threw it against the wall. The dogs rested their heads on their laps and it was so perfect that sometimes they wouldn't speak for an hour and then Murray would say something that didn't involve girls or sports and Jack would lift his hands in triumph.

Jack wanted to be around Murray for no reason other than to be around Murray. Murray wanted to be around Jack because Jack was earnest and he'd never met anyone earnest.

This was because Jack didn't just think; he was thoughtful. He spent 90 percent of his time focused on how someone else was experiencing the world. And then he met Murray and Murray knew everything . . . except that he mattered. And Jack couldn't help himself. It was like the universe had given him the ultimate challenge of loving someone who hated himself.

*   *   *

Things went wrong just before Anna entered the story.

One night the guys didn't make it to the bar. They were out in the yard after a long day of work. A few guests and younger staff members joined them at the bonfire. Jack was his usual self—a tiny bit drunk and waxing poetic about important matters. Murray poured two shots of whiskey into Jack's beer when Jack wasn't looking and sent Jack to sit on a fallen log with a girl named Theresa, the gorgeous red-haired daughter of this season's cook. Theresa's best friend was visiting from Florida, a pretty girl named Sunshine. Murray was immediately smitten.

Theresa and Jack made out until Jack threw up, and then they made out some more because Theresa was obsessed with Jack and Jack was too drunk to think about anything other than the melting polar ice caps and women's rights. "Seriously, it's your body. I hate politics," he'd said, literal tears in his eyes.

They ended up in the kennels, Jack's pants at his ankles, Theresa telling him it was her body and she wanted him to use it. He didn't like the taste of her mouth, but he kept that to himself. She smelled a little bit like she'd spent the day chopping onions with her mother. He smelled a little bit like Natty Light, so he wasn't exactly in a position to judge.

The next morning he couldn't tell who had used who, but the guilt made it hard to get out of bed. He'd crossed a line. Theresa actually liked him, and truth be told, he couldn't stand her. Which made him feel extra guilty. He held a belief that he was supposed to like everyone except racists. But even being around Theresa grated his nerves. Far as he could tell, she had a negative opinion about everything.

He shouldn't have slept with her. He shouldn't have even sat on a log next to her. He couldn't even remember why he did. Was he trying to be nice? Had Murray told him to? Later, they talked about it on the ride into town for dog food. He looked at Murray and said, "Dude, we've got to stop this or somebody's going to get hurt."

Fate had a sense of humor. Right at the peak of his guilt, Anna texted. They had met one night at a seedy bar in Luxor and talked about Saint Augustine saying, "Oh Lord, help me to be pure, but not yet," over an old-fashioned. She'd gone on to tell him about her job at the high school. How she was trying to get eyeball to eyeball with as many at-risk kids as she could and remind them that they were loved.

Bourbon, saints, and saving. She was his type.

She'd turned Jack down cold. But she'd gotten his number.

She was having a lonely night and a fight with Starr about her father, which meant she'd had three old-fashioneds and couldn't get that Saint Augustine quote out of her head. Jack worked at the Lodges; he'd told her this detail that night at the bar. He was off-limits, according to Starr, which was exactly why Anna texted him. Parents shouldn't outlaw anything. The moment they do, they light a beacon. And children are like flies. They love the light to death.

ANNA: You still think you can handle a girl from Luxor?

JACK: Absolutely. Name the time and place.

ANNA: How about tonight? Pizza? The old drive-in at 8?

JACK: I'll grab a pepperoni from the gas mart and meet you there.

The timing sucked, but Jack didn't question it. Not for one minute. Anna was the girl.

There weren't many drugs better than Murray.

But Anna was better in a single glance.

The problem was, he'd already lit Theresa's pilot light. She wanted more; he wanted less. As quietly as he could, he ghosted the cook's daughter. When he wasn't with the dogs or Anna, he climbed on a tractor and farmed. The acres he worked for Mr. Portage were in the best condition they'd ever been. He built raised beds, planted asparagus, broke and tilled ground for private gardens for all the owners. And when Jack was done with those projects, he started on the fences. There was hardly anything Jack hated more in the world than fence work. By the time he looked up that summer, Theresa was gone-gone and he and Anna FaceTimed every night until they fell asleep.

* * *

Jack falling in love was a problem for his best friend.

Murray sat in the kennel alone, throwing the tennis ball against the wall, hating the woman from Luxor who stole his best friend. He and Jack were still friends and coworkers, of course, but things were decidedly different. Anna was Jack's person now. And he didn't seem to want to bring her around the Lodges.

Murray endured five long, lonely years of the Jack and Anna show before Jack announced, "I'm engaged and I'm putting my cabin up for rent," at a staff Christmas party. He didn't even tell Murray ahead of time.

Murray knew what he had to do. One phone call to Theresa.

Theresa showed up at the staff gate of the Lodges with a little boy in the back of her van to pick up her check, ready to do Murray's bidding. This check was double the amount that made her go away in the first place.

Murray had always known if Jack found out he had a son, he would leave the Lodges for good. And likely for Florida, where Theresa grew up and was determined to raise Jack's son. Now, thanks to Anna, Jack was leaving anyway. First, his cabin. What next? His job? How long before Anna convinced him to move to a bigger city where there was more work?

Whenever love is desperate, you can expect stupidity. Murray didn't have words or explanations or rationales; he had feelings that were bigger than his understanding, and he acted on them. You will likely hate him for this, but people do it all the time.

Murray took his chance to get two for the price of one.

Theresa and the kid out the door. And Anna right behind them.

One little confession from Theresa to Anna and Murray figured he and Jack would be back in the kennels before the end of the week.

CHAPTER 23

ON THE DAY OF THE breakup, Jack was sitting on his couch, scrolling on his phone, daydreaming about Anna. She sent a selfie that morning of her shoveling snow, and he loved the way she looked in a beanie. Her dark hair was like silk against the white puffy vest he'd bought her. He wanted to peel off her clothes one layer at a time and make love to her in front of the fireplace.

A scream jolted him out of this fantasy. Anna's scream. From right outside his window.

Endorphins surged through Jack's body. He threw open his front door, expecting to find her bleeding to death or being attacked by a coyote. Never, not once, in the seconds between Anna's initial screams and using her words, did Jack assume he might be the cause of her panic.

With Anna, he'd been as close to perfect as he could be. He had kept only one secret from her, and that had been unavoidable. When the mother of the woman you planned to marry threatened you, you listened. And honestly, he got it. The protective lie. Kids from Luxor had short childhoods. They were jaded and brilliant and old souls. If they weren't, they died or got eaten up by drugs or swallowed by poverty. Jack created safety, and that let Anna's inner child come to the surface. With him, she asked for help. With him, she dreamed. With him, there was art and hope. Jack knew her childhood would catch up one day, and he planned to hold her when it did.

"It's okay," Jack said and ushered Anna inside. "Whatever it is, it'll be okay." He tried to fold his body around her.

Anna recoiled. The tears, the rage . . . he'd never forget her misshapen face at that moment. She slammed something into his chest and said seven words he heard in all his nightmares. "You're not who I thought you were."

She spun and left without closing the door.

The shock Jack experienced was like a giant had picked up his whole person and slammed him through a block of ice and into an arctic sea. "Wait!"

There was snow on the ground. He wore only boxers and his feet were bare; the tiny snow crystals ate through his skin like shards as he chased her. He watched helplessly as Anna launched her engagement ring at the stock pond. It skimmed across a thin layer of ice.

"I don't know what's going on," he cried honestly. "Anna, please, I don't know what's wrong!" he yelled at her truck as she drove away. His cheeks were wet, the tears freezing to his skin.

Then he opened the envelope and read the letter.

Anna,

Jack's lying to you.

Give him this picture of his son and tell him this is the last time he will ever see him. That's his punishment for being a terrible human who won't take care of his child. Good luck with that when you're married.

Theresa

There was no doubting the validity. Jack's son was his carbon copy.

*   *   *

Bloody feet. Bloody heart.
Jack became a man all over again.

*   *   *

Broken and in shock, Jack ran straight to the kennels in his boxers and bare feet. Murray and the tennis ball were there, as Jack knew they would be. Jack punched the wooden walls until his fist was bloody and doubled in size. Murray didn't stop him. He watched quietly, taking in the sight, and said calmly, "Forget her and go put some clothes on. It's freezing."

Jack tossed the envelope into Murray's lap. "She's . . . I'm . . . Theresa." He couldn't make the words come. He was a father. He was a father and his son was—he held the photo to the light—beautiful. If you'd asked him before that moment how parental grief worked, he'd have said he didn't have a clue.

In an instant, he knew. Like he'd downloaded a file into his soul. He'd lost more life than he'd ever lived.

He'd missed his birth and cake on his face at one and diapers and fevers and photos and chicken pox and . . . and . . . and he'd missed everything.

And then there was Anna.

She thought he missed all that on purpose.

Murray jammed the letter back in the envelope. "That's some serious stuff, dude. Theresa who?"

Jack tried desperately to jog Murray's memory. "Sunshine's friend. Her mom worked here. Please go ask Noah to look up her last name."

Jack didn't even know his son's last name. Or his first name.

The hurt came all over again. He changed fists and walls and began to punch.

Moments later, Murray returned from Noah's office, dusted the snow off his boots, and threw a huge camouflage coat around Jack's shoulders. "No forwarding address. Sorry, man," he told Jack as he zipped him in and pulled the hood around Jack's ears. "Dude, if you think she was telling the truth, why don't you take a week or two off? Go chase her down or make up with Anna. I'll feed the dogs for you."

Jack wanted to scream, *I don't want a vacation. I want to meet my son. I want to make this right.* He left Murray, and over the next week he visited his parents, who were now living in Canada full time. Hoping they might remember something he didn't. "Who?" they asked. "Theresa," he urged. "Red hair. Her mom was one of the cooks at the Lodges. About five years ago."

Workers came and went from the Lodges every season. As expected, his mother stared into space for five seconds and, when she couldn't recall a face or name, told him, "Son, if we tried to remember everyone you dated five years ago, we'd have a list longer than Santa's. Those weren't your best days."

Thanks for the reminder.

He didn't tell them about the boy, his son. His mother knew something was wrong. But because Jack was so prone to deep feelings, she never guessed that this time the feelings matched the size of the event. She told him, "Don't get distracted by another bleeding-heart case, babe. Focus on Anna."

"We broke up," he admitted, and let himself fully sob.

His mother wrapped him in a huge hug and said, "Oh, honey," which was exactly what he needed, and then she added, "I worried this would happen with a girl from Luxor," which was exactly what he hated.

His mother was always two things: the most loving woman he knew and a narrow-minded woman from Bent Tree. If you wanted the first, you accepted the second. Pride aided her adaptation of his failed engagement, which she spread far and wide through Facebook and text messages to her former coworkers. "Jack's ex was so dumb she couldn't tell the difference between *pawn* and *pond*. She launched her engagement ring into the lake and she's still sitting on the dock waiting for money." She laughed like this was the funniest thing she'd ever said. Inevitably his father would agree and say, "Thank God Jack dodged that Luxor bullet."

✻   ✻   ✻

What did it matter where someone was from?

Everything.

Nothing.

✻   ✻   ✻

Growing up is the process of taking all the downloaded truths and beliefs from your environment and deciding which of them you want to claim as your own. So while Jack rejected his parents' and grandparents' prejudices, he bought wholeheartedly into their long-term commitment strategies. He wanted what they had. Rock-solid companionship. A love that had the opportunity to wrinkle with age.

A love that lasted longer than a mortgage payoff. He wanted to know who would write the epitaph on his tombstone.

And that was gone.

He was out of their golden anniversary club before he even tried to join. Out of a legacy of Higgins sons loving Higgins fathers. That shame snuggled up to the rest of his shame like one of his pups settling in for a long nap.

* * *

Jack tried to make sense of Theresa's letter and couldn't. There had been zero contact between them since the summer Theresa left the Lodges. If Theresa had reached out, told him about the baby, he would have taken care of his son. Period. He'd have been scared to death, sure, but he'd have been in love. He was already in love and all he had was a photo.

Theresa never gave him the chance. So why send that letter to Anna? Why lie? Why turn up now?

To hurt him?

To do to him what he'd done to her? That was the only reason he could conceive and so he blamed himself again and again.

Jack couldn't find Theresa online. He even tried looking for Sunshine from Florida on Facebook, and that was the dumbest way he spent ten hours of his life.

Eventually he turned his futile investigation toward the Lodges, wondering if there was any chance Theresa had come back here looking for him. With Noah's help, Jack scanned every bit of security camera footage they kept.

A day before Anna dumped him, a navy minivan pulled up to the staff gate, off the delivery lane, and parked with the engine running. The camera lens had a layer of gravel dust that made the image smudgy. The angle wasn't great either. The driver was hidden behind the glare of the windshield and Jack started to advance to the next video. Then Murray appeared, and he decided to watch more.

Jack's friend jumped the staff gate and slipped on a frozen puddle. He ended up on his butt. Scowling, he dusted himself off and approached the passenger side of the van cautiously. There was no sound to the video, but Murray's mouth moved as he kicked icicles hanging from the running board and tire frame. After an animated exchange on Murray's part, he removed an envelope from his back pocket and tossed it angrily into the passenger seat. For a split frame, the driver, a woman, leaned into the camera's view.

She had bright red hair. And the same angry mouth.

Jack tasted onions and summer.

Theresa.

*　*　*

Jack showed Murray the footage and Murray denied this was Theresa. He claimed the driver of the minivan was a lodge vendor who was supposed to bring flowers to Lavinia Collins. They argued about her contract and delivery time. That was all. According to Murray, Jack was grasping at straws. *"Every redhead in the world isn't Theresa Carson,"* he told Jack.

Jack walked away telling himself that Murray might do some whacked-out stuff, but he wouldn't lie to Jack about his son.

Murray overdosed that night.

Murray never told Jack why and Jack never told Murray that when he went to the hospital to check on him, the minute the automatic doors of the lobby shut behind him, Noah cuffed Jack's shoulder and said, "Shut up about that girl Theresa. She's gone. Anna's gone. You want to lose Murray too?"

Jack became a man again.

A man who shut up. A man who showed up for Murray.

And also a man who stayed up late googling *Theresa Carson*.

If only Murray had given Jack her real last name.

*   *   *

Like I said, there is no short history on who Jack, Murray, and Anna are to each other. And the length of their future has yet to be determined.

CHAPTER 24

ANNA AND JACK ARE IN step and completely silent as they walk the corridor between Murray's office and the Orlov Lodge lobby. Their predicament is less than ideal. On that they can agree without speaking.

As a distraction, Anna reads the gold-plated placards mounted beside the guest rooms they pass. Each name is an owner or a family member. The walls are decorated with enlarged wildlife photos displayed in barnwood frames. Eagles. Bobcats. Ducks and geese. All by the same photographer, Matthew Crain. They suit the mood of the building perfectly. What doesn't suit is the musty smell.

"We should get some air in here," she says.

Although she didn't mean to give an instruction, Jack reacts as though she issued a command. He spins quickly, retraces their path, and opens the window at the end of the hall. Fresh cold air gusts through the narrow tunnel and hits the back of her neck. Anna takes a long, deep breath. "Thank you."

"You're welcome . . . boss."

"Please don't do that. This isn't my fault."

He shifts his baseball cap higher on his forehead and then down again before he says, "You're right."

They need common ground to get through this. Softening her voice, she says, "You were close to Noah. You okay?"

"Yeah," Jack says. "We weren't as close lately. I guess we got busy. Or maybe I got busy."

"Happens to the best of us. I'm sure he knew you loved him."

"I hope so," Jack says.

Anna takes a step that she never imagined possible. She reaches out and takes Jack's hand, which stops him in his tracks, and says, "Jack, he knew."

Common ground isn't a thing you stand on; it's a thing you make through vulnerability.

CHAPTER 25

FOSTER WAITS FOR ANNA IN the lobby. She has been gone long enough that Foster is growing restless. Gary the raccoon sits leashed and chewing on the couch's leather ruffle at her feet. Foster scrolls through her files on Anna. She rereads every text she and Starr have exchanged. Then she texts her husband.

> FOSTER: Hey, babe, it's happening.
> GARY JR.: Anna?
> GARY JR.: Did you break down and demand for Starr to introduce you?
> GARY JR.: Wait! Did you punch Starr? Are you texting from jail?

This is her husband's attempt at humor. He, better than anyone, understands the cost of gaining access to Anna via Starr.

> FOSTER: No. Not even close. She came to me.
> GARY JR.: So she knows?

FOSTER: Nope. Murray hired her to work the Royale.

FOSTER: Also, I'm bringing home a raccoon. Talk later!

She stows her phone in her Louis Vuitton clutch, knowing it will fill up with messages from Gary.

* * *

Anna is incredibly grateful to see Foster waited for her. And just as happy to see Gary the raccoon sleeping at her feet.

Foster dusts off her designer jeans and stands. Anna has time to notice what she didn't previously. Foster is pocket-size. The top of her blonde braids come to Anna's chest. She's not willowy like Anna; her build is stout. Anna admires the muscles in Foster's chest that the V-neck shirt and open cardigan display. If someone had come along and whispered, "I think she's the star of a television show," Anna wouldn't have doubted it one bit.

"Is there anything I can help you do?" Foster asks.

Anna says, "Maybe," as Jack answers, "No, ma'am, we're here to help you."

Anna cringes at her mistake. This woman is an owner. She should not think of Foster as a friend even though she wants to. Laughing with Foster has been the best part of her day. The only time she's truly exhaled since the gunshots woke her before the alarm.

"I liked her answer better than yours," Foster tells Jack.

"He's probably right," Anna says.

"I hate it when men are right, don't you?" Foster speaks directly to Anna, as though Jack isn't there. "My husband is rarely right so I don't have to worry about it too often at home." She gives a wicked grin and a wink that say more about her sense of humor than throwing shade at her husband.

Anna swallows the comment that could have been made at Jack's expense. Something like, *I hate it when men lie.*

Nothing gets by him. He acknowledges her restraint with a sad smile.

"Hon-*ey*." Foster drips the word into the room and looks between Jack and Anna and then back to Anna. "Oh, you two are yummy. I'd give you a bottle of wine to hear that story." Her finger dances through the space between Anna and Jack and she repeats, "Yummy."

"Mrs. Portage," Jack interrupts, presumably to keep Anna from oversharing or to make Foster stop saying *yummy.* "If Anna and I can't get you anything, we have an urgent matter to handle down the road."

"Go on! And, Anna, when you return from that *urgent matter,* please let me know a little more about Mr. Bright's unfortunate circumstances. Gary, my husband, not the raccoon, says I'm nosy as a starving anteater." Foster smiles brightly, lofts the raccoon into the air, and prances from the room.

"She's a delight," Anna says to Jack when Foster walks out of the building and in the direction of a Land Rover.

Jack grimaces. "I don't know whether it's good or bad that she likes you."

* * *

The November air smacks them hard on their way out of Orlov Lodge. They both shiver instinctively and Anna buries her hands in her coat pockets. She pushes her fingers through a hole in the seam.

The cold flesh of her thighs is shocking. Winter is near. So is nightfall.

She should ask Jack to borrow a better coat. She wonders if he still has the old gray Carhartt hanging in his front closet. Is Leader's leash hanging on a hook by the door?

Careful, Ryder, she tells herself.

Beside her, Jack tilts his face to the granite-colored sky. His nostrils flare in an adorable snarl. "She called us *yummy.*"

"She did indeed."

"Are we . . . yummy?" he asks innocently.

"I hope not," Anna says. "Now, let's find this donkey and get this crazy day over with."

Smiling, Jack uses the handrails to propel himself down the steps three or four at a time. He lands gracefully at the bottom before Anna starts moving. Unfortunately, Foster is right: he is yummy. He seems to have aged at a different rate than her, which is mildly annoying. Women do the heavy lifting of moving humanity upward and to the right, and what do they get? Wrinkles and eye bags. And what does Jack get? The energy to float down three sets of steps without losing a single breath.

Anna arrives at the concrete pad under Orlov Lodge and joins Jack. Their stomachs rumble in conversation with each other as they walk toward the vehicles. The toast Anna scarfed at breakfast has given all it plans to give.

"We'll stop at the staff dining hall after Noah's," Jack says. "I'm starving too."

If the dining hall is a paid thing, Anna doesn't have long to decide how much she wants Jack to know about the pathetic depths of her financial situation. She checks her phone. Waylon hasn't texted back.

What will she answer when he does? *Hi. I work for you now.* Maybe he'll be in the dining hall and she can tell him in person.

Twenty thousand dollars for a week of work is an answered prayer, a miracle, and yet Anna has no idea how to afford the next ten days. Should she have asked for an advance? Or clarified the schedule? Her mother has medical appointments next week. Is she fired if she drives her? There's too much she doesn't know.

At least tomorrow's work list is doable. Checking freezers, accepting wine deliveries, stocking firewood, and confirming the amenities requested by guests are all skills in her wheelhouse. She has handled forty teenagers in detention. How bad can hunters be?

One step at a time, she tells herself until they reach her truck and its empty gas tank and another wave of fear strikes. Anna blurts out, "We need to take yours."

"No biggie," Jack says and changes course. "Lavinia wouldn't want me to leave my truck along the sidewalk anyway." He catches her looking anxious and says, "Ryder, I said *no biggie.* You don't have to cry about riding with me."

"I'm not."

Anna doesn't feel the tears on her cheeks until she wipes them away. When she put on her humble britches and drove across the Ohio, working directly with Jack wasn't a consideration. Now she is his boss.

If it weren't terrible, it would be funny.

✳ ✳ ✳

Anna lifts herself into Jack's truck and gets sucked into a time capsule of pleasant smells and textures and memories. Peppermint gum in the console. Hay and dog food in the back. Smudgy nose prints cloud the windows. Muddy paw smears on the seat, door panels, and glove box. Thoughts of the spaniel make her instantly happy. Anna and Leader shared this seat many times, with Leader getting the better end of the deal.

"Sorry about the mess." Jack swipes his hand across the leather. Like that one action would clean the truck.

"No biggie, Higgins," she replies.

Each turns to gaze out their own window so the other won't catch them smiling. They are betrayed by the tiny squeak teeth and lips make when they raise the corners of their mouths. Neither comments, but they each take a very deep breath and relax.

After everything, they still make each other laugh.

And that is fairly yummy.

* * *

They are four miles from Noah's cabin, but it will take fifteen minutes to get there.

When Jack and Anna dated, Jack drove her all through the property, pointing out the various lodges and cabins and blinds. He talked endlessly about his childhood. Endlessly. You would have thought he was documenting the story for posterity. Every time he launched into Old-timer Jack—what she liked to call his story voice—she imagined that one day they would have a kid and Jack would bore the crap out of them talking about *the good old Bent Tree days*.

She wonders if he does that with his son now. Has Jack found a way to make things right with Theresa? She wants that, she thinks. After all, she's grown up without a father and knows that particular stab of abandonment. The questions it creates. *Why wasn't I enough for him to stay? Am I not lovable? What did I do wrong?*

Besides, if she doesn't want reconciliation for Jack, her argument for leaving crumbles.

There is no innocuous approach to that topic, so she doesn't ask.

People come and go. The closer the connection, the longer the emotional investment lasts. Unfortunately, Anna and Jack have been, as Starr likes to say, "close enough to wear the same pair of underwear in two different places." That is close indeed.

In Anna's heart, under all her anger and disappointment, which have admittedly cooled since their breakup, thinking about Jack making things right with his son makes her root for him.

Some things haven't cooled. Like the desire. She tightens her grip on her thighs and gives herself a pep talk. *Settle down, Ryder. You're here for twenty thousand and nothing more.*

"It's about five more minutes to Noah's place," Jack announces as they leave the main road and settle into a turtle's pace on the dirt and gravel service road. The more formal part of the property is paved. A guest can arrive at any of the Lodges in a Corvette and not scrape. After you pass the kennels, the gravel starts and the maze begins.

"How is Leader?" she asks, feeling nostalgic.

"About to have pups again."

"Is Pippa one of hers?"

Jack grins. "Oh yeah. The laziest she's ever had. That dog won't hunt for a bone in her bowl." He laughs and then looks nervous. "I sure hope this litter is more motivated. Pippa's an amazing pet, loyal as the day is long, but the money's better on the hunting end."

"You already have buyers?"

"For at least three, if she has 'em. No, I guess two now. Noah wanted one." Jack works the steering wheel nervously. "I can't believe he's gone." He swivels in her direction and lets his eyes land on hers. "And that you're here. This is weird, right?"

"Truly."

Worry creases his face. "You want to tell me more about Starr?"

"Yes, but not right now. Thanks for still loving her," she says.

"You know me. I still love everyone."

Anna smiles but lets Jack's comment go unanswered.

The forest thickens as they drive. The weeds stretch into the road-way like they're on a mission to take over. High above, an eagle pipes as it glides through the graying sky and perches atop a high branch of a dead oak. While she fixates on the beautiful predator, Jack swings into a hidden, narrow drive she probably would have missed if she was looking for it. Branches scrape the cab of the truck. The screeches make them both twist in discomfort.

"What is your favorite thing about Noah?" she asks.

"His accent, and then maybe that he thought he knew everything and it seemed like he actually did." Jack imitates Noah's Southern accent. "'This place ain't a park, Jack. It's a habitat. You know what I'm sayin'. We don't need a manicurist on the payroll. That's for a lady's toes, not the grounds of a river bottom huntin' sanctuary.'"

The accent is so thick you'd think it wasn't real.

The tunnel of foliage ends in a clearing with a raised hunting cabin. Probably no more than nine hundred square feet and at least fifteen feet off the ground. The backwater must reach here frequently. The exterior wood, in contrast to the dark evergreen giants surrounding it, looks white. The tan interlocking timbers are neat as a pin. Smoke rises from the chimney, reminding her that less than a fireplace of logs ago, Noah Bright was alive.

Jack cocks his head to the side as he stares at the chimney.

"What?" she asks.

"A couple of years ago Noah told me that when he died I should burn his house to the ground."

"Why would he say that?" She feels offended for the adorable cabin.

"Who knows. He was always a wild card." Jack parks and pitches Anna a set of house keys. "I'll look for the donkey. Will you put out the fire and check on the house? I don't know what Murray will bury Noah in, but you might search the closet for something."

Neither Jack nor Anna notices Topher Collins watching the cabin from atop an ATV parked in the woods.

CHAPTER 26

ANNA CHARGES UP THE DECKING steps two at a time, like she does at home, and catches her breath at the top. The wooden rail has a yellow hue and none of the screws are loose.

Had Anna looked closer, she would have spotted bloodstains near the bottom and more pooled in the grass where Noah hit his head and lay dying until the housekeeper found him bleeding out.

When Anna reaches the front door, she pauses long enough to text Starr.

ANNA: I love you. How do you feel?

Thankfully, the message goes through.
Three dots light the screen.

STARR: I feel with my hands. How do you feel?
ANNA: Like I should slap you. 🖤
STARR: Silly goose.
ANNA: Crazy duck.

Anna keys her way through the door and stops in the small entry-way next to a pile of Noah's boots. The interior is not at all what she expected from a man who lives and works at a hunting club. She is prepared for guns and dead animals, not books stacked along every wall, sliding this way and that. Dust gives them all a dingy look, but their spines are cracked and their pages worn. The only furniture in the adjoined kitchen and living room area consists of a TV tray, a metal gun cabinet, and a couch. Noah, bless him, does have a seventy-inch television mounted on the wall above the fireplace. The Netflix emblem is on the screen. The top profile name reads *Me, Myself and I.* There's also one for someone named Molly.

Molly, eh? Maybe Noah Bright had a lady friend. If so, Anna hopes someone informs her of his passing. She makes a mental note to ask Jack.

With a pitcher from the kitchen, Anna dumps water on the lava-colored logs in the fireplace. They sizzle and steam, and when they are completely cold, she opens the single interior door of the living room.

Noah's bedroom. His coverlet and pillows are thrown back and on the floor. Half a cup of coffee, a bottle of ibuprofen, and an open book lay on the little table next to the bed. In the corner of the room sits a pile of plastic sacks from Tractor Supply. They are filled with dog toys.

She tries the first of two closed doors and finds the bathroom. Long gray hairs clog Noah's brush. The toilet smells strongly of ammonia. Anna backs away quickly, suddenly feeling embarrassed for Noah. If it turns out she supervises a cleaning crew, she will send one over immediately.

Noah's closet is shallow and bursting with hunting gear for every weather condition. If the man owned a suit, she assumes it will be near the back. Anna wrestles through the heavy jackets, searching for something, anything, that isn't camouflage or flannel. Unable to reach the far-left side, she slides into the closet and uses her phone as a flashlight. She's trying to avoid tripping over his shoes when she slips on a nylon poncho and tumbles into the side wall.

The paneling gives way.

Anna finds herself lying on the floor of a small hidden space, the mock closet panel beneath her. The fall took her breath but did no serious harm. She stands carefully. Using the sparse light from the bedroom lamp and her flashlight, she notes the room is roughly six by six. One desk. One laptop. Dozens of files.

Anna peels a Post-it Note off Noah's laptop. A phone number. Her gut pings. Her curiosity is too great to ignore. She punches the numbers into her phone and hits Call.

A woman answers on the third ring. "Noah?" The voice is frantic and confused.

Anna waits for her to speak again.

The woman says, "I had a feeling you weren't actually dead. We need to meet about the product list before the auction. There's one rumor about enriched uranium. Another about missiles."

Uranium? Missiles?

The voice continues, "Is Jack going to help with the weapons auction or not?"

Jack?

Anna's heartbeat pounds in her ears.

"Noah, come on. Did you talk to Jack or not? I need to know which side of this he's on." There's a sudden silence and then, "Wait. Who is this?"

Anna hangs up.

The person on the other end of the line was Foster.

There's no time to process what Foster said or why she might be talking to Noah about uranium or missiles or Jack because her ex is on his way up the stairs. His pounding feet proceed him, and he calls, "Anna, hey! I'm gonna need some help with this donkey."

Anna slides the Post-it Note into her jeans pocket, puts the fake panel back in place, and shoves the hangers back the way she found them. "Coming," she yells and grabs at clothes. The nicest clothes Noah owned are apparently a sweater and a pair of cargo pants.

"Find what we're looking for?" Jack asks when she rejoins him in the living room.

"Obviously. Did you?"

Inside her heart, she's praying, she's rooting, *Please let Jack be a better man than this.*

She's sure of one thing: good men aren't mixed up in selling uranium.

*   *   *

Before you get too distraught, there is no uranium. There is only a rumor of uranium. Anna will consider the implications, obviously, but there's no need for you to fear for the end of the free world with her.

Your greatest fear should be reserved for an elementary school in Roseville, New Jersey.

CHAPTER 27

FROM THE DECK, JACK POINTS at the evergreen grove. "The donkey's that way."

"What exactly are we supposed to do with this animal?"

Murray had said to "take care of it," and now that the task lies directly ahead, the donkey seems higher on the problem list than she previously imagined. She puts everything else to the side and focuses. "Should I look for a rope?" she asks. Jack is great with animals, but unless this donkey is a miniature, they will need a way to lead the animal back to its barn or paddock.

Jack's arm shoots out and stops her from going inside to look for a rope. He gives her a look she can't interpret. Pity, maybe?

"What?"

"Anna. We're supposed to shoot it. That's what 'take care of it' meant."

"No. 'Take care of it' means, you know, make sure that sweet creature has food, water, and shelter."

Jack lifts his ball cap and scratches his forehead. "To you, yes. To me, sure. But Murray told me in no uncertain terms to put a bullet between its eyes."

Anna knows Jack hunts. Everyone around here hunts. The industry of the Lodges revolves around killing creatures and mounting the large ones on boards, but . . . a donkey. "How did the two of you ever get to be friends?" she asks.

Jack holds her gaze momentarily and then tugs the bill of his cap over his eyes. "We aren't as close as we used to be. Not since you and I broke up. I guess he's, well, that's another story for another day. Best advice: quit before he invites you to do something questionable."

"Like work with my ex?" she says, and tries to laugh but can't. "Why do you work for someone who wants you to shoot helpless animals?"

Jack shrugs. "Well, that's a new one. And there's also great dogs, free housing, money, purpose."

"Did you?"

"Did I what?" he asks.

"Do something questionable for Murray?"

Something involving uranium, she wants to say.

Noah is practically Murray's surrogate father, and according to Foster's admission on the phone, the older man has been part of a weapons auction in some way. It would have been logical for Noah to involve Murray, his protégé. Had Murray reeled Jack in?

Jack's shaking his head. "If you mean Theresa, that was a long time ago."

Anna is uncomfortable at the mention of her name and steers them back to the donkey problem. "Isn't it illegal to shoot things out of season?"

Jack laughs. "Anna, there isn't a donkey season."

"Jack." She mimics his intonation. "If you are going to shoot that donkey, I am not helping you."

"Just follow me."

Jack leads them into the thicket. The pines grow close together here, and they shove their way through the prickly branches until they are in more of a clearing. Ancient oaks rise hundreds of feet. Anna stretches her calves against a trunk and listens to the squirrels scramble after each other. She takes a deep breath. Memories and questions. This day is an audacious mind screw. Jack's feeling it too. He keeps catching her eyes in a knowing way.

They used to take trail walks. Not at Noah's, but in places that look identical. She'd forgotten the particular noise of tramping through the woods and how much comfort there is in breathing in wilderness and breathing out stress. And how frequently she and Jack had left bits and pieces of their clothing accidentally scattered through the woods.

"She's not much farther," Jack says. "Just across the creek."

"What do you think of Foster?" she asks to pass the time.

"She's a ballbuster."

"Is she a good person?" she says since she can't ask, *Were you two auctioning weapons with Noah Bright?*

"What counts as good these days?" is his answer.

On the other side of a dry creek bed, Anna spots Jack's previous path. Or maybe it's the donkey's. The lower branches are bent and broken. The sap smells earthy and rich. "You used to pick me up smelling like this and I always thought it was aftershave."

Jack doesn't turn around, doesn't comment. She immediately regrets her choice to say something personal.

He stops. "There."

"Oh." Understanding dawns in a single glance.

The donkey that killed Noah Bright, that Jack is supposed to shoot between the eyes, stands inside a lean-to shed that is painted bright pink. A wooden sign hangs over the gable: "Molly's House." Molly's roan coat is covered in a matching pink embroidered blanket with black letters that read:

DON'T SHOOT ME.

NOT A DEER.

I'M NOAH'S PET.

"Well . . . hell."

"I know," Jack says.

"She has her own Netflix profile. So if you were going to shoot her, you totally can't shoot her now."

"I know that," Jack says. "But I can't not shoot her either. Murray wants her dead."

"What if we leave her?"

"And have Molly turn up in her bright pink shirt during the Royale?"

She understands the problem and therefore decides to declare more emphatically, "But you can't shoot her."

"There's not a place on the Lodges where I can hide a donkey that someone won't see her or shoot her."

"Then let's take her to the farm," Anna suggests.

The corn will be harvested soon. The entire field is fenced except where it meets the creek. Molly can hang out under the house or down at the barn or even beside one of the old storage buildings. She'll be lovely entertainment for Starr while she recovers from chemo. Not a dog, a donkey. Anna and Jack will save Molly's life and Molly will help save Starr's.

"What farm?" Jack looks left and right like there might be one hidden in the woods.

Anna's eyes narrow with annoyance. "Starr's farm. I'll keep her until we figure out a permanent solution."

"Your mother's sick. You don't need more to take care of. Especially not a wild beast."

Molly, the murderous wild beast, must have decided Anna and Jack mean her no harm because she leaves her highly decorated lean-to and saunters toward them, head down, utterly submissive. She's between the size of a pony and a Great Dane, and when she lifts her head to look at them, she puckers her lips and hee-haws playfully.

Jack shakes his head in disbelief. "Aren't you a thing?"

Molly brays again and lifts her front legs like she's queen of a parade.

"No wonder Noah kept you," Anna tells Molly as she strokes her nose and the hair under her head collar. "What happened this morning? Did you get scared, sweet baby?"

＊　＊　＊

Molly had been scared. If Anna and Jack could have skipped backward in time and watched the scene that led to Noah's untimely death, Molly's actions would make sense.

Noah was a man of many surprises.

He had secret files and secret rooms, and when it was very late and he was lonely, he secretly shopped online for his pet donkey. His house was a decent distance from where the organized hunts occurred, but more than one hunter got a wild hair and headed his way. Noah couldn't stand the idea of Molly being hurt. He ordered the personalized pink coat and would never admit to anyone that he got carried away with the embroidering. His biggest secret, his biggest surprise, was he planned to let Molly sleep in his living room during the Royale. The pink lean-to was nice, but the living room was nicer.

The trouble was the deck stairs. Molly hated them.

Noah spent the last month of his life teaching Molly to face her fears. The donkey was brilliant, and she loved Noah, but she was scared of two inconvenient things: wooden steps and gunshots. With Noah's schedule, they didn't have much time for her training. The Royale was too close and Noah too overworked. Plus, his knees didn't operate the way they used to. He managed a couple of extra trips up and down a day, but not much more.

He and Molly had started working right as the sun came up. He'd taken the day off and he wouldn't sleep until Molly was inside.

Molly made it three-quarters of the way up the steps, Noah behind her, urging her rump. This was what it took when she was being stubborn, and Molly was incredibly stubborn this morning.

Five high-caliber gunshots.

In quick succession.

Noah's ears perked up at the caliber, at the closeness to his house.

Molly's reaction wasn't curiosity. The donkey brayed, reared, and launched her powerful back legs. Her right hoof caught Noah between the eyes with enough force it lifted the hundred-and-seventy-pound man off the steps.

Into the air.

Into gravity.

Noah Bright fell nine feet and slammed his head into the bottom railing. There he lay, Molly beside him braying and nudging, until the housekeeper came for the day's garbage pickup.

* * *

Jack has a high success rate on small problems. Coaxing a stubborn dog, bringing a dying plant back to life, explaining to a renter there isn't a pizza place who delivers to the property. Even re-bottling an expensive bourbon. He's unstoppable. But the large ones: Murray. Theresa. Anna. He's zero for three.

Anna's job and this donkey, this is both large and small.

The donkey leans her long, solemn face into Anna's neck and lets Anna stroke the length of her brown ears.

"This sweetie pie isn't dangerous," Anna declares and touches her nose to Molly's nostrils. They breathe in tandem.

What a strange day.

Jack found Foster Portage a leash for a raccoon.

His grandfather's best friend died.

His ex-fiancé became his boss.

And he has one big-ass decision to make.

* * *

Jack has no way of knowing that what he does with Molly will change their lives.

He's thinking as fast as he can through options. Follow his boss's instruction, shoot the donkey, and refresh Anna's hate? Betray his boss, his oldest friend, hide the donkey, and renew some trust with the former love of his life?

The stakes are high no matter what he decides.

If Murray finds out Jack and Anna didn't follow his instructions, he will . . . what? Fire them both? Surely not. Except, in the weeks surrounding Gleb's visit, Murray grows radically unpredictable. The entire staff walks on eggshells. Everyone knows that for eleven months of the year their job is the Lodges and in the twelfth month it's to get Gleb Orlov back on a plane before their boss shoots a person instead of a bird.

"Jack, please," Anna coaxes. "Let's drive her to the farm. If Murray finds out, I'll tell him I pulled rank on you."

Murray will never accept that explanation. But Anna is in love with this damn donkey. Plain and simple. In the animal kingdom, love at first sight occurs all the time. The odds increase dramatically if you have possession of a donkey wearing a pink blanket, owned by a seventy-something-year-old man who paid extra to have her name embroidered.

"Okay," he agrees. "But there are security cameras at all the gates, so we can't get her off the property in the truck without Murray finding out. Here's what I'm thinking . . ."

And that is how Jack and Anna and Molly end up on a boat, crossing the dark waters of the Ohio River.

CHAPTER 28

THROUGH A PAIR OF BINOCULARS, Topher Collins watches Jack and Anna attempt to load a donkey onto a speedboat. The donkey wears a pink coat and the stitching on the side says she belongs to Noah. Topher smooths his mullet and shakes his head in disbelief. The rumors about the donkey must be right.

What are Anna and Jack doing? Drowning it in the Ohio? Topher wouldn't put it past Murray. The sycophantic psychopath has a weird reason for everything.

The other thing that concerns Topher is how Anna and Jack maneuver around each other in perfect fluidity. From the looks of it, the young couple is back together. What an annoying day. Why is that kid here?

Kid is the wrong word. Anna isn't in pigtails anymore. She must be, what? Thirty? He's lost track since Waylon gave up on Starr all those years ago. However old Anna is, she shouldn't be at the Lodges. With Gleb coming to the Royale, Noah dead, and the missiles MIA, Anna is another complication Topher doesn't need.

He takes a long sip of his watered-down Mountain Dew. The sugar coats his tongue. The calming effect begins immediately. Under the deep influence of caffeine, Topher remembers something Noah told him once in a duck blind.

"You don't hide million-dollar shit among diamonds. You hide it with other shit."

He thinks again of the Post-it Note. Of his brother. Of Anna. And the words form a picture that makes sense.

M crates?

Lodges or Luxor?

Waylon's ex?

Topher would bet money that Noah stored Gleb's crates on the other side of the river. And since Waylon's name is on the Post-it, they are probably at Starr's house.

He'll find out tonight.

CHAPTER 29

HERE IS A PARADOXICAL INCONVENIENCE for someone who lives with shoreline on three sides of her property: Anna loves water and hates boats. Hates them. Always has. And they are part of the landscape. The river's lined with them. There's even an upside-down johnboat that hasn't been water worthy in years resting beside one of Starr's outbuildings.

On their third or fourth date, Jack borrowed a speedboat and invited her on a ride to Paducah. He'd been giddy with the idea. "We'll dock downtown and get some great food and walk around. There's an art gallery I'd love to show you. A proper date for a beautiful woman."

Anna thanked him and politely refused. He assumed she couldn't swim until she explained, "I swim like a fish; I have a thing about boats."

Jack saluted. "Heard. No boats, oh Captain, my captain." After that, they sat on docks, swam in lakes, and watched the sunset over the Ohio from the deck at her mother's house, but they never boated.

Until today.

If you need the courage to climb into a boat, a donkey wearing pink certainly helps. Molly also helps remind Anna how much fun it is to be with someone you love.

Used to love.

Still love. (There's the honesty.)

And still, what? Hate? No. She doesn't hate Jack. Not anymore. But she does hate how many years of her life she lost because of him. She doesn't want to lose any more. Her mother likes to say, "Between every two humans is a space, and what happens in that space will tell you all about what will happen between those two humans." She had followed up that lesson by suggesting there was a lightning storm in the space between Anna and Jack. "Girl, you two sizzle."

They had. Back then.

Right up until Theresa's letter ripped away the fabric of who Jack was and created a new Jack.

So it doesn't matter how much Anna loves Jack; she isn't a fool. She walked out of his life before he walked out of hers. And yet they are still . . . what had Foster called them? *Yummy.* Trust and electricity aren't mutually exclusive.

There on the boat, with Molly braying at the stern and Jack steering toward their inlet that backs up to the farm, Anna sees his goodness all over again. He's smothered in it. And then she thinks about what else Foster said.

"Is Jack going to help with the weapons auction or not?" And then, *"Noah, come on. Did you talk to Jack or not? I need to know which side of this he's on."*

Absorbing the fact that Bent Tree is home to a weapons auction doesn't come quickly.

Anna lives in Luxor, not in the plot of a spy novel. If you take the Choir Girls off the table, the most sensational things that happen are heartbreak and tax evasion. She probably would have written off the uranium as a misunderstanding except the Department of Energy produced enriched uranium at a nearby plant for years. The site closed but still carries a full cleanup staff. Under those circumstances, pilfering uranium isn't totally out of the question, but it's still far-fetched.

Selling guns isn't. Read the news on any given day and someone is doing something horrible with a weapon they hadn't been allowed to purchase legally.

She forces herself to sit with Foster's words. The picture isn't hard to construct.

There's a weapons auction in conjunction with the Royale that Foster and Noah know about. Jack either has been invited to help or was going to be invited to help.

Help do what? Stop it or start it?

Her first voice says: *Jack is good. He is rescuing a donkey for me.*

Her second voice says: *He fooled you once before.*

CHAPTER 30

JACK BEACHES THE BOAT ON the small landing area at the back of the Ryder farm. The grounds are untended and overgrown. There aren't ruts on the shoreline anymore, and uprooted trees lay where there was once a well-trodden path.

Jack wants to ask Anna if she's okay. If he brings up her fear of boats, she'll be embarrassed. Instead, he sneaks several looks and determines that when they get Molly settled on the farm, he will boat over to the Lodges, get his truck, and return with real food. Anna is way too skinny.

"What?" she asks.

"I was thinking about how I used to be covered in mosquitos down here and you'd never even get a bite."

Jack holds his breath, afraid that was the wrong thing to say, but Anna laughs. "You're sweeter than me," she concludes.

In the early stages of their dating life, Anna met Jack at the creek because Starr wouldn't let him on the property. This beach was their savior until Jack won Starr over.

Jack's ability to keep his mouth shut paved his road to trust with Starr. She gave Jack his own key to the property. Some days, when

Anna was at work and Jack had the day off, he came over and sat with Starr or worked his way through her chore list. He loved those days. His own mother was . . . he could never put his finger on the words. Judging him? Examining him? Starr seemed to accept him warts and all. She knew all about his wild days in far more detail than he'd ever shared with Anna. She might be the only person in the world who understood why he loved Murray and how infuriating it could be to love someone so complicated.

And likewise, Jack knew some of Starr's hidden past. They frequently debated whether they should tell Anna how Starr's past overlapped with the Lodges'. The longer they kept quiet, the more they believed nothing good would come of her knowing.

Some of the accrued trust between Jack and Starr should still exist, he feels certain. Even though he broke Anna's heart, he's never broken anything between Starr and Anna. And he could have. Starr knows that.

Anna says, "Hey, any ideas on moving this donkey? I'd like to be done with work sometime this century," and Jack realizes he must have been staring at the water for a long time.

The fiberglass sides and railing of the boat are waist-high. They had a heck of a time coaxing Molly aboard in the first place. She ate all of the carrots from Noah's fridge on the way over and now they have nothing to dangle.

"Move around on this side of Molly," he instructs. Without a thought, he tucks Anna behind his back and grabs Molly's lead. "We'll force her."

The moment the halter tightens, Molly rears and bucks. Jack and Anna move in tandem with the scared animal, narrowly avoiding Molly's rear hooves.

Anna pats the animal's flank. "Take a deep breath and stay right there, baby."

"She can't stay on the boat," Jack says.

"She's had a bad day."

"Tell that to Noah."

That sobers them.

The process takes so long that Jack nearly decides to set the boat afloat. Maybe that would count as honoring Murray's wishes.

It's Anna who lures Molly onto land. Talks her off like she's a child having a breakdown on an amusement park ride. "Let's go right over here and settle down," she says. "That's good, baby. It's not so bad over here on this side of the river. I don't care what all those Bent Tree ogres told you. You're going to watch over Starr for me. She's going to love you."

With Molly finally chomping on weeds, Jack looks down the long-rutted lane in the direction of the farmhouse. The deck lanterns twinkle above the corn. In daylight, Starr has a view of where they stand, and with the boat's lamps, she could see them in a heartbeat if she was at the window. "Is your momma gonna call the cops on me?" he asks, only slightly teasing.

"She's sleeping and you're here by invitation. Now, help me to the barn."

A gunshot pierces the air.

Molly freaks, rocking backward and then forward before launching her rear legs into the air.

"Easy," Anna says, moving closer. "Easy, baby."

She lurches for the lead and misses.

Another gunshot.

Two hooves smash through the air. They are so close to Anna's head that the breeze moves the wisps of hair by her ear. She falls backward into the tall grass. Jack's pulse is a racehorse as he reaches for her.

She accepts his hand up. "I'll get her some earplugs," Anna says.

Jack catches the donkey's lead. "Molly, my dear, you live in the wrong state for a gun-shaped fear."

CHAPTER 31

LAVINIA MAKES THE CALL SHE'S been dreading.

Gleb answers on the first ring. A series of traffic horns echoes in the background. Where is he again? New York? New Jersey maybe. Wherever it is, she's glad to be in Bent Tree. The only noise outside her window is gunshots.

"I heard," he says before she can speak. "My favorite informant texted after she found the body. Not my son, mind you. Useless."

She matches his lack of pleasantries. "Was it your doing?"

"I assumed *you* killed him," Gleb says suspiciously.

Lavinia picks absentmindedly at the skin around her thumbnail. "Hardly. You don't kill the mule carrying the luggage on the way *up* the mountain."

"I will miss him," Gleb says, which might be the most human phrase he has ever uttered.

"Me too," Lavinia says. "He was very useful."

"Indeed."

Satisfied they've grieved enough, Lavinia gets down to business. "We'll proceed, I assume?"

"Obviously. There's money to be made."

"Excellent. We'll be ready."

"Lavinia." His tone is cutting.

"Gleb," she cuts back.

"Noah received four crates that weren't in our normal inventory. You'll need to locate them as well."

Lavinia is surprised. Not about the crates. She's surprised Gleb's admitting they exist. She says, "Yes, I'm aware of your missiles," like they don't matter to her in the least. And then to keep the control, she says, "Never underestimate a woman, Gleb. She always knows what's going on in her house even when her children think they're pulling a fast one on her. And I regret to tell you that we will not be selling those this year. I don't start wars, darling. I arm common people who have the right to defend their homes. The crates will leave with you when you go."

Before Gleb can reply, Lavinia hangs up and calls her older son. As with the previous conversation, no pleasantries are exchanged. She begins with, "Have you located Gleb's crates yet?"

"Working on it."

"Find them now."

CHAPTER 32

THE LARGE BARN IS IN view, only a short hike from where they beached the boat. Except for Molly's crunching, they're quiet. At the barn, they hit another roadblock. Old rusted padlocks latch the large double doors and the main door. "Those have Starr written all over them," Jack says, wiping the rust from the locks on his jeans.

"You know it," Anna agrees. "I've never even been in here."

"You're kidding. Not once in your whole life?"

"I said I haven't."

"You aren't curious?"

"I never think about it."

"Oh, I'd have thought about and I'd have climbed right up there"—he points to the loft door, which is not padlocked—"and been in that barn in a heartbeat."

"Well, I think we established years ago that we disagree on principles."

"Did we?" he asks, as honestly as he asked on the day she left. "Maybe if you heard my side of the story—"

"Jack, not now. Just climb up there and come back with something that will bust the lock. Molly needs a shelter for the night, and we need to be done with this and find some food."

He climbs.

The going isn't easy, but his fingers fit between the vertical wooden slats. He works his way up, hand over hand, until he reaches the loft. The door creaks on its hinges but opens easily. Jack hauls himself over the top and into the barn with a little grunt.

Hay and mice are his first smell and thought. When his feet hit the wooden floor, little creatures scurry into their corners. Jack turns on his phone flashlight and takes tentative steps forward. The loft wood seems firm as long as he stays on the timbers. There should be a ladder somewhere along the eaves. "I'm fine, by the way," he yells playfully through the opening to Anna.

"You see anything?"

"Hay. Hay. More hay."

The barn's full of square bales. Worst-case scenario, he'll throw out four or five bales to get Molly started on something other than Starr's cornfields and they'll figure out a more permanent shelter tomorrow. There's no rain in tonight's forecast.

"That's great," she says.

Jack misses his next step. The wood beneath him explodes.

CHAPTER 33

HER MOTHER FELL IN THE shower six months earlier. Anna had been drawing in the living room and nearly levitated from the couch to the tub. Starr was fine. Or maybe that was the start of the cancer. But on that day she'd picked herself up and laughed about having more wrinkles than a Shar Pei puppy.

That had been a sliding tumble onto fiberglass. Jack must have fallen at least ten feet. And landed on what?

"Jack!"

Thankfully, the vision in her head—of Jack impaled on an old tool—is quickly set aside. "I'm okay. I think." His voice is breathy and pained, and closer to her now that he isn't as high in the loft.

Anna turns her ear to the crack between the barnwood and listens for him to say something else. Her heart's racing. "What can I do? How can I help?"

Jack doesn't answer.

"You landed on hay?" she asks hopefully.

"Sort of. I'm not . . ." His voice drifts.

"Jack!" She doesn't know how long she waits for an answer. Long enough that panic cuts into her.

"I need you in here," Jack says, something peculiar in his tone.

Without a thought of safety, Anna climbs. The tread on her boots slides on the aged wood. The going is much slower than Jack's ascent, but she's strong enough. Thanks to push-ups and yoga and working with hellions at the high school. Sweat beads across her forehead and runs down her neck and back. When her fingers close on the final board and she swings her body through the loft door, she screams with exhausted relief. "Almost there. Hang on," she calls as her eyes adjust to the barn's darkness.

Jack hasn't said anything else since he asked for help, but she hears noises below. She spots the broken wood where Jack fell through. "How do I get down?"

His lack of answers raises her panic again.

Praying she doesn't misstep, she tiptoes toward the eaves until she locates a ladder. She scrambles down quickly and hops off the last rung. Shadowy shapes go from the bare ground to the loft ceiling. The hay smell is overwhelming, and as far as she knows they don't use hay for anything. Light trickles in from the few cracks in the wooden siding and the edges of the ceiling where an exterior security light has kicked on at twilight.

"Jack? Answer me."

"I'm up here."

Anna follows his voice, stepping over and onto the towering bales, hoping she doesn't twist her ankle trying to reach him. The bales are slick and many are disintegrating. Maneuvering on and up them in the dark proves challenging.

"Hey," Jack says from directly above her. "Give me your hand and I'll help you."

She does as he asks, hoping she doesn't hurt him. Out of breath but at his side, she runs her hands along the edges of him, checking frantically for damage. Later, when they are inside, she will spot bruises and cuts, but for now he seems intact.

He clasps her hands in his. "Hey, I'm okay."

"You said you sort of landed on hay. I was worried that—"

"I landed on hay and—" Jack turns his phone's flashlight toward their feet and stomps the heel of his boot downward. It slaps against something solid. Beneath them is a slick white floor.

She bends to sweep loose hay and finds a metal D ring anchored to fiberglass.

"It's a cabin cruiser," Jack says.

"We're on a boat? You landed on a boat?"

"You look as shocked as me," Jack says and tosses several bales to the side to reveal built-in deck loungers. The leather has been eaten through by animals, the stuffing removed.

"Do you think it's stable?"

To her horror, Jack jumps. He lands and nothing moves. "It's wedged in this hay tighter than corn nuggets in my dad's stomach after an all-you-can-eat buffet."

"Thank you for that visual."

"You're welcome."

They are on the rear lounge deck. Presumably the outboard motor is behind them and the cabin somewhere in front of them. With the dark and the hay, she can't tell the scope of the vessel. Based on their distance from the barn floor, the craft is a decent size. Which means the cabin beneath them is quite large.

"Your mom ever mention this?"

"No."

The Ryders don't own a boat. Or at least not in her lifetime. While the boat beneath them isn't new, it's too modern to have come from her grandfather's era of owning the house.

If Jack hadn't fallen through the loft and disturbed the hay covering the roof of the cruiser, the boat would have stayed hidden. Even in daylight. Even if someone stared directly into the barn. Anna guessed there were hundreds of square bales blocking the visibility from the ground.

"There's more." Jack points at a narrow little path where he's thrown hay to either side. "And it's not good."

At the cabin door, Jack uses the sleeve of his shirt to cover his hand and lift the latch. "Don't touch anything," he warns and steps in front of her toward the heart of the cabin.

"You're scaring me."

"Good. This is the scariest thing I've ever seen."

Audio File #921

Beck, over the course of your life you're going to meet great people and terrible people and people with the same consistency and flavor as tofu. I try to be great. I'm pretty consumed by it, to be honest.

And then there's you. My beautiful anomaly.

There's no doubt about it: I have not been great with you. If someone asked you about me, you'd likely say terrible things. I don't blame you for that. If you're listening to this and you've spent your life hating me, I want you to know I understand.

Sometimes great people are terrible and sometimes terrible people can be great. This paradox is one of the most confusing things about being alive.

I want to undo my past, not undo you. Undo the moment where I somehow wrote myself out of your life. I don't even know the moment. I can't figure out what I did that made your mother believe I wouldn't help you or love you or support you. That moment has to be there somewhere. If I knew, I would fix that part of myself.

Sometimes I tell my friend Murray that forgiveness doesn't need to make sense to everyone. It needs to be given so you can move on with life. But what do you do when it's yourself that you can't forgive?

I'm sorry, Beck. I'm so very, very sorry.

I wonder if all fathers feel this way.

CHAPTER 34

DRIED BLOOD. EVERYWHERE.

Not that Anna can identify the dark substance at first glance. The paneled walls are stained with splatters that seem more like the set of a horror film than where a horror actually occurred. The once-white leather interior wears a blackened burgundy crust. The sitting area and the kitchen are splattered as well. There's a smear on the walkway where someone has been dragged.

She hasn't spoken. Can't. The truth registers.

Someone died down here.

She opens her mouth to tell Jack and nothing comes out.

You don't have to believe in ghosts to experience the thinness of the veil. The scene before Jack and Anna is so undisturbed that hardly anything separates them from the final party that took place in that cabin.

Glasses litter the tables and bar. The impression of bodies stays etched into the leather. Blood spills across the white interior.

Bile coats Anna's throat. She squeezes the muscles in her mouth and holds everything down. "We shouldn't be here," she says, but doesn't move.

Jack holds the phone out in front of him to guide the way forward, deeper into the cabin. He casts enough light on the floor that she spots a set of tracks through the smears. Large adult boots and a child's bare footprints. Both smudged in the bloodstains.

Hand in hand, they cross the kitchen and seating area to arrive at the boat's rear bedroom. The yacht is luxurious, but this particular sleeping cabin is built into the bow and only accessible by climbing a step and scooting onto the mattress from the foot of the bed.

There's more dried blood on the yellow coverlet.

"Look," he says.

She isn't sure what she's supposed to see. The ledge that surrounds the bed is covered in women's clothes. A purse lays open, its contents scattered. Photos are framed. A few have turned over. There's makeup and tanning lotion bottles along the ledge. A very flat pillow and a stuffed animal are undisturbed.

He points at one of the silver frames. "That's a photo of you."

She gasps at the sight of herself. There she is, likely on the deck of this very boat. At twenty-five or so, lounging in the sun and waving at the camera. She wears cutoff jeans and a navy-and-white-striped bikini top. The water around her is aqua blue. Anna doesn't remember that swimsuit. And she certainly doesn't remember the boat.

"That's not me."

"Please," he says. "You can tell me."

Anna rips Jack's phone from his hand and leans as far as she can toward the photo without touching the bed. There are tiny orange numbers near the bottom of the photo. The date.

"That's not me," she says, relieved that she isn't losing her mind. "I was, like . . . two years old when this photo was made."

CHAPTER 35

STARR RYDER WASN'T ALWAYS A mother.

In fact, she never wanted children.

Children were anchors. Her own mother made that clear. *"I wouldn't be stuck here if I hadn't gotten pregnant with you,"* Hattie Ryder used to say. Not when she was drunk. Hattie never drank. She spoke her cruelties over toast and eggs because she woke up every day of her life feeling the heaviness of motherhood, and by breakfast it had to go somewhere.

Every teen who grew up in Luxor planned to leave. Mothers warned their daughters not to get knocked up. The girls chorused the classic replies: "I'll never get myself pregnant like you did." Extra emphasis on *you*. Those same girls wrote speeches for class titled "One Day I'll Live in Paris" or "How I Plan to Change the World." They put spare change in coffee cans labeled *Get the Hell Out of Here Money*.

When it came time to leave, there were never enough quarters in the can.

Those girls became women who wished they were still girls. Then they had their own little anchors with diapers and curls.

Just like their mommas had.

Some of the young people sold their bodies to get out. The men to the army. The women to men they thought would be rich. Most returned to Luxor in worse shape than they'd left. The town didn't teach them how to live anywhere else.

Starr was one of those. The dreamers. The leavers. The hopers.

She got a job cleaning houses in Bent Tree by stealing a Bent Tree license plate off a restaurant wall. When she crossed the river into Kentucky, she steered her father's Ford into an old cut-through road and swapped the plates. That one small change opened up the world of work. Her brain did the rest. She memorized the towns surrounding Bent Tree and expertly dodged questions when people played connect the family dots. "Oh, you're a Ryder. I know some Ryders over on Willet Lane." Starr laughed and said, "We're bound to be cousins, but my folks are on the other side of the county."

Her plan was to buy a boat and head to New Orleans, where she'd get a job for one of the large cruise ships like Royal Caribbean and clean her way around the world.

These were not stories she told Anna.

She also didn't talk about her relationship with Gleb Orlov, the handsome man she met at the marina. Gleb had been trying to negotiate fuel for an event at his lodge later in the fall, but Carl, the old man who ran the docks, only heard one out of every ten words since he climbed out of his tank at the end of WWII.

"You have to yell," Starr instructed Gleb.

Gleb wasn't a yeller. That was the first thing Starr learned about him. She watched, totally fixated, as Gleb leaned close to Carl's ear and spoke kindly. "If you fix this fuel for me, I will pay to fix your ears."

Gleb and Starr negotiated far more than fuel that day on the dock.

Needless to say, Starr never made it to New Orleans.

But she did end up with a boat.

CHAPTER 36

IN THE STOMACH OF THE cruiser, Anna says, "I can't breathe."

Jack knows how to move her.

They are upstairs, on the deck, atop the hay, and sliding to the ground in seconds. Jack kicks the aged wood beside the barn door until it splinters. He makes a hole large enough for them to wiggle through. When they are outside again, they lie side by side panting into the weeds like they've escaped a drowning.

Ten feet away, Molly lifts her head and brays at the sight of them. Her mournful call anchors Anna to the world outside the barn. Anna flips onto her back and checks for blood. Only mud from crawling out of the barn streaks her clothes. There is even a pinch of clover under her watch band and hay clinging to the woven texture of her sweatshirt.

But no blood. Dried blood doesn't stain anything but your memory.

When she closes her eyes, little footprints fill her brain. The prints of a three- or four-year-old? The toe smudges were so light they were almost nonexistent. When that child, whoever they were, left the boat, someone would have needed to hose their tiny feet off. The person wearing the big boots likely had that job. Those prints clearly belonged to an adult.

Anna wants to shove everything from the cruiser into a mental hole and forget she ever ventured inside the barn.

*   *   *

Time slides backward the way it tends to do when trauma is having a revival.

Anna focuses on the child's feet in Jack's story.

Ten little toes. In the picture Theresa shared of Jack's son, the child was barefoot. He would have been about the right size to make the bloody prints on the boat. She wonders if Jack is thinking of his son too.

Anna accesses the memory of the day Theresa came to the farmhouse like she's scrolling for the photo on her phone. It starts with Theresa throwing the letter at her chest.

Then the stinging slit on her index finger from ripping open the envelope.

The words that undid Anna's future.

The boy, Jack made over.

Maybe it's the death cloud hanging over them or finding herself in a horrific experience with her ex-fiancé, but losing Jack's son in the way he did suddenly feels like a personal loss to Anna. Like many women, turning thirty transformed her biological clock into an alarm. For the last few years, the piercing shrill of her abdomen means she thinks about babies. And she stops herself from thinking about babies. She doesn't ever want to think about babies. And she only wants to think about babies. Starr's cancer compounds the longing.

Her mother might never see her become a mother. Lying there next to Jack, thinking about his son, makes her question her decision-making skills all over again.

If Jack had come to her and confessed he had a son whom he'd been caring for in secret, she would be a mother now. She and Jack would have married and been parents as much as Theresa would have let them. Of this, she's sure.

Anna's good with kids. She knows how to throw them in the air and tickle their rib cages to get a full belly laugh. How to kiss a boo-boo and dust off a bottom and say, "You're okay. Keep going." She knows how to use silly voices at bedtime and tuck blankets until a child is a burrito of sleep. Scaring away monsters, buying stuffed animals, lacing a string through a paci so it doesn't get lost—she's done them all.

If he was their boy, she'd pause every night at the door of his bedroom and say, "Night night, silly goose." And Jack's son would singsong back, "Night night, crazy duck." They would have been a silly goose, a crazy duck, and an old hoot owl. Because of course Jack would have eaten up the opportunity to spin his neck in odd directions and hoot from his belly.

But that's not what Jack did. She'd gotten that wrong about him.

What else has she gotten wrong about the people she loves?

* * *

Jack's voice brings Anna back to the present. His gentle, "Hey, tell me what's in your head right now," sounds as scared as she feels.

She faces him. His stomach lifts and falls with deep, deep breaths. How many times have they lain next to each other, hoping silently for an invitation? How many trembles and shudders belong to Jack touching her? How many kisses?

"What are you thinking?" he asks again.

"You'd never believe me." She hardly believes herself. But trauma is a zipline from one place to another. "What about you?"

"I can't get that blood out of my head. Someone must have died on that boat."

Anna feels screams in her inner soul. Who came aboard to drink that wine and died before they picked up a glass? The tragedy tightens her chest.

Anxiety squeezes and squeezes until Anna isn't sure she can get a deep breath. She understood the violence immediately, the same way she understands there is only one person who could have hidden that boat. Anna glances toward the farmhouse and half expects her mother to be on the porch.

Jack follows Anna's gaze and pushes up on his elbows. "That was Starr in the photo."

"Yeah."

"Do you know much about that time in her life?" he asks kindly. Like he's trying not to imply her mother is the one who manifested all that blood.

Anna isn't stupid. Her mother had a before. Every mother does. "No," she says honestly. "But, Jack, I do know her. She's my best friend. And whatever happened on that boat, she couldn't have . . ."

"Unless she was protecting you," he suggests.

That rang true. If someone tried to hurt Anna, Starr would put a knife through their heart and hit it with a sledgehammer for good measure.

Jack says, "Has she told you more about your birth father than she had when we were . . . ?"

Anna huffs. "No. She never talks about him."

In the year after Waylon left, Anna got curious about her biological father. Her mother always had dates, partners, nights out, but Waylon was the only one who came through the locked gate. The only one who knew Anna as a child. After he dumped Starr, Anna came right out and asked Starr if Waylon was her real dad.

"No, my love. And you don't need a father when you have a crazy duck like me. Right, silly goose?"

"Right," Anna said to leave the conversation.

But once Anna started thinking about her dad, she couldn't stop. She begged for facts the way children pester their parents for early Christmas presents. Starr matched Anna's persistence for months. Finally, Starr threw up her hands and said, "Fine. Fine. Fine. Your father hated pickles."

That was a Monday.

On Tuesday: "Your father had a small scar in the smile line to the right of his mouth."

Wednesday: "He was the worst driver I've ever met."

Thursday: "He had a great laugh but he was always serious."

"Mom," Anna asked on Friday night. "Where is he now?"

"Oh, my silly goose, I'm so sorry, but your father died when you were very young."

Anna curled up in her mother's lap, twirled the fake pearls of Starr's necklace, and said something Starr never forgot. "I'm so sorry, Mom."

"For what?"

"That you lost someone you loved."

Starr smooshed her nose against Anna's until they were both cross-eyed and said, "Oh, silly goose, I chose you and I'd choose you again and again and again and again and again to infinity and over the moon and back again with a loop around Saturn for fun."

At the time and in the years that followed, Anna told herself a story about that conversation. *Talking about my father hurts my mother, so I won't talk about my father.* But now, having discovered the photograph on that bloody cruiser, she sees Starr's statement much more like an either-or. *I chose you.* If her father died a natural death, would her mother have used that particular language?

Questions tumble out of Anna in a rush.

"You know her, Jack. How would she hide that boat in the barn? Like, physically? How could she stack hay up that high? She's not a big woman. Is this why she's so private? And is this why I've always hated boats? Was I there? Are those my footprints? Did I bury this? How do I . . . ?" Anna puts her head between her knees. "What am I supposed to do if we find out my mother, like . . . killed my father?" She exhales and then screams into the dirt until she's dizzy.

Jack doesn't shush her. Or try to fix things. He touches her shoulder and squeezes to remind her she's not alone. The warmth and weight of his hands is familiar and grounding. They stay that way until she is calmer and her breathing is easier. Then he asks one more question. "Do you remember that boat?"

She presses into her memories. Into her childhood. "No."

"Then here's what we know. Your mother said your father's dead. She is fiercely protective of you and wildly private. You have a cruiser covered in blood that someone made every effort to hide. That doesn't automatically mean those footprints belong to you and it certainly doesn't make Starr a murderer, but this isn't something we can ignore."

He's right about everything.

CHAPTER 37

AT ANNA'S INSISTENCE, JACK MOTORS home alone.

He would have asked to stay if Starr hadn't called. She'd fallen next to the couch and couldn't get up. He heard Starr laughing deliriously in the background. Anna being Anna had said to Jack, "I have to take care of her. Will you come in the morning?" Then she touched his face, his right cheek. "You're going to have a bruise. From where you fell. You should ice it."

"Go," he said and promised to return at 7:00 a.m.

She left him at a run.

He's docking on the Bent Tree side when her text comes through.

ANNA: Got Mom into bed. Not lucid enough to question about the barn.

JACK: Don't talk to her alone.

ANNA: Because she's dangerous? I literally carried her to bed.

JACK: No, silly. Because if you're going to do hard things, you shouldn't do them by yourself.

JACK: Consider waiting until after her treatments???

Three little dots appear. Disappear. He watches them come and go for twenty minutes, like they're a movie. In the end, she says, I'll wait until you're with me.

Day Two

CHAPTER 38

WE RETURN NOW TO THE potential future of the Roseville community. To measure its likelihood to make the cover of *People* magazine.

Corey William Turrent.

It's 5:00 a.m. and Corey has spent most of the night walking back and forth between his father's house and Roseville Elementary like he's on an airport conveyor belt. This was his school. His neighborhood. Every crack in the sidewalk. Every mailbox number. Every teacher and person in the front office. He knows them all.

Corey's father is the principal.

And while Albert does not have multiple personalities, or dissociative identity as the disorder is called today, he's at least two men to Corey. There's the revered leader who fights for competitive wages and a new playground, followed by a state-of-the-art school building. And there's the man who did not call the ambulance when Corey was nearly beaten to death in the school bathroom.

That injury—three sneaker stomps to the head—was not something Corey recovered from physically or mentally. The damage to the frontal lobe was devastating.

There is a reason for most stupid things.

For the son, it began medically and became revenge.

For the father, it's pride and justification.

On the day of Corey's attack, Albert found himself caught between his love of success, which protects and provides for many children, and the protection of his own child. The sneaker stomper's father was and is the largest private donor in school history. His name: Preston Rose. The same Rose family who built the town and runs its government and employs Albert's father on its fiscal court.

Rather than hold his son to his chest, sob, and promise to make things right, Albert looked at his bandaged child and said, "Corey, why didn't you fight back?"

Corey thought about that question for years.

He is ready to fight back now.

* * *

Noah Bright is dead and Murray doesn't know there's an auction.

Albert Turrent is on his way to Bent Tree, currently stopped at a Buc-ee's to refuel and buy merch for his wife.

And Anna Ryder is a couple of hours away from agreeing to help with the auction.

The stars are aligning for violence.

CHAPTER 39

BEFORE LONG, NEARLY EVERYONE WE'VE met will wake up and be consumed with the same task: locating four crates of missiles.

But not Topher Collins. He will still be asleep while they scurry and worry and dither and dather. He found the stored missiles exactly where Noah's Post-it suggested they'd be. But it's another thing he found that had him dialing his mother at 2:30 a.m.

She answered immediately, like she'd been waiting. "You've located them?"

"Yeah."

"Where?" Lavinia asked when he didn't volunteer more information.

"In a stall in a barn on Starr Ryder's property."

He waited on Lavinia to tell him good job. To ooh and aah over his brilliance. She didn't. Not even a crumb of encouragement. He was slighted but moved on. "What do you want me to do with the products?"

"Bring them to me."

"Okay."

She's his mother, so she heard his hesitation. "What aren't you saying, Topher?"

"We have another problem." Air gurgled in the back of her throat—a sign of her anxiety—and he said, "Mom, I'm standing on the *Juneau.*"

"The what?" Had it been a decent hour of the day, she would have understood and screamed.

Topher said, "Oh, only the boat Waylon was supposed to sink so we don't go to jail for accessory to murder."

Lavinia dropped more than one f-bomb before she concluded, "He drove it to Starr's. Waylon looked right at me and said he'd taken care of it and then he drove it to the whore's house on the other side of the river. I'm going to kill him."

Topher explained the way the boat was wedged into the barn and how there was no easy way to destroy it without burning down the barn. Which would draw attention and questions they didn't need prior to the Royale and the auction.

"You're right. After the Royale, I think it's time to call in an anonymous tip to the Choir Girl tip line. Thirty years is a long time for a crime to go unsolved. Those poor families need closure," she said with mock sympathy.

"He'll point at us."

"Yes, he will, but you and I will be long gone by then." Then Lavinia explained the exit strategy she'd had in her back pocket since she started selling weapons.

"Are you saying we're out?" Topher asked.

"We are out."

CHAPTER 40

BENT TREE, KENTUCKY, IS A place of ones. One gas station. One lawyer. One main highway. One small restaurant named the BeeGee. One school. The only things that don't come in ones are churches and hair salons, and there are far too many of those to count. As such, there is only one undertaker in the entire county.

Leroy Elmes never would have made it in a town of twos. He is far too awkward to look at or speak to. Now, the little old ladies adore his bowl haircut and above-the-ankle suit pants, but young women take one look at the clothes and his pasty skin and think, *Pedophile*.

Leroy is neither adorable nor a pedophile. He is simply an undertaker without a lick of emotional intelligence who happens to play in a Beatles tribute band twice a year. Undoubtedly fantastic if you are dead and need facial reconstruction. But to the living, he hands a tissue and a bill in the same conversation without understanding why families wish they could stuff him in the casket with their loved ones.

Murray knows Leroy because everyone knows everyone, and Leroy knows Murray because a short, crooked-nosed rich kid is a hard thing to hide in a county of strapping, confident rednecks.

Year after year, Leroy and that damn bowl cut arrive at the Royale kickoff party and drink until he has an excuse for not being able to shoot straight the next morning. The thing that separates Leroy from the other handful of local attendees is Leroy never pays. Or rather, he is never charged. Gleb comps the undertaker a ticket to the events.

Murray once asked Noah why they didn't charge Leroy, and the man said Leroy's presence gave them more control of the narrative if something tragic happened during a hunt.

That explanation clicked for Murray. "Leroy handled the Choir Girls."

"Exactly," Noah says. "For you and me, he is an asswipe and an ass saver, eh?"

After that, Murray steered clear of Leroy.

When he phoned the day before, the undertaker bragged that he had a date and was unavailable until morning. Murray doubts this, but he's fine to wait. He falls asleep on the couch, exhausted from his all-nighter and grief, and doesn't even hear his girlfriend come home.

* * *

He awakes with the awareness that his father arrives soon. Murray has twenty-four more hours to prepare Anna for the Royale. At least she and Jack took care of the donkey. Jack sent him a text late last night.

JACK: Deed done. What time tomorrow?
MURRAY: You and Anna start at 8:30.

He doesn't want Jack and Anna spending much time together, but he needs Jack to show her the ropes. He'll be off with the dogs and the hunts the moment the Royale kicks off. Immediately after the

Royale, Murray plans to fire Anna for some made-up incompetence. The hardest part will be to find a way to blame Jack for her dismissal without Jack finding out, but he'll do it.

He has zero intention of losing Jack again.

*   *   *

Murray arrives at Mercy Regional and finds Leroy's hearse parked by the morgue door. He twists his hands around his steering wheel, dreading the task ahead. On cop shows, they always depict a scene in a morgue with a body on a sliding aluminum slab. Murray breaks out in a cold sweat at the thought. Noah's voice fills his head. *"Everybody dies, kid. As long as you didn't kill 'em, things are simple. When you kill them, things get complicated real fast."*

Murray gets out of the car and drags his heavy body forward. Thirty minutes later, when the paperwork is signed and the body loaded, Leroy attempts to make conversation. "You look a little green. How's your father?"

"On his way to Bent Tree. He should arrive tomorrow morning."

"I assume we'll wait until after the Royale for Noah's services?" Leroy asks.

Tears prick at Murray's eyes. "The staff will want to come, and I need them doing their jobs until Sunday departures. I also need to consult my father. Noah was family. Is that a problem?"

Leroy lifts his shoulders. "I can keep him on ice as long as you pay the freezer bill."

That's all of Leroy he can handle. Murray's brain zooms in and out. He says, "Take up the bill with Dad," in a clipped voice.

"I always do." And then Leroy scans Murray up and down and says, "He prepaid for you too, you know?"

That wakes Murray up. "I'm sorry. What?"

Leroy chuckles to himself. "Gleb paid for your arrangements the night you tried to—" Leroy draws a line across his neck with his index finger. "I guess that means I don't have to meet him here to pick you up one day. I'll pack you up in the stretch Mercedes and that'll be that." Leroy delivers this news with no emotion. There is no way to know if he's trying to piss off Murray or if this is his idea of conversation. He adds, "He said that would save him the flight."

Murray's blood shifts from frozen to boiling in a second. Without thought, he shoves Leroy into the side of the hearse. The breath whooshes from the skinny man's mouth on impact. Murray raises his fist. He has no words, just rage.

"Go ahead," Leroy says. "I'm happy to turn your anger into more freebies. Heck, this might even get me into the auction for free."

"What auction?" Murray demands.

"Oh. You don't know. Wow. Good luck with that now that Noah's dead."

Murray's anger is white-hot. It has been so long since he wanted to beat someone, genuinely beat someone until they looked like meat. He feels that rage, owns and contains it, and steps back, releasing Leroy. With a cold death stare, he says, "You're going to tell me everything you know about this auction."

"Why would I do that?" Leroy increases the distance between his body and Murray's clenched fist.

"Because if you don't, you'll end up needing your own one of these." Murray taps the hearse. He doesn't sound evil. Far from it. The disconnect of emotions is more threatening than the anger.

Leroy tells Murray everything he knows.

CHAPTER 41

WORLD COMPLETELY UPSIDE DOWN, OR as some might say, at long last, right side up, Murray makes two phone calls before he goes into the office. The first is to Gleb. *You are a mean son of a bitch*, he tells himself. *You tell your father what's what.* "Hey, Dad," he greets.

He is off to a bad start.

"I arrive tomorrow," Gleb answers, already sounding bored with the call. A bar scene buzzes in the background noise. Jukebox Nirvana. Beer rushing through the tap into a highball glass. Muffled orders of whiskey on the rocks. It's 8:15 a.m. in New York. Gleb says, "Today I will drink my grief away and tomorrow you'll be at the landing strip at 9:00 a.m. to meet me."

"Lavinia told you about Noah," Murray says.

"No. I expected to hear from you, but your little girlfriend texted first."

He ignores the guilt trip rather than apologizing, which shows improvement. "Leroy has the body. It's taken care of." Murray flips an egg in the pan. He has stopped by his house to eat and change clothes. He takes a deep breath. "Dad, Noah read me in on the auction. We'll be ready without him." Wow, he says that like he's reading from a script. Most likely because he practiced all the way home.

In truth, Murray understood the mechanics of the auction, but none of the logistics. Leroy hadn't known anything about where the weapons might be stored on the property. He'd only been able to give Murray an idea of the inventory from the invitation he received from the auction account. Somewhere there must be at least a hundred crates of automatic weapons. And if Murray is guessing correctly from the strangely coded advertisement Leroy showed him, there are missiles or bombs as well.

Gleb's laugh is low and Murray almost misses the pleasure of his father's satisfaction. "Solving problems instead of making them. I barely recognize you, Merkoul." His father takes a long, audible sip and then silence and then, "Are you calling to tell me how you convinced Lavinia to go along with selling my special crates?"

Unsure of how to play this, Murray must guess. "Topher's taking care of that part. He says she'll come around"—he gambles again to prove he is in the know—"on the missiles inventory. The money is too good."

"Ah," Gleb says, and Murray relaxes his shoulders. "You've seen the four crates I added. You must have been very impressive for Noah and Topher to include you."

Murray doesn't gloat. Not when he needs to bait his father for more information. "Dad, Noah said there was a breach somewhere on our end. Who do you trust the most after Noah? Lavinia and Topher or someone else?"

"Lavinia and Topher will not betray us. Gary Sr. could be a wild card."

The last time Murray laid eyes on Gary Portage Sr. the man was being spoon-fed orange Jell-O by his wife. They said it was a complication of long Covid, but Murray believes the cognitive damage is permanent. "He's not in the driver's seat anymore. Do you trust Gary Jr. and Foster?"

Gleb groans. "Everyone is aging and dying. Aging and dying. Blah, blah. Bring Lavinia to the airstrip when I arrive. We will go over the details together." Gleb skips over any mention of Gary Jr. and Foster and asks, "What else did Noah say about the breach? Is it related to the stolen missiles or the usual inventory?"

"Noah thought it was the missiles." Murray can't resist a touch of revenge. "Actually, he was investigating Leroy. I'll take care of him."

Gleb orders another whiskey sour from his bartender and rants about how hard it is to find good help.

Murray can't think of a way to get Gleb to tell him where Noah stored the missile crates without giving away that he lied about seeing them. Murray will have to locate them himself. Noah was forgetful. Somewhere in his office or home, there will be a note. He's sure of that. The man has more Post-it Notes than 3M.

"I'm sorry about Noah, Dad."

"Yes. Yes. Well, I'm proud of you at least."

Murray has waited his whole life to hear that phrase.

Of course it's undercut when Gleb adds, "Don't screw up or I'll cut off your dick and serve it to pigs."

Father and son laugh together.

But for very different reasons.

✳ ✳ ✳

Fathers cannot give up on their children without risking that one day their children will return the favor.

*　*　*

Murray's second call is to Anna. He checks his watch. It's 7:30 a.m. She isn't scheduled to start work for another hour. He doesn't care. Somewhere at the Lodges are four crates of missiles. He knows he can't cover that much real estate without help. Jack, Murray's normal go-to problem solver, might turn him in. He can't risk Saint Jack Augustine making an appearance on this one.

But Anna. Murray wagers he knows how to acquire her help. But that ask needs to come before she meets up with Jack.

Too late.

Jack has been at the farm since before sunrise.

In fact, when Anna receives Murray's call, she's sitting beside a barn that hides a boat that has the power to ruin his life. Jack is not ten feet away, sitting beside Molly, brushing her coat. Both of them are avoiding eye contact with the hole next to the barn door. Both of them think about what lies on the other side.

"Congratulations on the donkey," Murray says to Anna.

"Thanks. I'm heading in to work soon. I got the to-do list you sent for the day."

Murray cuts to the chase. "Anna Ryder, what is the worst thing you have ever done?"

"Excuse me?" Both the intimacy of the question and the use of her full name unnerve her.

"Are you a good person?" he asks.

"Mostly."

"If that's true, it should be easy to admit the worst thing you've ever done."

There's dead air while Anna thinks. Maybe about where this is leading. Maybe about the answer. Finally, she says, "Probably lying to my mother."

Excellent. He could work with a liar.

"And do you still love my friend Jack?" he asks. "Might I suggest this is not the time to lie."

"Is my previous relationship with Jack an HR problem?"

Jack's head snaps up but Anna waves him off. *"No big deal,"* she mouths to Jack, even though her heart is racing.

"HR?" Murray laughs at the idea. "No. No. It's not an HR problem. But I'll pay you a thousand dollars to answer me honestly. Do you still love my friend Jack?"

The line is quiet.

"Yes," she says. "I do."

"Good. Now, I'm going to tell you the worst things I've ever done and afterward make you a onetime offer."

"Okay," Anna says.

"I sent Theresa away and I paid her to write that letter to you. Jack found out he had a son when you showed him that letter." Murray hears the catch of Anna's breath. "So the deal is this: I'll trade you Jack's son's location for your silent and absolute cooperation this weekend. No one ever knows what we do. Not Jack. Or your best friend. Not your therapist or your priest. Your mother or your father. Not now. Not twenty years from now. No one. So tell me, Anna Ryder, do you want the job or would you like to spend the rest of your life ruining Jack's future?"

This is not the worst thing Murray has done, and it isn't even the worst thing he's done to Anna and Jack, but it's the first time he's admitted his own selfishness. He altered the course of their lives. This should have made him sad. It doesn't.

"Yes," Anna says. "I'll do whatever you need."

"Good. That's what I like to hear. First, you will convince Chester to be a guide for the Royale. Then you will go to Noah's office and search for anything that has the word *auction, crate,* or *missile.* I'm looking for the location of four deliveries that would have been made to Noah last Monday. Send me photos of whatever you find. If you don't find anything in Noah's office, go through his truck, his ATV, his house. Hell, the entire property. Get me a guide and find me those crates. You got it?"

Anna moves away from Jack and lowers her voice so he won't hear her ask, "What exactly am I supposed to tell Jack I'm doing?"

"That you're looking for Noah's phone. I have it so there's no danger you'll find it. And, Anna?"

She is so mad she can barely speak. Her "yes" is almost inaudible.

"Should I use additional threats to guarantee your allegiance or can I count on our arrangement?"

"You can count on me."

"Very good."

Audio File #1221

Beck, one day you're going to fall in love. Maybe with a woman. Maybe with a man. It'll feel like you bit clean through a jalapeño and ran your tongue over the seeds. Every taste bud comes alive and starts kicking. You can't turn it off no matter how hard you try. That's what it's like, except instead of it happening in your mouth, it happens in your soul. It's fresh and flavorful and burns like fire.

Yep, being in love is the best and worst thing that will ever happen to you.

I was in love. Unfortunately, not with your mother. Your mother and I happened at a party. Not a pretty origin story, I'm afraid. And I think me being in love with Anna is why your mother left without telling me about you. Or maybe she didn't know she was pregnant when she left that summer. But when she found out, Beck, she could have come back at any time and asked for help.

Instead, she waited years. Why did she do that?

I didn't deserve what your mother did to me, and neither did you.

I'm a good person, but sometimes I'm afraid that if I saw your mother again, I might kill her. Maybe we all have darkness in our hearts. "Where can my heart find refuge from itself?" Saint Augustine said.

I doubt he ever wanted to kill someone, and that's why he's a saint and I'm a sonless father.

I think I'll delete this recording.

CHAPTER 42

ANNA HANGS UP THE PHONE a different color. She is grayish-green and frozen in place, her eyes wide and stony like a deer's. Murray has that effect. Jack has been on the receiving end more than once and it isn't fun.

"His bark is worse than his bite," he tells Anna, hoping to comfort her. "He's always a bear when his father's coming to town."

Anna holds her same vacant expression. "I'm not so sure about that."

"Does he suspect Molly's alive?"

Anna grunts, hating the fact that she needs to lie to Jack. "No. He wants me to spend the day looking for Noah's phone. It's missing and there's information he needs for the Royale."

"So you're looking sad because you wanted to spend the day with me instead?" he jokes.

She did. But that's not why she shoves her phone into the pocket of her jeans so forcefully she rips the end of her nail to the quick. Anna wants to punch something. Or cry. Or drink.

More than anything she wants a time machine so she can go back and tell her younger self that Jack didn't abandon his son. *"His bark is worse than his bite."* No, Jack, his bite is infected.

Murray set up Jack.

Murray took his son from him.

Murray stole Jack from Anna.

And now Anna works for the bastard. And is supposed to do something illegal on his behalf? Molly saunters over and nudges Anna's arm. "I'm the jackass," she whispers to Molly, who brays her agreement.

If Anna tells Jack now, she fears he might drive over to Bent Tree and kill Murray. That solves nothing. She will tell him, but not until she has the location of Jack's son.

Murray screwed the wrong person.

* * *

They walk side by side in the dirt rut leading from the barn to the house. In order to avoid Jack inquiring more about her conversation with Murray, she says, "Tell me about how plastics are ruining the oceans or why I should be taking vitamins or what's happening with the ice caps these days. Spill the tea on your favorite soapbox."

Jack lowers his head and kicks at a weed. The dewy blades attach to his boots. "Actually, I haven't read the news in years."

This astounds her. When they were together, Jack woke early enough to drink three cups of coffee while he scrolled through various accounts.

"Yeah," he explains. "I hit a point where the pain of knowing was bigger than the hope of solving anything."

"So you stopped caring?" she asks, struggling to understand. Jack's activism is quintessential Jack. Or it was.

"'Course not. I decided to limit how much I brought into my sphere of caring."

"Okay." That makes sense. "And what's in your sphere now?"

"The dogs. My family. Declining the general state of loneliness at work."

"There's the Jack we all know and love."

Jack lifts the collar of his sweatshirt to his lips and hides his face before speaking into the fabric. "Did you know the surgeon general issued a warning about loneliness? It's killing people. Like, as much as smoking. That sounded crazy at first, but then I thought about my life and I started talking to people." He pokes his head out and looks at Anna with his huge, eager eyes. "It's been my own little experiment. I'd find a way to bring up loneliness and see what people said, and gosh, Ann, it's everywhere."

He dropped the vowel. Ann, not Anna. And it warms every part of her.

"What's the center of your loneliness?" she asks.

"A little boy who looks like me and the woman I planned to spend the rest of my life with."

CHAPTER 43

WHILE JACK AND ANNA ARE at the barn, two vehicles park beside the farmhouse.

The first to arrive was invited.

Starr answers the front door in a T-shirt and jogging pants that are several sizes too big. She immediately pulls Foster against her chest and squeezes the woman with so much warmth and love that they both sigh in deep satisfaction. "Come on in, darlin'."

While Anna was helping Jack with the donkey, Foster called Starr and explained, "I did not break our deal. Anna showed up at the Lodges and helped me rescue a raccoon." Which is how Starr got the tea on Jack and Anna and Anna's new employment situation.

The mother thinks of a million corrective things to say to her silly goose, but in the end she settles on thank you. There's only one reason her daughter would go to the Lodges and that's to pay for her treatments.

It's one thing to be known for actions.

It's another to be known in your intentions.

Starr can only hope her daughter will give her the same forgiveness when she realizes everything she's kept from her.

Foster picks up a glass duck figurine and spins it in her palm as she watches Starr try to lift a glass of water to lips. Sensing the tension, she guides the straw to Starr's lips and says, "I see you freaking out. Don't do it. Anna's going to be fine."

"If she starts to remember . . ."

Foster cuts Starr off, assures her. "She'll have us both. And Jack. I have a feeling he's not going anywhere either."

"You've got to get her away from the Lodges," Starr says.

Foster doesn't answer. Her instinct isn't to Bubble Wrap Anna. She wants the truth and has no illusions that the truth will make anyone safe. But she will protect Anna at all costs. There is no way to explain that to a mother, though. A mother will always believe no one can provide the same level of protection as she can.

And no one feels more guilty when that protection fails.

* * *

The two are in the living room waiting on Anna to return from the barn, watching an *NCIS* rerun they've both seen many times but never together, when the second knock comes. This time at the back door.

Starr can't exactly spring into action. Every movement is slow, even pushing the quilt off her lap and placing her phone on the table. Foster offers to send whoever it is away, but Starr snatches the cane Anna placed by the sofa and plods forward over the worn gray carpet. There is only one person who comes to the back door, and she finds her heart nearly in A-fib at the thought.

Through the little rainbow-shaped window of the oak door, she spots him. The massive, ruddy man, who is not her type and precisely her type. Her breath catches at the sight of him the way it always has. He is loaded down with more bags of groceries than she can count.

Wheezing, she opens the door, braces against the jamb, and says, "She called you, didn't she?" She tries to say these words without smiling, but her lips creep upward with every syllable.

"Something like that," Waylon says. He is also smiling. Until he notices the cane and his eyes tighten with worry.

✳ ✳ ✳

Starr's going to let him in.

Waylon can already tell. His heart pounds. Two parts anticipation, one part fear of that cane. The last time they were in close proximity she broke his nose.

"I come bearing gifts," he says and lifts the bags to eye level.

"I see that." She steps aside with the help of the cane and he can't help himself, he kisses her cheek on the way by. "That's awfully brazen of you," she says, but he felt her cheek press against his lips like she was returning the gesture.

He hopes she stays in this mood. Hard news is better on a full stomach. So he starts unloading groceries and setting out milk and biscuits. "How much bacon should I make?" he asks when he comes to the sack with all the breakfast meats.

"Well, Anna went for a walk with Jack . . . to the *barn*"—Starr lifts an eyebrow—"and Foster's in the living room. So, you know, just our usual crowd today." She snickers.

Waylon keeps his back to Starr and continues emptying the grocery sacks onto the counter and into the fridge to hide his reaction.

Foster's here. Jack's here. Anna's at the barn. Maybe the reckoning has started already.

"Breakfast for five instead of three. Got it," he says. "What's wrong with you, pretty girl? You got the flu?"

"Something like that." Starr collapses at the table without cussing him.

He should have known then that she doesn't have the flu, but it hasn't hit him yet. He's too clouded and distracted to think straight. He taps his heavy boots in rhythm with the song in his head, whisks eggs, and starts the bacon.

Starr coughs as the grease tickles her nose. "I won't be able to eat. But that smells divine."

"I'll make you," is Waylon's only reply.

She is a pale stick figure and her once-spotless house is a mess. The microwave's broken. He'll replace that as soon as the Royale ends. In a single scan of the room, he finds other projects to tackle. Warped linoleum. Mold eating the ceiling around the light fixture. The ice maker sounds like a beaver in a woodpile. He decides that if Starr kicks him out after she has recovered from whatever she has, he'll hire someone to do the work. Let her be mad. He doesn't care anymore. She's been mad for years.

He wants to fix something. He wants to fix her.

He wants to show up like a freakin' knight who has been away at war instead of a coward who returned years too late.

From the looks of her, she needs him as badly as he needs her.

CHAPTER 44

WAYLON'S TRUCK AND A LAND Rover are parked under their house.

Anna breaks into a run. Jack's on her heels, saying, "That's Foster's car," when she throws open the front door of the farmhouse and screams, "Mom!"

For a split second, she's afraid her mother is dead. That's the only logical reason for people to be in their house. And yet her mother, Waylon, and Foster Portage are seated in the living room chatting about the Indiana Fever. Waylon makes a little sense. Foster makes none. Unless she traced Anna's phone yesterday.

The woman is dressed in tight-fitting athleisure wear pants, an oversized army sweatshirt, and tennis shoes Anna has only seen on Instagram ads. Foster's hair is in a high ponytail and there's the remnant of a milk mustache on her upper lip. She offers Anna a warm, disarming smile that seems to say, *You'll understand in a minute.*

"Hey, silly goose." Her mother's voice is so weak it's barely there.

Anna cocks her head in exaggerated surprise and says, "Hey, crazy duck! You've got *company.*"

"Uninvited," Starr whispers, but she doesn't look upset. She glances past Anna at Jack. "You've got company too. Should I call the cops?" A pleasant grin stretches her lips to their widest point.

"Not this time," Anna says.

Jack sheepishly lifts his hand in greeting. "Hey, Starr."

They are officially in a twilight zone.

Awkward stares are exchanged. Everyone seems to be asking, *How did we get here?* No one volunteers an answer, so Waylon hefts a paper plate of bacon from the coffee table and says, "We were in the kitchen making breakfast, and this one"—he squeezes Starr's leg—"slid right out of the chair onto the floor."

"Do we need to meet with her doctor? Or call someone?" Foster asks.

"No," Anna says and plays back the woman's voice from Noah's closet. *"We need to meet about the product list before the auction."* "But could you all maybe give me a minute here alone with Mom?" She tugs a St. Louis Cardinals blanket off the back of the recliner and tucks it around Starr.

Foster, Waylon, and Jack ease toward the kitchen. Jack lingers at the doorway and uses hand gestures to see if he is allowed to stay. If she needs him.

Oh, how this simple kindness makes her want to tell Starr about the biggest screwup in her life. How she misjudged Jack. And wasted her life. And now she's mixed up in a game of chicken with missiles to make things right.

Anna kneels next to her mother and lifts a water cup and straw to her lips. Starr sips and her eyes close when she swallows. The effort seems enormous.

Starr says, "I am having a very strange dream about our favorite exes redeeming themselves." The joke, while appropriate, has none of Starr's typical fire. Cancer is a thousand small thefts of energy.

"Mom." Anna strokes Starr's hair and realizes it hasn't been washed in several days. How long has it been since Starr had the stamina to shower without help? Two weeks? A month? Anna refuses to break down. She keeps her voice low. "There are two things you need to know. I got a job at the Lodges—"

"Foster told me." Her mother's voice is sharp and weak. "Silly goose, you don't have to do that for me."

"Yes, I do, and it's a shit show we can talk about at another time. But now, we need to talk about the barn."

Starr's eyes flicker open. Her pupils dilate. "Don't go in the barn." She lowers her head onto the pillow and says, "It's private property."

These are frail whispers, but Waylon pokes his head into the living room like he heard.

"Anna," Waylon says. "Let her sleep."

There's a note of something in his voice. Warning? Fear? Protection? Whatever it is, it gives him away. Waylon knows about the barn's secrets. That means she has a second source to question when she finishes with Starr. She says, "Waylon, I need a minute," with just as much authority as he used and he leans back into the kitchen. She listens until she hears him pull out a chair at the table and scoot in before she lowers herself carefully onto the couch cushions. She rests a gentle palm on her mother's cheek. "I've been in the barn, Mom."

Tears eke to the corners of Starr's eyes and roll off her nose onto the couch between them. She presses her cheek against Anna's hand. A fever boils her skin. In a minute, Anna will get up, wet a washcloth, and drape it over her forehead. But not until she has said what she needs to say.

"I've seen inside the cruiser, and if you did something, I don't care. I love you and you're my mom and I know you and I'll always want to know you. No matter what. I don't know why that boat is hidden in our barn or why it's soaked in blood. I only need to know how to protect you the way I'm sure you've protected me."

The tears come harder then. The puddle on the couch grows. Neither woman speaks.

Mothers and daughters. What a conundrum of complicated emotions. It would be a wonderful thing if they could age into a relationship of equality. Just two women. But Anna suspects that even if she lives to be a hundred years old, she will filter her life through the lens of Starr Ryder's love and hope for her life. Girls are delivered into the world at birth, but rarely do they live outside the womb of their mother's approval.

There are moments, though. Glimpses of equality, usually brought on by trauma. This is one for Anna and Starr.

"Who hurt you, Mom?" Anna isn't sure why that's the question; it just is.

The tears grow larger. "Not me," she sobs.

"Who then?"

"Her name was Jenni."

Anna turns Jenni's name through her mental Rolodex and finds no one. "Say more. How did you meet? Who is she? A friend? Coworker? Lover?"

"The auction." Starr's words slur. The energy required to stay awake is extinguished by the effort of her deep emotions.

Anna massages her mother's cheek, hoping to coax more from her. "What auction?"

Starr shakes her head. "Don't ever talk about the auction, baby girl. We can't. But that's where I met Jenni."

"Okay. No auction. What am I supposed to do about the barn?"

"After I die, show Foster. She'll know."

"Mom."

Anna wants to say, *You aren't going to die. You're going to live forever. I need you. Why is Foster allowed to know things you won't tell me?* But she is her mother's daughter and chooses another path instead. She says, "Waylon wants to sleep with you," and her mother replies, "Well, of course he does. Who doesn't want this sexy body? Now, let me sleep, silly goose."

"Only if you promise to eat."

"I'll eat if you forgive that beautiful man of yours." Then Starr is asleep.

CHAPTER 45

ANNA DRAPES THE COLD WASHCLOTH over Starr's forehead and tries to decide what to make of her conversation with Starr. The name Jenni catches in the spiderweb of her mind. Who's Jenni? Better question: Who hurt Jenni? Did Jenni die on the cruiser? What's her tie to the auction? What's Starr's?

One thing solidifies. This auction Murray is pulling her into, for which Noah moved missiles and who knows what else, and which Foster and Jack are connected to in some way, has been going on for decades.

From the kitchen window, Anna watches Waylon, Foster, and Jack on the deck lean against the weathered railing. Foster points at something on the river and they all laugh easily together. As Anna opens the door, gunshots echo across from Bent Tree. Molly brays loudly from the barn and kicks her hooves in response. "That's probably my husband," Foster says. "He was heading out to get a few rounds in when I left."

Jack says, "The sky will sound like a war for a week. Every hunter who arrives will be getting more than a few rounds in. Poor Molly."

"Gary the raccoon seems to hate them too."

Waylon whistles. "You have a raccoon?"

Anna steps out on the porch and answers for Foster, "Yes, that's our meet-cute." Then she shrugs and says, "Mom's sleeping."

"That's not the flu, is it?" Waylon says.

Anna shakes her head. The wind kicks up and dried leaves blow and crackle across the decking boards like tumbleweeds. A bucket that once held an aloe plant turns over. Anna rights the pot and says, "Foster, join me in the kitchen? Jack, I'll meet you at your boat in five minutes. Waylon, if you'll stay here and walk me to the creek, I'll tell you about Mom's condition."

Dismissed for the second time in ten minutes, the guys head down the steps and Foster opens the door and gives an *after you* gesture.

Back inside, Anna discovers all the groceries and food Waylon has on the counter and the water boiling on the stove. Her stomach growls at the sight of the food. She went to bed hungry the night before.

Foster pours oats into two bowls, adds a generous helping of butter and cinnamon, and sets them on the table next to the bacon. "Tuck in," she says to Anna like Anna is the guest.

Anna experiences a sudden cascade of discomfort at the state of their house. Foster came from money. Meanwhile, Anna has been washing dishes with only water for the last two months because she doesn't want to spend ninety-nine cents on soap. Foster probably eats bagels and lox or eggs Benedict and freshly squeezed juice, not quick oats.

Not that it should matter. Why should she care what Foster thinks of her? She doesn't.

But of course, she does. Anna found the jeans she's wearing in the ten-cent bin at the Samaritan's Purse. Meanwhile, the soft fabric of Foster's sweatshirt makes Anna want to reach out and pet the sleeve. The disparity of Anna's life feels too obvious.

Too embarrassing.

Too on display.

Anna likes Foster. The woman is bold and confident. Like Starr. Anna doesn't know anyone her age with those qualities. Luxor isn't exactly a factory for confidence.

"I'm sorry I can't offer you coffee," she says, unable to hide her shame. "There's probably some in one of those bags, but I don't have time to make it before work."

"Oh, I hate hot drinks. I'm not Mormon. I just don't find them refreshing. And in case you're worried about all this"—she throws up a hand and spins her index finger in a circle to indicate the kitchen—"I grew up in thirteen different foster homes, which is how I got my name and my attitude. That should keep your eyeballs level with mine. There's no room for shame with me. I'm the first to say I can't stand a rich bitch, so I'd appreciate if you'd not look at me the way I look at my mother-in-law."

Anna nods appreciatively, surprised by Foster's background and her ability to read minds. "I want to know why you're here. Why my mother seems to trust you. Did you come with Waylon, or is there another reason?"

Foster works the corner edge of a new *People* magazine between her thumb and forefinger. There's a caginess to her energy, like she's deciding how much to trust Anna.

"Your mother called me."

That explains how Foster made it through the front gate and door. Anna slides the magazine across the table out of Foster's reach. "Why did she call *you*?"

"It's complicated."

"Uncomplicate it."

"I will if you will." Foster meets her gaze. "You're the one who called me yesterday. The person I mistook for Noah. I tracked your number, Anna. Phones are much easier to identify than they used to be."

Anna's gray eyes widen as she considers her options. Murray's threats are still fresh in her mind. She decides to fire back at Foster. "Whose side are you on?"

Foster's eyebrow arches in a wicked curve. "Man, I like you. If you swung toward girls, you'd be my type. Have you ever thought about that before? Like, who your type would be if you were a lesbian? I'm not hitting on you. I'm married. I'm only saying . . . you're ballsy and bold and that makes me feel less lonely, because I'm ballsy and bold too, and not many people like that about me. Or at least that's what my therapist says."

Anna doesn't blush and she's mildly flattered. She takes the compliment with a nod and drops some sarcasm at Foster. "Did you mean to say that if you were a lesbian, you'd hit on yourself?"

"Basically, yes," Foster says, and the two bust out with inappropriate laughter, which they stifle when they realize they might wake Starr.

"Okay," Anna says when she catches her breath. "You were explaining your side before you tried to change the subject."

"Was I?" Foster asks coyly.

"You were, and I don't have much time."

"Can you get me into Noah Bright's cabin?" Foster counters.

"What does that have to do with my mother calling you?"

Foster repeats the question, this time with more intensity.

Anna eats a few spoonfuls of oats. "I can, but I won't unless you give me a reason."

"Some time ago your mother made a decision to trust me. I'm hoping you'll do the same. To explain that to you, I need to poke around Noah's cabin."

"Is this for your podcast?" Anna asks.

"Yes, but let's also say I'm on a passion project."

"Okay. Now, are you hoping to sneak around Noah's for good or for bad?" Anna isn't sure she can trust Foster's answer, but she's hoping her face will tell her more than her words.

It's a good tactic.

Foster answers with total conviction. "For good. And now, how did you get my number?"

"Poking around Noah's cabin," Anna says, raising one eyebrow.

"Then you already know Noah was meeting with me to take down the auction?"

Anna arches one eyebrow, hoping Foster takes that as a yes. Inside, her stomach squirms. Foster Portage has a plan to stop Murray.

"Excellent," Foster says, a gleam in her eyes.

Anna agrees to meet Foster at Noah's later. "Don't bring Jack," is the last thing Foster says.

CHAPTER 46

ANNA'S BRAIN BURNS WITH DISCOVERIES.

Years ago Starr got caught up in something illegal at the Lodges. Anna's not sure this is a problem she can fix, and she's not used to running into barriers she can't overcome. Luxor might not teach you advanced math, but there's certainly an education in resourcefulness and resilience.

Broken heart? Move on. Students in trouble? Find them options. No money? Work harder. Get a new job. Go. Do. Go. Do. Always a solution.

But this. This is a jigsaw puzzle with pieces sprinkled across a large field. Rather than focus on everything she doesn't know, she fixates on the two largest pieces in her hand.

A past crime on a boat.

A future weapons auction.

Her mother is connected to them through a woman named Jenni? She'll start her search with a single name. And she'll make Foster tell her more at Noah's.

CHAPTER 47

LAVINIA COLLINS IS GETTING A pedicure. She doesn't understand Southern women who don't have a foot-care routine. Not when the swampy heat makes it impossible to wear closed-toe shoes for eight months of the year.

She admits varicose veins present a challenge. Is she calling more attention to her aging legs and their unsightly trails by highlighting her toes in her favorite fall color, Static Nails Liquid Glass Lacquer in Bordeaux? She doesn't know because (a) no one would dare tell her, and (b) if she missed her weekly appointment with Caroline, the aesthetician will check the paper for Lavinia's obituary.

Today was supposed to be a morning of pampering: a Tervis full of champagne and orange juice and her phone playing meditation music recommended by one of her favorite podcasters, maybe even a pop into Talbots for a new blouse.

Things are not going according to plan. Not since the phone call from Topher in the middle of the night. She's been awake since, working on a solid exit strategy. There is no other choice. Not with the *Juneau* still in existence. Lavinia bites into her knuckle until there are teeth marks.

She has never trusted Waylon in the same way she trusts Topher—that much is already evident from her succession plan—but she never imagined this level of betrayal. And for what . . . that whore from Luxor? Starr Ryder is a plague. And once again, she and her daughter are endangering Lavinia's legacy.

Lavinia hadn't planned on selling guns for a living; she'd thought Avon or Mary Kay, but it turned out she didn't have the skin or patience to host parties for women. If she wanted childish behavior, she would have had more children. Two was at least one too many, but Martin had been too drunk to put on his condom and she ended up with a second baby less than one year after the first. At least they were boys. She initially called Waylon her Irish blessing, but he certainly hadn't blessed her waistline or her vehicle choices. One kid was car territory. Two put you in a minivan for fifteen years.

Lavinia and her late husband were in the gun-trafficking business longer than they've owned Little Lodge. Their first auction, down on the Texas border, was how they made a down payment on the waterfront property in Bent Tree. That was before the Orlovs and Portages built lodges and the property transformed into a destination. The Lodges came together like a small theme park, one Southern attraction at a time. Tracts of land were added every year as previous surrounding land owners died or caved to the pressure.

Lavinia believes deeply in the work. She participates in capitalism and freedom. Protecting yourself is a basic human right.

She uses the yearly Royale as a cover event to host one of the largest weapons auctions in the world. You have to have three things to hunt: land, a weapon, and the Second Amendment. Lavinia gathers all three essentials and caters to everyone who cares about them.

The model is simple. Her remote team acquires—steals and

buys—weapons from Central and South America up the rivers on barges, and Lavinia sells them to a bunch of folks who fit one of two categories: those who can't legally buy a weapon and those who don't want the government to know how many weapons they buy. Lavinia loves the money, but it isn't her only objective. She once let an older woman in Bent Tree trade four thousand canned products and a quarter of cow for a particularly lethal handgun.

Gleb and Noah started as buyers. They had so many ties and connections they were partners by the third year. Business boomed. And there were no blips until Gleb got them all tied up in the Choir Girls hoopla. It has taken Lavinia decades to rebuild trust in the industry after that disaster. And now, with Waylon's unbelievably stupid choice, the fiasco is potentially right back in her lap. There are Collins family fingerprints all over that cruiser.

That said, she's not sure what to make of the fact that Waylon has stored the *Juneau* for more than twenty years—gosh, it has actually been thirty—and he and Starr never used it against anyone. Is there a chance he kept the boat for another reason? Does Starr even know it is there? Is Lavinia worried over nothing?

She thinks of his earlier phone call. His offer to help with the auction crates. That could have been a genuine offer to get back in her good graces, or he might be building evidence against her and Gleb about those stupid missiles.

This is all very untidy, and Lavinia is no longer a spring chicken. The business doesn't excite her the way it did when her husband was alive. When they were young and passionate about their rights. You couldn't walk fifty feet on their property without hitting a Don't Tread on Me flag. Oh, those were the days. Her eyes mist at the memory.

"Is this hurting you, sweetheart?" the woman massaging her toes asks when she sees Lavinia's tears.

"Not at all. This is just a terrible wine selection," she says of the glass in her hand.

The woman who is not Caroline rolls her eyes and says, "It was the $8.99 bottle at Big Jim's."

Lavinia goes back to her retirement thoughts. Yes, when she adds up the facts—Noah's death plus the *Juneau's* existence plus Waylon's betrayal plus stolen missiles—there is no other choice. If only one of those conditions existed, Lavinia could handle things. But four anomalies signal disaster.

Much like her younger son, she feels things coming to a head.

*　　*　　*

The woman scrubbing Lavinia's heels warns her the next part might tickle. She has a cheese grater in her hand. Lavinia hasn't been able to feel her heels in years. "Good luck, darling," she tells the woman and reaches for her phone. She dials Topher.

"Yep," he says, his typical greeting.

"The nosy guide. How did that play out?"

"Handled," he says and takes a loud slurp from his cup. He has always been a noisy eater.

"You're sure?"

"Yep."

"And you've changed the location of the other item from Luxor to Bent Tree?"

"Yep. I even hid one crate of *inventory* at Murray's in case we need more compliance from the little bastard."

"Very good," she says. "So, tomorrow night, Portage Lodge, cabin 20, at 10:00 p.m. for the auction guests?"

"Yep. Right after kickoff ends. Like usual."

The Royale kickoff always begins with a shrimp boil on the lawn. A rowdy, joyful occasion. There's more testosterone at that party than in any UFC fight. Male bonding and boasting. She sighs when she remembers they always break at least one table.

By nine, those with auction invitations will start to slip away toward their various rooms, claiming they want to get an early bedtime since the first Royale hunts start at 4:30 a.m. the next day. They'll show up at cabin 20 for the main event of the evening, ready to raise their little white shotgun-shaped paddles.

"The slides are ready?" She usually handles the slides herself.

"Yep."

Two things have made the auction a success. The presentation and the photos. They made a rule early on that the auction and the products would never be in the same place. During the auction, buyers are shown photographs. Money is then transferred on delivery and delivery is staggered throughout the year. When a delivery is made, a photograph is taken of the purchaser holding the product. They are then asked to sign the photo with the following phrase, "I own this such and such." Copies are made and stored in various deposit boxes spread across the South. In her opinion, they are ridiculously hard to catch because they are careful and everyone has equal incentive to keep their mouth shut.

Lavinia's feet are wrapped in warm towels. She loves this part of the pedicure, but it never lasts long enough. "Then you don't need anything from me?" she says to Topher, relaxing into the chair with her iPhone. She needs to book private flights and activate her household staff in Cuba to prepare for their arrival on the day after next.

"Nope." Her son slurps his drink again. "Not unless that body floats. Okay, I'm gonna take a nap."

Lavinia eyes bulge with annoyance. Even if there's money left on the table, her sons are clearly too stupid for her to stay in the biz. She will never wear prison orange, and she can't imagine giving up her pillow. Can you pay a chiropractor to come to a prison?

Lavinia doesn't want to find out.

CHAPTER 48

FOSTER LEAVES THE FARMHOUSE WITHOUT saying goodbye to the guys.

Anna and Jack are supposed to be at Stockton Lodge at 8:30 a.m. to supervise the table setup for the kickoff lawn party the following day and then go see about hiring the guide Murray wants. Chester something.

Jack jogs ahead to see Molly. He isn't saying it out loud, but he's growing antsier by the second about them being late to meet Murray.

Anna promised her time with Waylon will be fast, and she hopes it is. They walk side by side. Waylon feels shorter, but of course he isn't. Anna's merely taller. Their strides match each other now. Maybe that's what growing up gets you: the ability to look down on the people who used to carry you to bed.

"Thank you for bringing food." Her eyes suddenly feel soggy at the edges. "I wasn't sure how I was going to feed her."

To her surprise, Waylon has tears in his eyes too. "How bad is it?" His voice quivers.

"The worst," she says, but of course he already knows.

That's how it is when someone's face was once your favorite face on the planet.

Anna explains Starr's condition, the money situation, Anna's dismissal from Luxor High, and the hard drive to the other side of the river yesterday morning. It feels good to let loose of the story. When she reaches her introduction to Foster and Gary the raccoon and how Murray subsequently hired Anna to be Noah, Waylon stops in the middle of the corn row, puts his hands on his hips, bends double, and laughs. "Only you." He straightens, the amusement fading, and looks her straight in the eyes. "I'm going to take care of your momma so you can quit."

"Oh, Waylon, we both know you can't do that."

"I'm leaving the family business. And I think you, or you *and* Jack"—Waylon meets her gaze briefly with a flash of happiness—"should too."

"You're leaving for real?"

Waylon looks back in the direction of the farmhouse and shoves his hands into his pockets. He looks lost and found at the same time.

"I'm out," he says. "I'm righting my wrongs and starting over with your momma. I've got enough money saved to take care of us. I've put up with too much from my family and I'm done."

Anna thinks her mother would enjoy overhearing this conversation. She suspects that in the lower chambers of Starr's heart, she never gave up on Waylon. He hurt her, but he also loved her fully. And that is a hell of a thing.

The kids aren't usually the ones dishing out "I'm proud of you" to the adults, but Anna does. And then she adds, "'Bout damn time."

"I have your blessing?"

She snorts. "Uh, Starr Ryder owns her own blessings. If you convince her, you've convinced me."

Waylon reaches for Anna. His hands are monstrous on her lean shoulders but gentle as he squeezes her. They stand like a coach and player for long seconds, eyes eating into each other. The only thing larger than Waylon's wide baby blues is his belt buckle. She thinks he'll say something about Starr's sickness. Instead, he says, "The Orlovs, my family, hell, the Royale itself, it's no place for you. I'm not your father, Anna, and you're a grown-ass woman, but please don't go back there."

"I can't leave yet."

"You started like three hours ago. You owe them zilch."

"Waylon," she protests and breaks his contact by stepping decisively backward. The corn is at her back, tickling the skin beneath her sweatshirt. How much should she, can she, tell him? Is everyone at the Lodges in on the auction? If so, would exposing Murray take Waylon away from her mother again? "I just can't," she finally manages to say.

"How about I pay you whatever Murray said he would?"

"It's not that," Anna says. "I mean, it is, but it's not. I'm righting my own wrongs."

"Fine. Do it on this side of the river."

"That might be the first time in history someone from Bent Tree said Luxor was the solution."

"Dammit, Anna, don't make jokes. I'm telling you Gleb's dangerous and you need to stay away from him. And I don't know what Foster's playing at, but you're all going to get burned if you take on Gleb."

"Gleb? You mean Murray's dad?"

"Yeah. Gleb and Noah structured the entire hospitality business of the Royale and the Lodges. Half of what they do isn't legitimate. You gotta get out."

Waylon's fists clench, his eyes bulge, his jaw flexes. Anna takes another step back and her feet sink through the tilled earth between the cornrows. A mouse crawls out of a nearby hole and scampers away. She says, "I understand that. And as soon as the Royale ends, I'm out."

Waylon wiggles in his navy fleece Royale logo vest like he aims to take it off. Instead, he slips his arm out of his sleeve, then his side holster, and drops a small pistol in her hand. "If you won't quit, take this. I don't want you around Gleb without a weapon."

Anna shoves the gun at him. "I'm not taking that. Gleb doesn't know me from Adam."

Molly hee-haws and Waylon and Anna turn momentarily toward the animal. If Waylon has thoughts on Molly's presence, he doesn't share them. Anna watches his eyes track from the donkey to the barn; his chin lifts as he looks to the open loft door and then lowers his gaze to the hole near the ground that Jack kicked out with his foot.

"That's not true." He reholsters the gun. "He'll know you the moment he sees you."

She sighs dramatically.

Much later, when she looks back on this conversation, she'll be embarrassed about that sigh. How stupid it was. She'll wonder what would have happened if she'd just taken the gun.

Waylon slaps his hands together and holds them in the prayer position. "Anna, you look identical to your mother. And trust me, he knows her."

"How?"

"That's for her to say. But listen, everything in that barn over there goes back to Gleb Orlov."

"How do you know?"

"Because." He cocks his head decisively to the side, like he's deciding on something. "I'm the one who carried you off that boat covered in blood. You want to know more"—he holds out his phone—"call Murray and quit."

She fires back, "How about I call the police instead?"

He doesn't seem alarmed or threatened. "The police will find out plenty, I'm sure, but that will hurt your mother and they won't be able to answer the questions that will keep you up at night. I can do that. And I will do that, but I can't do it if you're dead. You've got to walk away from the Orlovs before the Royale. Understand?"

Jack appears, his face beet red from running up from the creek. "Anna, Murray's losing his shit. We need to go. Sorry, Waylon," he says.

Waylon's phone is still outstretched. He's waiting on Anna's answer.

She gives him the one he least expects.

She walks away.

After all, she is her mother's daughter. He's lucky she didn't break his nose.

CHAPTER 49

LYING CONSTIPATES JACK'S BRAIN, WHICH usually means a lie isn't worth the headache.

His grandpa used to say, "Let your yes be yes and your no be no. Like the Good Book says." That phrase made a lasting impression on young Jack. Grandpa also told Jack that he talked so much he could start an argument in an empty house.

Which made no impression at all.

In the ten minutes it takes Anna and Jack to cross the river, Jack makes up his mind to lie anyway.

He walks into Murray's den-like office and throws himself on a leather ottoman. Dog hair poofs through the air when he lands, and then he sees Pippa wearing the tarantula costume and he bellows, "Ah, yeah," like he's an excited child.

Murray throws the pup into the air until they are nose to nose. "Daddy's little spider. Nice touch," he tells Jack.

"Hey, it's Gleb week. I gotta do something to take your mind off things."

"Like these?" Murray peels open an Amazon box and lifts the lid. He can't help but grin at the contents.

Jack already knows what's in there. One hundred yellow tennis balls. His only question is, should he turn the box upside down to make Murray forget his freak-out, or will that agitate him by losing more time? Jack opts to leave the box upright and steals the coffee cup off Murray's desk, takes a long sip, and proudly announces, "Man, we rolled through things yesterday. The donkey. Anna's tour of the Lodges. The freezers. They're all clean except for the Stockton. You want us to stick with the lawn party setup this morning?"

Jack worries the truth is written on his face and his oldest friend will see right through him. They've done none of these things.

"I'd like my coffee back," Murray says as he collapses into his chair with Pippa. "Would you like your own cup?"

Jack shakes his head. "No, thank you. That gasoline you drink is awful."

Anna refuses a coffee offer too.

She hasn't spoken since they left the farm. He's not sure if it was the boat ride or something Waylon told her or whatever Murray called about earlier, but Anna is rattled. More rattled even than she looked last night after they discovered the cruiser in the barn.

Ten years ago, Jack would have pressed her. *Is it your mother? Waylon? The blood in the barn? What are you not telling me?* Silence scares him and sets his empathy on fire. It's like his brain screams, *Fix. Fix. Fix.*

These days, silence still scares him, but taking from Anna scares him more. He wants conversation, not coercion. He wants her to give rather than for him to take. Love is patience and he chooses love.

"Impressive work on the list," Murray says. "We might be on time after all."

"We're going to crush this," Jack says a little too enthusiastically.

Murray squints. "You definitely don't need coffee."

"Uh, you look like you should drink another three pots," Jack says. The circles under Murray's eyes have darkened since yesterday. There's an unnatural part to Murray's hair and an uncomfortable amount of grease. That means Murray is stressed. He can't keep his hands out of his red silk when he's anxious. "When was the last time you slept?"

"I tried last night, but . . . Noah," Murray says and shifts in his chair. This disturbance wakes the spaniel, but only long enough for her to paw at one of the costume spider legs. Then she slides her head into the crook of Murray's arm. "Oh, to be a dog," Murray says absently and scrubs the pup's head.

"I'm really sorry about Noah," Jack says.

Murray affixes his eyes on Anna. She stands across the room at the doorway, her tall, lanky body leaning against the wooden frame, her head bent toward the floor, her eyes vacant. Murray says, "Bad mood, Anna Ryder?"

Jack has no idea why Murray uses her full name, but he answers for her. "That's my fault. We skipped breakfast."

"Well, get your girlfriend some food and then get me a guide. The lawn party should be a breeze."

Jack ignores the girlfriend comment and says, "Which lodge is Chester supposed to guide for?"

"Portage."

Jack and Murray roll their eyes in unison.

"He'll have Gary Sr. with him," Jack says aloud for Anna's benefit.

Murray leans back in the screeching chair, tugging Pippa higher onto his chest. The pup stretches against him and licks his neck as he says in his high-pitched fake voice, "And you know, that man can't find rubber ducks at the carnival, can he, Pippa girl?"

Pippa snuggles and wags. Jack avoids snickering along with Murray even though it is a well-documented joke that Gary Portage Sr. is the worst hunter of the Royale. And that was true long before his mind went. If he didn't own a lodge, he'd never be allowed to hunt here. His son, on the other hand? Junior once hit a bumblebee at a hundred yards. A damn fine marksman.

Jack asks, "Anything else we should know? Anything that might sway old Chester to say yes?" Knowing a dollar amount would tell him how much leverage he had to make the hire.

Instead, Murray says, "Oh yeah. He's the one who found those women years ago."

"Which women?"

"You know, the dead ones. The ones on Mayfield Creek."

CHAPTER 50

MURRAY'S A FIRST-CLASS WEASEL.

Anna spotted his weaseldom the day before and ignored it for the money. What sort of man tells the woman he's hiring to be perfect to be paid for her work?

She hates herself for saying yes to Murray and yet, if she hadn't, she wouldn't have the opportunity to find Jack's son. Giving her ex-fiancé back the last five years is impossible. Giving him a future with his little boy isn't. She'd been stubborn, stupid, and untrusting when Jack said he had no idea what Theresa was talking about in that letter, and he'd been telling the truth. The reckoning consumes her.

Fixing this is worth whatever risk Waylon is trying to protect her from.

In Murray's office, she watches the men speak to each other like she's standing on a hillside peering down at an arena. Murray has showered and shaved and lacquered himself in Old Spice. *Skeevy* is the first word in her head.

Jack is all Jack. Tennis balls and dog Halloween costumes.

It took everything she had to keep her mouth shut as Jack lied through his teeth about their accomplishments. Even as he lied, she saw how much he loves Murray. They have their own rhythm, their own sparks.

Chemistry isn't always packaged with morality. An earnest kid and a narcissist can get swirled together like milk and coffee. Anna will return to this truth many times in the future. She will stare at her Jack and know that he is also Murray's Jack.

That one tiny part of him will confound her. It will also make her question herself. What strange magnetic forces of her heart are attracting her opposites?

For now, she stands silently in the office. Aware and jealous.

Rage oozes out her pores. Murray has done so much irreparable damage to his best friend, and Jack has no idea the short man's smug glances and use of Anna's full name mean he's toying with her. Testing her. Daring her to say something.

Murray knows she won't. And not only because she wants his son's address, but because she left Jack and he stayed. It's her guilt that keeps her from screaming, *Jack's mine, and I'm his, and you can't take anything else from us, you inconsequential little fuck!*

There are rational thoughts too.

Like why would Murray do this to Jack? Is there more to the story? Is the child even Jack's? Or was that a lie too? There is also a chance Murray is a psychopath. Waylon implied that Murray's father killed the Choir Girls. Is there "like father like son" violence in his blood?

The notion catches in her throat.

This is every bit as dangerous as Waylon claimed.

As she's considering this, she realizes Jack isn't talking anymore and Murray's ushering him past her into the hallway. She follows and Murray steps between her and Jack. "She'll be right out and you two can use all your persuasive talents on Chester James," Murray tells

Jack as he closes the door. Loud enough for Jack to hear, he adds, "I need her to fill out paperwork for the direct deposit."

That part turns out to be true.

But there's more.

He raises his arms—she assumes to take her wrists, but instead he holds his palms out in an innocent gesture. He speaks in quick and concise phrases. "You're mad at what I've done. At what I'm asking you to do. I don't blame you. If I knew only what you know, I'd be furious with me too. But stop and question if there's a chance I'm protecting him. Look at us. We're brothers. I was here before you got here. I'll be here after you're gone. I was here after you left." He punctuates the final *you*. "I'm not trying to hurt him."

Her eyebrow arches. "Jack doesn't need protecting," she hisses. "And hiding his son from him definitely hurts him."

"I don't expect you to understand how dangerous the Lodges is, but I can tell you this: it's no place for a kid to grow up. I'm trying to get Jack out of that danger without my father hurting him or someone he loves. Which is why, Anna, I need your help."

Anna's not ready to accept this answer. She fires back, "If you're such a good Samaritan, why give me the address in exchange for information about the auction?"

"Oh, I don't know . . . Because I don't want to go to prison. I can't search this property by myself and I can't ask Jack to help me, so, yeah, I'm using you and no, I don't feel bad about it. But I am not hurting Jack or his son; I'm saving his fucking life and don't you ever question that again. We need to find four crates of missiles or my father will start killing people again."

Murray's argument catches Anna off guard. It has a logic that is not at all psychopathic. In fact, it sounds more like something her mother might say if Anna was in danger. That makes it ever so much harder to know what to do next. "You honestly believe Jack is mixed up in your father's auction?"

"I hope not. But someone around here is. And my father is throwing Jack's name around. You get me that information and I'll not only give you your precious address, I'll make sure Jack's name is nowhere near this. Double-cross me and I'll take you down with Gleb. Deal?"

"That's not a deal; that's a bribe."

Murray lifts one shoulder in a tiny shrug. "Doesn't matter. You'll do it."

"Okay," she says, and leaves him smiling like the Cheshire cat.

Audio File #1387

Beck, it occurred to me that you might google Bent Tree, Kentucky, and stumble onto our darkest story. I feel like it's my job to tell you that Bent Tree is perfectly safe now. Whoever killed the Choir Girls isn't local. The murder is linked to another case in Texas. You'll see as you keep googling. I don't want you to worry about visiting me. I promise I won't let anything happen to you. Bent Tree is not a dark place to grow up.

That morning was dark, though. If you were to get interested in the case—so many people do—I should tell you that I was a kid when it happened. The morning the bodies were discovered, my granddad and I were on Mayfield Creek too. That's the name of the beach where the murderer staged the bodies.

Granddad ran one of the reporting stations for hunters participating in a competition. It was four to five miles inland. When he motored out that morning from our dock, I went along like a shadow. I'm guessing we boated by the scene around 4:55 and neither of us heard or saw anything.

The police were nice when they talked to us. Never treated us like criminals. It wasn't like you see on television. They asked questions and then made sure we didn't want to talk to the pastor of our church. I probably should have. I had nightmares for months. Not because

I saw anything on the beach. I didn't see a thing. But a couple of years later, an older kid at school showed me a picture and I couldn't get those dead women out of my head.

Your brain plays tricks on you about stuff like this. I've been to Mayfield Creek a lot since then and I've seen those stories on the internet, so sometimes I'll picture the scene like I was there.

I wasn't. Being on the water always made me sleepy and it was stupid early. I tried to tell the cop there was a white cruiser on the water, but Granddad told me I fell asleep the moment I got in his boat and I dreamed the thing up. The cop wrote that down, and every now and then you'll see a reference to it online. *The Unknown Cruiser.* I feel guilty over that.

Granddad and I never talked about that morning as I grew up. A day or two before he passed, they pumped him full of morphine to reduce his pain and he babbled about saving me from a choir. He was very distressed. It took me several hours to piece together that he was talking about that terrible morning on Mayfield Creek.

I kept saying, "Granddad, we're fine. No one hurt me that day." Eventually the nurse came in and changed his dosage and he settled down. I don't think he ever stopped feeling guilty that I was close to a murderer. Our last conversation was more peaceful. He moved on from Mayfield Creek to our other favorite topic: dogs. In his very last moment on the earth, a huge smile lit his face, and he gave my hand a little squeeze and said, "Juno."

That was his dog's name. She was a beautiful stark-white Pyrenees with the sweetest face. One failure of this audio journal is there are no images for you to see. If there were, I'd paste a hundred dog images here.

My best advice, if you google Bent Tree and get an eyeful of crime photos, is to follow Granddad's example. Pull up another window on your browser and search for photos of Pyrenees puppies. Dogs can't solve murders, but they sure will fill your mind up with love.

CHAPTER 51

PRIOR TO FINDING THE BODIES, Chester James met one of the Choir Girls.

Not that he realized it at a helpful time for the investigation.

This would be a very different telling if he had.

* * *

Chester is one of those rare guys whose integrity and transparency have thousands of witnesses. People love him. And rightly so.

When the Rolland County Sheriff's Department recorded Chester's testimony, he swore to tell the truth, and he kept his promise. He shared every godforsaken detail from the shrill alarm until he beached his boat on Mayfield Creek.

Sheriff Bailor asked, "And did you recognize anyone?"

Chester's emphatic and horrified "No" convinced everyone listening. He explained seeing the blood and forcing himself to check each woman for a pulse. He told the officer how he held his breath and looked away as he touched their cold necks. The nine faces were completely blank in his memory.

Imagine you glanced at a church choir on Sunday morning. Six hours later, would you know who was standing in the second row, three people from the end? Or would you only remember they all had on robes?

He came across as exactly what he was: a victim.

One of the federal guys recommended a therapist and Chester went. That helped. He started sleeping through the night again. Eating. Talking. As long as he avoided the media, he healed. Unfortunately, when new officers joined the case, they were sure he'd remember something new. He never did. Instead, they gave him details he never wanted to know.

Their names.

Their histories.

Their photographs.

He was forced to grieve their faces.

Each time Chester dutifully agreed to help. He'd cry, and when he could form words, he'd say, "I'm sorry. I want to help, but I don't know anything new."

Genevieve Lockwood was one of the nine names.

That detail passed right under Chester's nose because by the time Chester met Genevieve, she had shortened her name to Jenni. And by the time Jenni appeared in the photograph, she looked different enough that Chester didn't recognize her as the woman he gave his virginity to in a dark bathroom in a Luxor bar.

*   *   *

Jenni Lockwood came from Texas to work in Bent Tree. She had a seasonal job cleaning at the Lodges. The money was good. The job brainless. Bleaching toilets and washing sheets beat the prospect of living with her strict parents after graduation.

Plus, the Lodges paid the workers in cash and the hunters sometimes paid them in jewelry their wives didn't wear anymore. The girls on the crew griped about this, but mostly they drank cheap wine and laughed in their bunk room about the stupidity of men. Their goal was to move between Bent Tree and Gulf Shores and never pay taxes for anything.

The first year they worked at the Lodges, Jenni and the girls piled into cars and drove across the bridge to Luxor to blow off steam. One of the locals told them about a hole-in-the-wall honky-tonk called Wild Willies. Turned out, the dive bar was rough and ready. And charming, if you didn't mind a layer of dust on the 1970s beadboard trim. The woman at the door didn't check their IDs, and Jenni had the best pizza she'd ever put in her mouth.

It was there, on a dark dance floor, that Jenni met a hunter named Chester.

Her life changed forever. What little of it there was left.

* * *

Chester's grandmother taught him to line dance in her kitchen. First she'd make him wash the dishes, then they'd turn on one of the Georges and boot scoot until *Dateline* came on. Those were some of his fondest memories.

After she died, Chester found the closest line dancing joint. A dark little place in Luxor with cheap beer, George Strait classics, and pizza. A perfect Thursday night. He thought he'd only go once. Drink a beer, tip his hat to his grandmother's memory, and that would be that.

He saw her from across the room.

Jenni did not dress like his grandmother. Didn't dance like her either. Her round cheeks hung clear out of cutoff jeans and they flexed perfectly as she grapevined and do-si-doed. She wore bright red cowboy boots that hit halfway up her calves. Legs for days. She was tan with thin, chiseled arms that suggested she worked hard, though they never talked about her work. Her face was heart-shaped and she wore sunglasses to hold back her hair. Chester loved the way her long, brown hair curled at the nape of her neck when she was sweaty from dancing.

By the end of the season, they'd torn up the dance floor and accidentally ripped one of the towel bars off the wall in the single-seater bathroom. Twice. The manager made a joke about it that made Chester blush.

She was his first sexual experience.

He was her first example of true kindness.

Neither of them regretted a thing.

They had one fantastic summer and parted ways without a good-bye. One Thursday evening she didn't show up on the dance floor.

Chester never saw Jenni again.

Not until a podcaster named Foster Portage arrived at his Marsh Lake home and laid nine photos on his marble-top bar.

"Chester, I've got a bartender from Wild Willies who says you were a Thursday-night regular back in the day. And as luck would have it, look at this." She slapped down a tenth photo. "That looks like you and Genevieve to me."

Foster's ace was a low-quality image of Chester and Jenni perched on barstools, toasting drinks, Jenni's lips on Chester's cheek. Foster lit into Chester with accusatory sarcasm. "Gosh, my copy of the police report doesn't mention a word about you knowing one of the victims. Why is that? Seems like if you were in a relationship with one of the Choir Girls and you found the bodies, that was relevant testimony. Anything you want to say?"

Chester, ever polite, held up his hand to indicate he needed a minute and then walked casually to the sink and threw up.

*　*　*

If you measured the grin on Chester's face in that photograph of Foster's, you might guess the photo was taken the night he and Jenni broke the towel bar at Wild Willies. You'd be right.

It was also the night he'd gotten her pregnant.

And although Jenni and her child returned for three more summers to Bent Tree, she never breathed a word to Chester. Never returned to the bar in Luxor. She thought she saw him once, riding a four-wheeler across a field with a rifle across his lap, but that was as close as they came to bumping into each other. Bent Tree was small, but there were people in the county who stayed in their pockets of land and rarely left. That was Chester.

You might ask why a woman would do such a thing—keep a baby from his father.

And the truth is, Jenni wasn't thinking about Chester one bit. He was a guy in a bar who could line dance. She liked her life. Craved her freedom. Loved the money she made drifting here and there. Sharing her kid with a man who planned to stay in Bent Tree felt far too confining. Her dream sounded like two Ping-Pong balls bouncing among Texas, Bent Tree, and Gulf Shores. And back again.

She didn't live long enough to regret the decision.

CHAPTER 52

MARSH LAKE IS A PURE Bent Tree legacy.

These days the property's reputation is generated from the wildlife photography of Matthew Crain. Bald eagles and cranes mostly. Plenty of magnificent landscapes too. Those photos are on everything, from the cover of the telephone book to the walls of the fiscal court to the area directly above Jack's mother's couch. Those few pixels are the only access granted.

Jack, on the other hand, has his own code to the property's security system and is allowed to come and go as he pleases. On the drive, he tells Anna about Chester and the dog he sold him three years before. A runt. Same litter as Pippa. Sweet as could be. Before the purchase, Jack warned the older man and his wife that the spaniel they chose wasn't a hunter. Chester said, "Fine by us. We don't do much hunting anymore." But then he paid Jack a pretty penny to train the dog on basic skills. During that time, Jack came out to Marsh Lake daily. Early in the morning, when the grass was still swampy and the flowers were shy.

"So Chester likes you?"

Jack pokes out his lip thoughtfully. "Yeah. He does. We, like . . . dude bonded, I guess."

"Like with Murray," she says under her breath, but he chooses not to respond. She says, "Well, it sounds like a high probability he'll say yes to our offer."

"I don't know. I got the feeling he wanted to leave everything connected to the Lodges behind."

"Because he found the bodies?"

"I assume so, but it never came up when I was training Margie. Margie's the spaniel."

"Yes, thank you for the clarification. I assumed you weren't training his wife." She growls at herself for snapping at him. "Sorry. That was douchey. I didn't get much sleep."

"You're forgiven," Jack says and wonders exactly how much he's already forgiven her. It seems like more than he meant to. "Anyway, the former owner of Marsh Lake, this man named Turner Lottenmeir, was the one who started the competition Chester was in when he found the bodies. Lottenmeir was a retired newspaper tycoon from Washington, and according to Granddad, he used Marsh Lake and the competition to stay relevant among the DC crowd."

"People from DC came to Bent Tree?" Anna sounds incredulous. "I don't remember you talking about this before."

"I hadn't met Chester yet, but you know people from all over the world come to the Lodges." No matter how much Jack explained, Anna never bought into the popularity of hunting culture. "Back then, Turner used the competition as a way to get a bunch of deep pockets in one place and then he spent a week lobbying for his favorite candidates while they hunted. It would probably be going on today if Lottenmeir hadn't died. Marsh Lake is a crown jewel. After we top this ridge, you'll see."

Jack speeds up and the entry to the property comes into view.

The beauty is unmatched and wild with life. The imperfections of nature—weeds that look like flowers, growing red vines, leaves of every shade of orange—make every sightline perfect.

"Welcome to Marsh Lake," Jack says and lowers his window beside the security keypad. The large black gate inches slowly backward and Jack winds along the driveway, waiting for Chester's house to spring into view.

A dog runs at them barking. Margie is mature now and very much the same spotted brown spaniel he remembers. Jack keeps the window down, calling to her, and she runs with them all the way to the front circle drive. Margie waits impatiently for him to exit the truck. One pat on his chest and she's in his arms. "I remember you." Their noses smoosh together in a way that makes Anna break the frown she's been wearing since they left Murray.

Chester James appears on the porch, squints, and then waves. "Jack! Good to see you."

"You might not say that in a minute," Jack says, a hint of mischievousness in his voice. "I've got a proposal for you."

"Already married, my dear boy." Chester flashes the chunky onyx ring on his fourth finger. "But I'm flattered."

Jack remembers this about Chester. How he moves through the world with an inviting ease. "You can't turn me down that fast," Jack says. "Not when I've got your baby in my arms." He spins the sweet spaniel in the air. "Isn't that right, Margie?"

Behind Jack, Anna's shadow closes in on him. He offers her Margie's head to pat, hoping to bring a smile to her face. She talked on the way here, but he suspects most of her thoughts didn't make it to words.

He's still waiting. Not pushing.

Chester, on the other hand, is talking. Saying something about his talent for telling people no and how he's built a career out of the word. "Wouldn't be able to afford this place if I didn't, Jack. I guess you could say I've got a talent for . . ."

Whatever Chester has to say next is lost in a jaw-dropped stare at Anna.

CHAPTER 53

AFTER DISCOVERING THE CHOIR GIRLS, Chester James pivoted his life away from Bent Tree, Kentucky. No more line dancing. No more ducks. No more camo. He sold his rifles and stowed his boat. He chose a life without bullets and blood. A life his grandfather never imagined for him.

The move started with a college application to Western Kentucky University. Four years later, degree in hand, he followed a girl to New Jersey, where he became a financial analyst for her father's global aerospace company. They married and honeymooned in Italy. A good year became a good life that yielded great money and a solid marriage. No children. And not very many friends. But neither Chester nor Lauris would have said they were lonely or restless. They busied themselves with work, volunteering, and social obligations. The years slipped by like a ball of ice melting in a glass of bourbon.

The only things Chester kept from his old life were a hatred for his alarm clock and a country accent his clients found charming. When the Choir Girls showed up in his dreams after another podcaster or reporter brought the case back into his consciousness, Lauris shook him awake and kissed his neck. "You're okay," she said to ground him, because she knew where his brain was. He never hid the reason he left home, and Lauris never pushed him to return. Although she sensed how much that rugged place and his loving grandparents created the sweet husband he was. For that, she loved Bent Tree before she ever laid eyes on it.

When Chester's mother died, Chester and Lauris traveled south for the beautiful service in the small country church where Chester had accepted Jesus. His father wasn't well enough to leave the nursing home, but there were reunions with old friends and hunters. All of whom regaled Lauris with stories of Chester's hunting prowess.

Noah Bright had even said to Lauris, "Your husband was the best guide, best shot, ever born in Bent Tree." Chester had kicked back in his chair, laughed, and said, "A million years ago, maybe," but the compliment landed in soft tissue.

After they left the cemetery on the day of the funeral, Chester drove Lauris through the river bottoms and backroads of his childhood. Much to his surprise, Lauris expressed discontent with her father's concrete universe. Later she'd say that she fell in love twice in her life. Once with Chester. And again with Bent Tree.

"We should move here," she declared, tears rolling down her cheeks. "You can work remotely. That would put you closer to your father's nursing home in Paducah. I've had years of living near my parents. You should have that chance too. Besides, I've never seen you smile this much. You miss this place. Admit it."

Chester said, "The only thing that would get me back here is Marsh Lake, and that place will never be for sale."

Chester didn't know Lauris hired a Realtor to watch the property. She called the day after the funeral and made her wishes very clear. "If it ever goes on the market, we want it."

The next year Lottenmeir died and Lauris bought Marsh Lake for Chester.

"A vacation house," she said, eyebrows dancing at her husband when she presented the deed. "Who needs Hawaii? We'll make our own paradise."

They had. It took about four million trips to Lowe's and there was no telling how many packages Amazon lost trying to find their gate, but they were here full time now. They mowed their own grass and planted another hundred bulbs every fall so they could sit on the porch and watch spring paint them a private universe.

Turned out that Lauris loved fishing nearly as much as she loved Chester. They closed out most days with their lines swaying in the water, waiting for a fish to hit the bait, their sweet Margie sleeping beside them.

Moving home taught Chester that what happened to him as a young man, discovering the Choir Girls, wasn't better or worse in Kentucky or New Jersey. The haunting traveled. Some days the murder was the size of the sun; others it was a molecule he couldn't see.

When he lays eyes on Anna, the haunting comes alive.

"Jenni," he says.

Anna doesn't speak, even though it's clear he's addressing her.

Jack interrupts, "Chester, this is Anna Ryder."

The girl's face holds him in two worlds. He's back in cowboy boots at Wild Willies. He's on his porch staring at a young woman who reminds him so much of Jenni he can't breathe.

He'd had a similar reaction to Foster Portage. Foster hadn't necessarily looked like Jenni, but she'd certainly reminded him of that time in his life. Untamed. Unmoored. She was cynical and outspoken. Bombastic and yet warm. Every woman Jenni ran around with sounded exactly like Foster Portage.

"Of course," Chester says, embarrassed. He tries to explain. "Never mind me, young lady. You look like an old friend of mine. It's a little uncanny how much you're a carbon copy of her. I apologize for my misunderstanding, but I assure you it was a compliment. My friend was beautiful and beloved."

"Thank you," Anna says.

"No. Thank you. Two visits in two months from people in your age group from the Lodges. I must be doing something right with my life. Or something very wrong," he jokes.

"Two visits?" Jack inquires.

"Yes, Foster Portage was here. Perhaps a month ago."

Jack scrunches his forehead and says, "That's weird, unless . . ."

Chester's eyebrows arch and his chest falls. He wags a finger at Jack. "You are correct. She came out to interview me for a podcast she's working on about . . . you know."

"Foster's working on a Choir Girls podcast?"

Chester bows apologetically. "Could I ask you not to let that cat out of the bag? I told her I wouldn't mention her latest project. You can imagine her in-laws won't be pleased. Now, my dear," he says to Anna, "would you like to come inside and sit down? You're looking a little peekid, as my granny used to say. I've got a glass of sweet tea with your name on it."

Anna waves him off. "I'm not normally this quiet," she says and attempts a laugh. "Mr. James, I need to ask you for an incredible favor."

Her voice is also from the past.

Not Jenni's. Or at least, he doesn't think so. But similar.

"It's Chester, and ask away."

"We're down a guide for the Royale, and my boss says you're the best."

"I don't do that work anymore. Hung up my hip waders, you might say."

Anna's heart-shaped face falls and Chester snaps his fingers as the gnawing memory comes into focus. "Wait. What did you say your last name was?"

"Ryder."

"Starr's your momma," he says with confidence. Starr and Jenni had been cut from the same cloth. The bartender at Wild Willies used to say if it weren't for their hair, one black as a raven and the other brown as a bear, you couldn't tell them apart. That was a stretch, but Chester agreed if you put them both in ball caps and a dark room, you might kiss the wrong one accidentally. No wonder he'd reacted so viscerally. Not Jenni's daughter, Starr's.

"Yes. How do you know her?" Anna asks.

"Oh, she used to work nights at a place in Luxor called Wild Willies. I line danced there back when my knees had a little more spring and we got to be friends. How is your momma these days?"

"Doing good," Anna says, but her face tells a different story.

Jack turns sharply to check on her, and Chester knows something she said isn't quite true.

Regardless, the old happy past looms.

Starr and Jenni sitting in a corner booth whispering about afternoons spent on Starr's boat. The drunken parties. All those guys from the Royale who tried to worm their way aboard in various ways. Oh, how they drove the men crazy. Drove Chester crazy.

"Did she make it to New Orleans?" he asks.

"I don't think so," Anna says.

"Man, she and Jenni used to spend hours on that boat of hers. For a while there I thought she might turn into a fish." He laughs at the memory of the two women in string bikinis with long-neck bottles in their hands and beach towels wrapped around their hair. The sun feels hotter on his neck than it has in years.

Jack and Anna step up onto the porch. Jack says, "Were you ever on the boat?" as he looks through the glass on the bottom level of Chester's house all the way to the lake.

"Maybe a time or two," he admits.

"Where is Jenni now?" Anna asks.

Chester's smile dims until deep lines crease his face. "She was one of the Choir Girls."

CHAPTER 54

ANNA WAS THREE YEARS OLD when the Choir Girls died. Too young to have remembered anything firsthand.

It doesn't matter what side of the river you grow up on—everyone knows the basics. There are documentaries, although she hasn't watched them. And podcasts. She tried a few of those because one of her favorite students said, "Ms. Ryder, you *have* to listen. You know that guy in Texas is sus." Anna never made it through more than one episode.

True crime isn't her entertainment vibe. Give her a beach romance or a celebrity memoir, please and thank you. None of that nonfiction crap Jack used to read all the time. Who needs to be reminded of humanity's capacity for evil?

Not Anna. And especially not when said evil is practically visible from her bedroom window. Her mother always agreed on this point. "We don't need that violent energy in our life, silly goose. *NCIS* is as dark as we get."

However, if she's pressed to make intelligent conversation around the topic of the Choir Girls, Anna will quote the Wikipedia basics. Nine women murdered somewhere, crime scene unknown, and their bodies staged on Mayfield Creek. The killer wrapped the women in bedsheets and tied them to posts in a weird pyramid formation. He—this was a presumption based on the strength required to move the bodies and drive the posts—wrote the word *sing* in blood on the white fabric.

The murder remains unsolved. A cold case with no persons of interest. If you bought the FBI agent who ran the initial investigation enough to drink, he'd tell you they never had a true suspect.

The case has a fascinating twist.

The same crime had been committed in Texas on the shore of the Trinity River that same year. Fewer women with different injuries, but the staging was precisely the same. Sheets. Posts. *Sing.* The same murders only months and states apart, right down to the bloody handwriting.

* * *

Two narratives about the serial killings emerged back then.

One: The murderer isn't from here. He's from Texas.

Two: A murderer from Bent Tree did this same thing in Texas.

Those from Bent Tree held on to the first narrative like it was a billion dollars.

* * *

The town's lackadaisical response to the Choir Girls is confusing. Annoying even. Unless you grew up knowing every person on your road. And their mammies. And their cousins. And their secret child from their high school drunken escapade.

The rule of small towns says terrible things only happen because someone is unlucky, drunk, or stupid.

Like ... a tire drops off the pavement followed by an overcorrection of the steering wheel, and *bam*, you're at a funeral crying, "I hate that road between Stallings and Bent Tree."

Like ... one teenager who dares a drunk classmate to cannonball through a winterized pool cover, and *bam*, he gets to watch his best friend wheel through the rest of his life.

Like ... a man swings a sledgehammer near the base of an old stone wall to speed up the demolition, and *bam*, he ends up buried in rubble.

These are misfortunes referenced over meatloaf and potatoes. Eventually you are allowed to chuckle at some of them while your partner kicks you under the table. All could be turned into either a sermon or a stand-up act.

However, if you want to sleep at night, you treat Mayfield Creek like a local ghost story.

When the topic of the Choir Girls comes up—usually stoked by the media or a stranger passing through—the most prevalent theory in Bent Tree is that the nine women were part of a sex-trafficking scheme gone very, very wrong.

And of course, someone is always quick to add, "You know the killer probably brought them across the river. We shouldn't be Luxor's dump site, but we are."

"The whole thing probably started in Luxor," someone else would say. "Couldn't be Bent Tree."

Anna resents every time someone perpetrates that preposterous story about her town. She longs to lash out, lash back. *Why do you assume poverty makes people violent?* Even though no one looks at her, at

Anna Ryder specifically, and says, "You're involved in this!" she feels culpable because she was born in Luxor.

Anna stares at her shoes. The old Converse sneakers that have carried her through the last five years. The canvas threadbare. A hole formed at the toe.

She feels the truth.

Beneath that hole are the same feet that walked through Jenni's blood on the *Juneau*.

CHAPTER 55

ANNA FINDS IT HARDER AND harder to be surprised. But the whiplash and then the cascade of understanding lands like a blow to her gut.

Starr and Jenni were friends. They likely met at the bar. At some point Starr said she owned a boat. Plans were made. Starr and Jenni liked a good party. And one day that party got interrupted by someone violent.

That doesn't explain the motive. Or why someone staged the bodies on the creek. And it certainly doesn't explain why Anna was on that boat when the murders happened or the connection to the Texas crime. It doesn't tell her whether Starr was there or how they escaped the bloodbath in the cabin.

It tells her only one thing for sure: she doesn't remember a damn thing.

Anna massages her temples so hard she thinks her thumbs might puncture the skin.

Waylon said he carried her off the boat.

He's carrying her in many of her memories, but when she searches for one prior to that Christmas with the firepit and Kentucky Fried Chicken, she comes up blank.

Chester looks as though he wants to comfort her and doesn't know how. His hand hangs in midair near her shoulder without making contact. He buries his hands in his chinos instead. "Are you okay, my dear?"

Anna contorts her face into what she hopes is a calm, normal expression. "No. Yes. I'm so sorry. That could not have been easy," she tells him.

"It was awful," Chester admits. "I've lived with the deaths all these years, but at a distance. Like this awful thing I happened upon. I mourned for families I didn't know, only to find out recently that I'd been mourning for myself as well." He takes a deep breath. "Jenni was a delight. We were young and"—a playful gleam overtakes his sky-blue eyes—"rambunctious. I had no idea that the Jenni I dated was Genevieve, the Choir Girl. Not until Foster showed me a photo."

"What photo?" Anna asks.

"I don't know where she got it. Had to be from someone back then. They weren't images I'd seen before. Maybe your mother gave them to her?"

"Maybe." A prick of jealousy snags at Anna's heart. That whole part of Starr's life has always been hidden from Anna.

Chester must register Anna's frown as disappointment because he says, "I have some photos from our summer together if you or your mom would like them. They were dear friends."

"I'd love that."

"Come on inside."

Chester's house doesn't have a hint of Bent Tree flair. The modern black-and-white, flat-roofed monstrosity is all concrete pillars and top-to-bottom glass on the lowest level.

Anna and Jack follow Chester inside and up a staircase next to an inground pool.

"Lauris refused to put the house on stilts," he explains. "We went back and forth about what could sustain a flood, and she talked me into a lower-level pool house." He gives a half-grunt that suggests he is actually quite pleased with the situation. "Unconventional but"—he rubs his hands up and down his abs—"it has been good to my core."

It has. Anna guesses Chester to be in his midfifties rather than his midsixties. A few nudges from his wife about cholesterol have gone a long way. His calf muscles knot as he climbs the concrete steps.

At the top, Chester gestures for Jack and Anna to find a seat at the large dining room table. He fills water glasses and disappears to grab the photos. Anna and Jack exchange silent awe regarding the home's decadence. "What did he do?" Anna asks.

"Financial stuff in New York."

Chester strolls back into the kitchen already talking. Anna realizes he's been sharing details since he left and they haven't heard a thing. ". . . We're supposed to go out on the *Juneau* for an afternoon. This was before Jenni disappeared from my life, actually. Several years before the murder. Anyway, her boss, Noah, called and demanded she work an extra shift or she'd be fired. We dropped the plans and I drove her straight to the Lodges. Later I found a Walmart sack in my back seat full of photos she'd had developed and a bunch of scrapbook stuff. I'm not sure why I hung on to them, but after Foster told me Jenni was one of the Choir Girls, I drove over to my grandmother's property and dug them out of the attic."

Chester unclasps two manila envelopes. Aged, molded photos and scraps of memorabilia scatter onto the place mats. Anna scans the contents. Trying to take the images in and piece together Jenni beyond the few details she knows: Her mother's friend. Chester's lover. A Choir Girl.

There's a graduation program. Note cards with teenage swoopy letters. Various photos of Jenni at different ages, made by different cameras and photographic technology. Anna's eyes land on what should have been an inconsequential photo.

Jenni, at nineteen or twenty, sitting on the floorboard at the side sliding door of a minivan. One knee folds over the other. The sun is on her face. NASA buildings fill the background. Brightly manicured grass holds a sign that reads "Houston Space Center."

She wears pink sunglasses and smiles widely as she lifts a can of Coke into the air like she's toasting the sky. Boxes and bags fill the van around her body. She barely has room to fit above the running board. Over Jenni's right shoulder is a Barbie Dreamhouse. All the traditional pink plastic pieces have been painted green.

Anna snatches the photo off the table.

"What is it?"

"I had a dollhouse like this," Anna tells Jack.

Chester leans over her shoulder. "Ah, I helped her unload this. One of the regular cooks at the Lodges had a daughter. Jenni picked the dollhouse up one weekend when she went home to Texas and brought it back for her. She was like that. Kind and generous with her stuff. I only remember because of the color. When I asked her why it wasn't pink, she said green went better with her G.I. Joes."

* * *

Green goes better with G.I. Joes.

Starr had said that too.

The flash of memory is incomplete. Ten seconds of a five-minute video. But Anna sees herself.

She's cross-legged in the luggage area of a minivan. The green Barbie Dreamhouse in front of her. Blue fingernail polish that she likely painted and then picked away. She raises the elevator for the four army men riding to Barbie's attic.

"Honey bear, finish your ice cream," comes a voice from the driver's seat.

"Can't we paint this pink? Barbie is pink," Anna asks.

"Green goes better with G.I. Joes," Starr says from the front. "Right, Moonie?"

Another voice. "Right, Starr."

There is so much happiness it floods the van. The kind of happiness that is only shared over memories and inside jokes.

"You ready to roll?" asks the voice of Moonie.

"Ah, give 'em a few more minutes to play. They should have called Texas the Long-ass State instead of the Longhorn State."

The memory's gone.

*   *   *

Jenni had indeed given the Dreamhouse to the cook. And the cook had given it back after Jenni found out she was pregnant. "Mine's grown out of it, and yours"—the woman patted Jenni's bump—"will love it."

"I think I'm having a boy," Jenni had said.

"Then you'll be glad it's already green," said the cook.

*   *   *

The rest of their time at Chester's table passes in a blur for Anna. Chester reclasps the envelopes and hands them to Jack. He promises to consider the offer to guide for the Royale. Anna never fully returns from the black hole in her brain.

Back in the truck, Jack says, "Ann, I need to tell you something."

CHAPTER 56

ANNA'S HEART SINKS WHEN JACK says her name.

"I've wanted to tell you," he begins, which is never how you want a conversation to start. "And now I don't have a choice."

Anna preemptively prepares for the worst confession she can imagine. Jack is in a serious relationship with Theresa and plans to move where she is after the Royale. And in that preparation, she knows for certain she never fell out of love with Jack. She'd just fallen into hate as well.

There's something worse, she realizes. Murray might be telling the truth. Jack could be involved in the auction. Selling illegal weapons. Maybe he got caught up in it a long time ago with his grandfather and Noah.

"The thing is . . ." He's silent for too long. The sentence stays unfinished.

"Hey." She touches his leg and then his face. The gesture is familiar and foreign. Her heart pounds wildly because the giant who has been stepping on her heart for the last five years has finally moved his foot. "You tried to tell me Theresa was lying and I shut you out. I promise, this time I'm listening. You can say whatever you need to and I'll deal."

He tightens his brow and massages his jaw. "The day we broke up, you screamed that I wasn't who you thought I was. In a strange way, you were right."

"No," she argues. "I was shocked and angry and disappointed, but I wasn't right."

"Hey, this is not about Theresa or my son. On that front, Ryder, you were totally wrong." He is teasing her and stalling. "That day, when you handed me the envelope from Theresa, I thought you were going to hand me this." He opens her glove box and pulls out another photo, not unlike the ones in the manila envelope on the back seat.

❊   ❊   ❊

No one prints photos anymore. They live inside the cloud or a device. But back then people were still printing photos like this one.

The one of two children. A girl and a boy in swimsuits. Pudgy and skinny at the same time, the way only children can be. Soaking wet. Hair wild from swimming. Cheeks all pink from the sun. They sit with their knees side by side on a purple lounger. Arm floaties pushed up around their elbows.

Anna recognizes them both.

Audio File #1458

Beck,

I've already told you all about Anna Ryder and how we fell in love. Here's something I haven't shared yet, and I'm not sure why.

I almost didn't ask Anna to marry me. I wanted to. She's smart and beautiful. When I'm around her, I never pretend. Son, that's how you know you're with someone worth spending your life with.

I had to ask myself a big question: Do I care more about the past than I do the future? I thought I knew, but it's harder than you think, Beck. The past is so known and trustworthy. The future scared the crap out of me. Still does.

Anyway, Anna's oddly connected to my employer, and Starr, Anna's mother, told me that if we married (and she hoped we did), then we needed to leave the Lodges completely. That wasn't an easy thing for me to stomach. My grandfather and I built the cabin I live in. We planed the wood ourselves. The process was painstaking and long and beautiful. It was the last thing I did with Granddad before he died. Well, more like he and Noah sat in their lawn chairs directing traffic and laughing at me. I knew absolutely nothing about carpentry when we started. The product we finished had Granddad's exquisite personality.

I feel close to him when I'm here. Close to my childhood and easier times.

Starr basically told me I had to choose, and for the most part she wouldn't tell me why. It has something to do with Anna's father. I've wondered a million times who Anna's father is. And that always makes me think about you doing the same thing somewhere. I wonder if your mother talks about me. If she has moved on. Do you have a dad in your life? On the one hand, I hope you do so very much. And on the other, I'm understandably jealous.

Anyway, Anna doesn't look like anyone I know from work. I've tried to identify her features in the men who might be Starr's age and I'm terrible at this. You look like me. If you ever see a picture, you'll know. The Higgins genes are a big, bold outline that anyone can pick out. I'm so glad for that. Not because I think I'm handsome, though obviously I do. But because it's the way I'm connected to you.

Starr thinks she's protecting Anna, and maybe she is, but her father should have a chance to know her. I mean, my favorite saint said, "There's no saint without a past, no sinner without a future." Maybe that means I'm blinded by you, but if I ever figure out who her father is, it's going to be hard to keep that a secret.

CHAPTER 57

HIS SECRET IS NOT THE auction.

Anna lifts the photo closer, examining every square millimeter.

"Anna, Starr made me swear I wouldn't tell you." Jack keeps talking. "And I made that promise with every intention of keeping it, but that was before you got a job at the Lodges."

"What is this?" She means, *What does this mean?*

"You need to quit," he says. "God knows I don't want you to. The last thing I want to do is push you away, but . . ."

"Why do you have a photo of us? And why weren't you allowed to tell me you did?"

Jack's been wearing his fear since last night when they discovered the boat. The dark circles under his eyes are the color of plums.

Anna forces herself to be measured. To think. To breathe deeply. She used the same tactic when she was working with a student in a dangerous situation. That gave her the distance to seek more information. "Walk this back for a minute. Start with the photo. With you and me and everything you know."

Jack throws his ball cap on the dash. "I don't remember this being taken or meeting you. I found it in my grandmother's album and showed it to Starr because I wanted to frame it for you, and she flipped out. She made me promise I wouldn't give you the photo and to tell her if you ever started to remember stuff from your early childhood. She said she was protecting you. She implied from your father, but you know how she is. It's hard to tell anything at all when she locks up."

Starr would lie to anyone about anything to protect Anna. Apparently, that includes Anna herself.

"There's no one in this photo but us," she says. "It's not like you've got a picture of my father. Why would she care?"

"I don't know. Because we're at the Lodges? Because maybe this is near the time you were on the *Juneau*? I'm not sure, but she was very clear."

"Starr told me my father was dead. Did she tell you he lived in Bent Tree? Or worked at the Lodges?"

"No, nothing like that. Only that if I loved you, I was to keep you away from the Lodges as much as possible and that you were never to be there during the Royale. When we were together, I made sure. But yesterday you were in front of me asking for help and I caved and put you in danger. Now, with the boat, and you starting to remember things, and Chester calling you Jenni, you can't work the Royale. Can't you see?"

Dangerous pieces slide into place.

Anna isn't merely footprints through blood; she's a witness to the murder of nine women. And someone out there doesn't need to be reminded of that possibility.

She replays Waylon's offer of his weapon. His declaration that Gleb was responsible for the blood on the boat. The lost murder scene. Nine women. Chester's Jenni. Eight others. Starr's friends, gone.

He didn't murder Anna. So that means either he didn't know she was there or he had a reason not to. She suspects that reason is biology. Maybe she's not in danger of being killed. Maybe she's in danger of being taken from Starr. That might explain why Starr doesn't want Anna at the Lodges or celebrating anything to do with them. Not even a sweet childhood photo of her and Jack.

"I'll quit tomorrow before the Royale starts. There's still something I need to do," she says.

"Something that's more important than your life?"

"Yeah," she says. "Actually, it is." She thinks of Murray and feels the set of her jaw. Realizes for the first time that they're likely siblings. She doesn't know what to make of that. She only knows her blood pressure spikes when she thinks of what he's done to Jack.

"And you're not going to tell me."

"Can't." Her pointer and middle fingers are in the air. "Scout's honor."

"You're not a Scout."

"Jack," she says, unsure if she's going to come out with her next question. She thinks it depends on how he looks at her and whether she can see his goodness all the way to the core.

His voice ripples with fear. "Yeah?"

"What do you know about a weapons auction during the Royale?"

CHAPTER 58

"ONLY THAT THERE IS ONE."

Anna's feet press against the dashboard so hard the plastic bends as she frames her next sentence. Here's the moment of truth. The one she can't come back from. "Noah never asked you for help?"

"Yes," he says.

It feels like someone clamps her heart and starts to squeeze.

Jack says, "I turned him down."

Anna exhales. "And Murray?"

"Noah claimed he's not involved. And Gleb basically hates him, so I doubt he would pull him in."

That satisfies her as truth. "He is now. Noah's death, I guess. And he says Noah told Gleb you're involved."

"How do you—?"

"One more question," she says quietly. "If I take information to the police about the auction, you're positive that you're safe?"

"I am *not* involved."

She believes him. "Your parents?"

He shakes his head, considering. "Granddad and Noah were close, but he's been dead for years and I just can't see him involved in this."

"Will this kill your job?"

"Probably. But I'll land on my feet. I always do." His voice is heavy with comprehension. "Will you tell them about the boat too?"

"Yes," she says. "Nine women. Their families. I'm telling. It's only a matter of when." Her brain whirls. She lets it spitball. She tells the truth that scares her. "The thing is . . . that crime scene is preserved for a reason. My mother hid me for a reason. I don't think Gleb Orlov knows that boat still exists. And I think I . . . I think he might be my father. And maybe that's why she's basically been hiding me too."

*　*　*

Anna has always had dreams shaped like Disney movies. Not the animated ones. The old ones with Shirley Temple and Hayley Mills. The ones where gruff men turn out to be loving softies in ninety minutes or less.

As a child, her mother popped an old copy of *Heidi* into the DVD player, and Anna waited with complete dread and joy for the grandfather to get his life together. He always did. Right there at the end.

Anna would cry and her mother would say, "Silly goose, there's no grandfather in our story. No white horses or rescuing knights. Just your kick-ass mother and all the love in the world she can give."

Anna always said she understood.

That never changed the longing.

*　*　*

"Do you want to talk about your father? About . . ." Jack tries out the name. "Gleb?"

"Not really." What she means is, not yet.

We all wish our fathers were good men.

Anna's unknown father has always been more like a mold made of plaster than an actual person. He was there once and made an impression, and that impression was made into a copy and that copy was hidden deep in her mother's secrets.

Now the unknown has a name. How is that supposed to make her feel? Mad at her mother for telling her he was dead? Maybe. But not nearly as mad as she is at him for being unknowable.

Jack nods thoughtfully and she asks, "Will you do me a favor today?"

"Anything." His earnest nature fills his face like a ring of light.

"Find out anything you can about Foster Portage."

Jack looks puzzled. "You think she's involved with the auction? Or you think she might know about the boat because of her podcast?"

There is so much mystery where Foster is involved. "She's definitely investigating the Choir Girls and Noah, and I want to know why and if we can trust her to help us. Starr trusts her, and she doesn't trust anybody who hasn't earned it. So I think we can, but she's one of the owners. She could be playing both sides."

"Do you trust your mother?"

"I think so." Irony hits her squarely in the feels. Not only had she been wrong about Jack's treatment of Theresa and his son, but she'd held him to a standard that no one else is made to meet. Hours ago, she sat beside her mother and asked if she murdered anyone and then proceeded to tell her it was okay if she did. That part was true. She loved her mother no matter what.

But Jack . . . She kicked him out of her life without a single conversation or explanation. She isn't sure why. She's aware that if she wants to let him back in, she needs to do more work than a simple apology.

"And Waylon?" Jack asks. "We trust him?"

She likes his use of *we*. "Absolutely," she answers. "Any crime he committed was to save Mom or me. That doesn't necessarily make him innocent, but he's not dangerous."

Gathering her courage, she asks, "While we're on the subject of trust, what about Murray?"

Jack is still and contemplative. He shifts his hat cockeyed and then squares it. "I don't *trust* Murray with everything. But I trust him completely in some things. Does that make sense? If he says Gleb thinks I'm involved, that's probably an accurate perception. Noah did invite me into the deal."

She says, "You love Murray?"

"Yes."

"More than me?" She winces that the question is out in the open.

"Different than you, Ann. Very, very different than you." He must have seen straight into her doubt. He says, "He's there when you aren't. Weren't. Before and after. He's an old friend and I don't have many of those. There's no one else in my life who sat in the kennels with me and Grandfather. No one else who taught me how to plant a garden or grill a steak. He's not perfect, not even close, but he was there and that matters to me."

"So if you found out he did something awful, you'd still love him?"

"Yes. Same as you love Starr. And I think . . . I think that's how real love is supposed to work. Present when people are inconvenient or imperfect." The corner of his lip raises in the way that tells her he is done with the conversation.

Anna hates Murray, and she suspects that Jack never will—even if he finds out about Theresa and Murray. So she asks herself a strange question. One that most humans don't stop to ask, especially when they think they're right about someone: *What does loving my person look like right now?*

The answer is shockingly simple. She lets it be.

"I'm so glad you have love like that in your life," she says and, without hesitation, leans over and pecks Jack on the cheek.

His hand lifts to the place she has just kissed and then he says, "Thank you for that."

And in that moment, they fall completely out of hate.

✻   ✻   ✻

"So now what?" he asks.

Good question.

"We get through this day. We do the work assigned." Anna leaves out the fact that she'll be looking for four crates of missiles, but does explain her arrangement to meet Foster at Noah's after she finishes Murray's errands. "We'll check in all day by text and then you can come to the farm tonight after work. Waylon will be there with Mom. I'll try to bring Foster, if I determine she's helpful. We'll make a plan together."

They drive back to Portage Lodge without saying much else. Both are deep in thought. When they reach the company truck she's to use, Jack hands her a map of the Lodges' property and his baseball cap. "Keep your head down, Ryder."

Anna tucks her ponytail through the back of his cap and then kisses Jack's cheek again and says, "I do think we should frame that photo."

And then she is out of the truck.

CHAPTER 59

GLEB ORLOV DIDN'T ALWAYS DREAM of joining the family business. He was a footballer. As a young man, he had the lithe body of
a goalkeeper. More caps and stops than his opponents. He was good
enough to sign with a Premier League and have hopes of playing on
his national team. Those dreams could not compete with his father's
authority.

His relationship with the sport of football isn't important except
for one tiny detail.

When his son, Merkoul, was very young, Gleb played a pickup
soccer game with some of his former teammates. In the first half,
a man three times his muscle mass slammed into him. In turn, he
slammed into the post.

They took him off the pitch on a stretcher.

Later that night, when Gleb woke in a hospital room, a doctor
explained his injuries. He suffered a very dangerous concussion and
another more sensitive injury. One that meant he'd likely never be
able to have children. And also, important fact, they discovered a
preexisting condition that meant it would always be difficult for him
to conceive. Not impossible, but highly unlikely.

"I do have a child," he said.

There were paternity papers. He'd confirmed it because he was suspicious.

"Well, count it a miracle," the doctor told him. "One in a million."

As soon as Gleb was healthy enough to walk out of the hospital, he got a second paternity test to see if he was a two-in-a-million kind of man. He was not. The next day he put Merkoul on a plane to Kentucky to punish his wife.

Murray's father, his real father, was not a man with soccer prowess. He was the beautiful red-haired taxi driver who drove around Gleb's unhappy wife.

CHAPTER 60

MURRAY CALLS MIDAFTERNOON TO CHECK in, and Anna takes the same tactic Jack did that morning. "Chester agreed to guide." The lie buys her time to collect as much information as she can from Murray about the auction and then meet Foster that night.

The day crawls by with no discoveries. Noah's office, work truck, and favorite duck blind are unfruitful. She snaps six or seven photos of notes that might apply and sends them Murray's way to appease him. After each one, she waits for him to taunt her. He doesn't. One text arrives midafternoon.

MURRAY: Thank you. Keep looking.

Why can't bad people just be bad all the time? she thinks. Nice and clear. Why send a normal text message? How is she supposed to interpret that?

All day she hopes to run into Foster or Waylon or Jack. No one surfaces.

That leaves too much time for her brain to stay on the mental roller coaster of Gleb Orlov. Is he her father? Did he kill the Choir

Girls? Could Murray be her brother? How in the world is she supposed to find missiles and stop an auction in less than twenty-four hours? She debates calling the police now and telling them everything, but that will be spun into a story about a Luxor girl telling lies about Bent Tree men and it will not get her the location of Jack's son.

By seven that night she's frustrated and angry and no closer to anything she's searching for. The only good part of the day has been texting with Jack. They stay away from serious topics and play a game from when they dated. He starts a semi-famous quote and it's her job to finish it. Playing with spotty Wi-Fi makes her far worse than she was half a decade ago. He sends Saint Augustine, E. E. Cummings, Martin Luther King Jr. Even some Dolly Parton. That one she knows. Her mother drilled Dolly lyrics into her like she was learning the Rosary prayer.

When it's finally time to meet Foster, Anna parks a quarter mile away on a gravel turn-in and jogs through the woods past Molly's lean-to. She reaches the edge of the woods covered in sweat and mud, but feeling in far better spirits. The exercise is a lovely dopamine hit.

There is no sign of Foster's Land Rover at Noah's. Anna runs across the lawn, up the steps, and shoves the key in the lock.

From somewhere nearby, Foster hisses, "Hey."

Anna nearly jumps out of her skin. "I didn't see your car."

Foster makes a point of looking over the edge of the deck railing and says, "I don't see yours either."

Anna turns the key and opens the door for Foster. "Murray told me not to be seen. What's your excuse?"

"I'd rather word not get to my in-laws that I'm meeting up with a staffer at a private cabin," Foster says.

"You don't want me to be your scandal," Anna teases.

"Exactly."

Anna leads the way into Noah's bedroom without turning on a light.

Inside the bedroom, she pulls the curtains and turns on her flashlight. "Okay, I'm here. You're inside. Tell me why my mother called you." She deeply suspects Foster could have gotten herself in here.

"First we search, then we chat."

The two women stare at each other. A tiny showdown ensues that Foster wins with a wink. Foster says, "Nice look," and Anna says, "Uh, you too." Since this morning, Anna has changed into tennis shoes, leggings, and a wide-necked sweatshirt. It's the poor man's version of Foster's outfit. Anna's still sporting Jack's ball cap and Foster has her hair in two braids. They're dressed for sneaking around.

Anna realizes Foster has removed all her extras. No makeup. No fake lashes. No pearls or diamonds. No Louis Vuitton. Just a tiny woman with a riveting smile.

Anna says, "If there's something hidden, it'll be in here." She shoves her way into the closet and through the false panel. Noah's secret office surprises Foster, but she says nothing. Together, they pull all the files out of the desk and take them back to the bed. The stack isn't large and most of it appears to be financial documents that aren't forthcoming if they're related to the auction or Noah's personal records.

"What are you looking for?" Anna asks.

"Noah promised me evidence about the auction. I need locations. Details. Something to shut them down."

"For your podcast?"

"Yeah," Foster says, distracted by the files. She flips through the labels quickly. "But there's nothing here. Nothing obvious, at least.

He said he had thirty years of buyers. A way to track down hundreds of weapons."

"So you're not investigating the Choir Girls like you told Chester James."

Foster laughs from deep in her belly. "Oh, I am. If I could, I'd opt for a public hanging of Gleb Orlov, that sick bastard."

A jolt rips through Anna's system. Should she tell Foster that Gleb might be her father, or will Foster stop trusting her if she knows?

"He killed my mother," Foster announces. She says this like she might have said dozens of other phrases: *Pizza for dinner. Iowa women's basketball is my favorite. Let's start a hobby farm.* The matter-of-factness is peculiar and effective.

"Who was she? Your mother?" Anna says and then feels terrible that her first response wasn't sorrow.

"Genevieve Lockwood."

"Oh," Anna says. And then another longer, "Ohhhhh." And then finally, "Jenni was your mother." Anna continues to stumble over her words. "Oh gosh, I'm so sorry, Foster."

"Me too."

"How did you find out?"

"Starr tracked me down."

"That's why she trusts you. She's known you all your life," Anna says.

"You really don't remember me, do you?" Foster's disappointment is at the surface and almost desperate.

Anna doesn't.

"I hid us, Anna. I hid us while he killed them all."

✳   ✳   ✳

One sentence strikes from earlier that day. Waylon said, *"I'm the one who carried you off that boat."*

Carried.

She didn't walk through the blood.

Foster did.

*   *   *

Foster Portage examines the woman before her, scans every feature in search of the little girl she remembers with blazing accuracy. She could not have picked Anna out in a crowd, not by looks.

But certainly by feel. Anna's energy is the same as it was at three. Helpful and curious. Foster felt it yesterday when they were rescuing the raccoon.

They'd been best friends by default. Their mothers were inseparable, and the girls were always in tow or sharing a babysitter. At Jenni's little staffer cabin, they played with the puppies and climbed big trees. (Even met a boy near their age named Jack.) On Starr's cramped boat, they played Barbies in the storage area under the bed and jumped off the railing into the lake with their tiny spotted swimsuits.

On the night the Choir Girls died, Starr was at work and Jenni had the girls. She told them, "You two play under here while my friends are over and I'll get you both big ice creams after they leave." The girls didn't need the bribe. They loved their hideout.

How magical it was to be a small and hidden creature in a world of adults.

Right up until the first gunshot, the first scream.

What Foster remembered very specifically was Anna crawling toward the gunshots and the light. Their Barbie tunnel was actually a

T-shaped storage area with an exit at the foot of the bed. Usually accessible by lifting the mattress. Meant to be a place for sheets or pillows or off-season clothes. As soon as Anna moved, Foster jerked her back and smashed her body against her only friend in the world and said, "Shh."

There they lay trembling until the boat grew quiet with death.

Even then, Foster wouldn't let them move. Their three-year-old bodies sweating through their clothes, their hearts almost exploding. They were brave enough to live, but not leave. And who could blame them? Foster had no idea how long they were there. Long enough they both fell asleep tangled in each other's arms.

When they awoke, there were voices again.

Men moving around. Men making a plan. Men dragging bodies up the steps of the cruiser.

The girls held their breath for so long they passed out.

Hours later, a big, burly man lifted the mattress and said, "You're okay. I gotcha both."

✻   ✻   ✻

A million tiny decisions.

The process of how someone becomes.

And who someone becomes.

The decision made that night by Waylon Collins separated Anna and Foster. One girl grew up with stability. The other grew up searching for it.

Finding each other again will change everything.

✻   ✻   ✻

They say nothing and then they start to speak at the same time. Neither manages a true word. Anna plans to say, "I don't remember." The words die on her lips.

Someone is on their way up the deck steps outside.

Foster freezes, eyes wide. "Hide."

They leave the files spread across the coverlet and hide in the closet as the front door closes in the living room. Anna pushes them into Noah's secret room and in tandem they lift the panel into place and ease their bodies against the fake wall.

There are at least two people in the house.

One male. The voice is mature and unfamiliar.

The other is female and Southern.

Anna holds her breath. Foster is close enough to feel her exhale. She presses her lips against Anna's ear and says, "Lavinia and Murray?"

Silently, Anna removes her phone from her pocket and checks for messages. The dim light casts Foster's face in shadows.

Murray sent five texts in the last hour. Each a single word. Anything?

One comes through, vibrating against her hand. Murray: Anything?

Outside the closet, the man and woman bicker. They cuss loudly about the state of the room and the stupidity of Noah Bright. Will they suspect someone was reading the files on the bed posthumously or will they think Noah left them that way?

Foster squeezes her hand. Tight enough Anna wants to cry out. Instead, Foster pulls their clasped hands to her heart to steady the shaking of Anna's body. Behind them the panel rattles ever so slightly.

✵　✵　✵

Here is the conversation the girls in the closet cannot hear.

"You asked me to come early. I came. Why? This is not my style."

"I'm out, Gleb."

Gleb laughs like he's never heard anything more hilarious. "There is no out. The auction will go on."

"Sure, but without us. We don't steal missiles from first-world governments. You've gotten reckless and greedy, and I'm not going down for your stupidity."

"You've gotten useless and incapable, Lavinia. Me, I rise to the need while you piss away opportunity and money."

"Noah's dead. Murray hates you. Your connection and control here are over."

"What about our son, Lavinia? Does he know who his father is?"

"Oh, screw you!"

"I already did," he says with an evil laugh.

Lavinia loses her patience. "Buy us out or——"

"Or what?" He grins, enjoying the challenge. He assumes he has the upper hand because he always does. Right up until she says, "Or I'll send the police to where your precious little murder scene is stored. Now write me a check."

"Oh, you must learn. No one threatens me."

Gleb Orlov means what he says.

✳ ✳ ✳

"*Gleb,*" Foster mouths.

Anna gasps and Foster presses her forehead against Anna's. "Shhh," she says as they try to listen.

The violence is too quiet for them to hear.

The quiet stretches. One minute. Two. Three.

After the fourth full minute, Foster can't wait any longer. She removes the small revolver tucked into the waistline of her leggings. That army sweatshirt hides it perfectly. *"You stay,"* Foster mouths at Anna. *"No matter what."*

The presence of the gun ramps up Anna's anxiety to another level. She can't get a deep breath, but she will not panic. The woman taps the screen on Anna's phone for a burst of light and whispers, "I've got you."

Anna asks, "But who will have you?"

And Foster nearly collapses from the love.

It takes all her gumption to say, "I'm trained for this." If this surprises Anna, she doesn't show it. She nods firmly and does the most unexpected of things: she presses a kiss against Foster's forehead and says, "Be safe."

*   *   *

One hour earlier, Lavinia Collins had been in her walk-in closet dressing for the evening. After some indecision, she chose a spectacular navy jumpsuit, lovely gold earrings that Martin purchased for their thirtieth wedding anniversary, and a pair of sandals that showed off her glorious pedicure. Following her meeting at Noah's, she planned to join Topher for a private dinner. Their last in this house.

Once Topher consumed several glasses of bourbon—the good stuff tonight—she'd tell him the Cuba plan. He would hate it. When she alluded to her exit strategy earlier, she knew he was picturing Canada. They had a lovely home on a hundred acres covered in caribou and snow. But that house and property existed in their financial records. The Cuba home did not. Topher would argue with her decision and then he would offer to kill Gleb. That might lead to a conversation about paternity, and she'd rather spend her life in Cuba than let things get that messy. So ideally he would be drunk enough to agree without having to get into the details.

She had one of the chefs preparing his favorite lamb dish. Lavinia had stopped by the kitchen more than once that afternoon to smell it roasting. Superb. She would miss their chefs.

Everything needed to look and smell and be perfect.

Or so she thought.

As it turned out, Lavinia only had one perfection left.

After Gleb Orlov squeezed the life from her neck, her white-blonde hair lay in a curtain around her face that was so perfect he swore at her beauty.

CHAPTER 61

ONE PROBLEM WITH BEING IN the Portage family for the last four years is how infrequently Foster has been in pulse-pounding situations. The only thing raising her heart rate over a hundred these days is Marco, her spin instructor. When Gary asked why she needed her sidearm to meet up with Anna, she'd actually thought, *Do I?*

"I don't," she told Gary with a coy wink. And followed that up with, "Feed the raccoon."

He laughed and she tucked the gun at the small of her back. Then he kissed her on the temple and said, "Mother said a Bentley arrived this evening and parked behind Orlov Lodge. If Gleb is on your agenda, you might want to pack more than that little thing. I'm out with Carter tonight."

"Don't drink too much," she told him.

"Don't kill him and get caught," he fired back.

They were good together, she and Gary. Equally good at pretending.

Not that they needed to be extremely good.

Gary's parents were so old-fashioned they never noticed their daughter-in-law had more chemistry with Gary's sister than she did with Gary. Nor did they notice Gary's proclivity to stare at his best friend's ass. Gary and Carter had been together since their college tennis days at Brown. The elder Portages remained clueless. Or maybe they ignored what they knew and hated. It was hard to say with conservative parents whether ignorance was bliss or bliss required ignorance.

Some days Foster actually felt married to Gary Portage. What was a marriage anyway? The person you lived with, ate carbs with, lamented eating carbs with, watched TikTok videos with. Most of Foster's married friends stopped having sex after their first kid. "It's too much of a hassle," her friend Leisa said. Foster remembered scoffing. This arrangement was too much of a hassle. Sex was . . . Foster wasn't sure she remembered.

The real Foster is inside her somewhere. Five years ago, when Starr tracked her down out of guilt and Foster began the pilgrimage toward her roots, she met Gary at a bar called Wild Willies. They'd fallen deep into friendship at first sight and had stayed up all night explaining their respective situations. By sunrise, they plotted a mutually beneficial plan. Gary would get Foster into the Lodges to investigate Gleb Orlov, and Foster would be Gary's arm candy so he could please his parents and his boyfriend. Marriage to Gary gave her a chance to take down the Orlovs. And she got to live like a very rich lady in the process. It wasn't enough. Not the money. Not even the revenge.

But Anna.

Finding Anna is worth it all.

* * *

She thinks about the fire in Anna's gray eyes. Its electricity.

How many times has Foster thought about Anna over the course of her life? A million times? Maybe more. Anna is the last memory that ties Foster to her mother, and now she isn't a memory anymore.

Foster already knows she will do anything for Anna.

Isn't it strange to know a thing like that? To connect. Or maybe a better phrase is . . . to integrate. Or to realize the thread of your life has already been woven through the fabric of someone else.

Maybe you've felt it too. Irrational and yet certain. Magical and yet the most human thing in existence. That moment when you know someone is your person. That they always have been and always will be part of your story.

That's what's happening inside Foster's heart.

Inside her brain, she knows she can get herself killed if she's not careful.

The situation beyond the closet has likely turned violent and might require intervention. Being a foster kid gave her grit. The army gave her gumption and training. Foster's military career was both decorated and deliberate. She finished high school and enlisted. The army paid for college, sent her around the world, kicked her up the ranks, and spit her out into the ATF, which she quit when she married Gary.

Bent Tree was a new mission, and taking down the man who killed her mother wasn't sanctioned by the government.

Hand on the knob, she says a quiet prayer for the Lord to save her queer little soul and bursts into the room with her weapon drawn, ready to face Gleb.

Lavinia lays in a heap on the floor, her glassy, open eyes affixed on the ceiling.

Dead. Foster knows in a glance.

The room is otherwise empty.

Foster checks for a pulse while keeping her eyes on Noah's bedroom door. Nothing pulses under Lavinia's skin. Foster clears the room, the bathroom, the living room. Heart pounding in her throat, she steps onto the porch and hopes her eyes adapt quickly to the darkness. She waits for a shot, but the night is quiet and the stars are loud enough she sees the entire yard, all the way to the surrounding forest. Not even a shadow moves.

"Damn it." The hissed words are full of venom.

Foster kicks herself for reacting slowly. In the closet, the idea that Gleb would kill Lavinia seemed far-fetched. The woman was the matriarch of the operation. There had been hundreds of other opportunities to do her harm. Whatever Lavinia used to threaten him must have worked.

Frustrated, Foster returns to the closet for Anna.

She finds her sitting cross-legged on the floor, staring at her phone. "Did you call someone?" Foster asks.

Anna lifts her phone to Foster and shows her the 911 keyed in, the call button untouched.

"Is Lavinia . . . is she—?"

Foster nods.

"What do we do now?" Anna asks.

Foster isn't sure about the best course of action. Should she call this in or leave Lavinia to be found? If the local police show up and investigate a murder, it will affect the auction. It might go on; it might be delayed. If it carries on as planned, she'll have another chance to stop Gleb. If it's delayed and Gleb slips away, he'll have all the time in the world to rebuild the operation somewhere else. Then there will be more guns in the hands of assholes who would use them to kill kids

and grocery store shoppers and people listening to concerts and . . .
She answers with steel. "We take him down. Which means I need
to make an appearance at the in-laws' so no one will think anything
about where I was tonight and then I'll come to your mom's and we'll
talk this through. Okay?"

"You were really there, weren't you?" Anna says. "With me on the
Juneau."

Foster isn't one of those women who prides herself on never crying. She owns a full range of emotions—raging bitch to sadness
cyclone—and her tears crest at Anna's question and drip down her
cheeks. "I was."

Without saying a word, Anna cups Foster's face and uses her
thumbs to wipe away Foster's tears. No one has ever done this. Not
one of her many temporary families. Not her military unit. Not even
Gary. The women stare without blinking, without looking away. Taking in the years and how they've each worn them. It is painful, and
yet, for the first time in a very long time, Foster feels . . . well, she
isn't sure how to wrap her head around what she feels; all she knows
is she's being seen.

And after being invisible for years, she feels something inside her
tear loose.

✳   ✳   ✳

This is not the last time these women will face death together.

But it is the first time they face life together.

✳   ✳   ✳

"What do I tell Murray?" Anna asks. "He knows I'm here."

"Tell him you didn't find anything."

"Okay."

"And you can't tell Waylon yet," Foster makes herself say. "Or Jack. They need to find out naturally. Whenever that is."

They part. Each of them at a run.

CHAPTER 62

WHEN ANNA REACHES THE LUXOR Bridge, she lowers the truck window and leans her head into the cold, whipping air. Her face stings. Her knees are bruised. There is at least one cut on her cheek and more on her arms and legs from where she tripped and scrambled toward her truck.

Noah's cabin plays on repeat.

Foster's confession.

The truth about who they were to each other and to the Choir Girls.

Lavinia's crumpled body on the floor. The overwhelming sadness she experiences for Waylon.

The bridge's rainbow-shaped steel cage rises on either side. The paint is peeling and the massive bolts look like bright buttons in the oncoming traffic's headlights. This bridge is visible from her bedroom window. Briefly she entertains what would happen if she crashed into the side. Would the steel and concrete hold? Or would she and the truck end up in the Ohio? Would her mother watch the truck hit the water from her chair?

"Jesus." She utters the name as a prayer, trying to get ahold of herself.

There isn't any good way to come down from the last hour. By the time she arrives at the farm, her skin is ice cold and her teeth rattle.

Jack's truck is parked under the house like he belongs to them. That brings a smile that boosts her spirits. She cuts the lights and her mother calls, "There's my silly goose," from the deck above.

Anna yells as normally as she can, "Good evening, my crazy duck!"

Jack leans over the decking, hands clasped, grinning nervously. "We were about to come looking for you."

That draws the tiniest of smiles from Anna.

Slowly she climbs, hoping the rhythm of home heals her before she reaches the top step. She arrives in time to watch Jack lift her mother from the deck lounger and tease, "I let you stay up and wait for her, but now it's bedtime."

Her mother giggles and drapes her arms around Jack's neck. He settles Starr against his chest. In the dark neither has a good look at Anna yet. Thank goodness, or else the spell might break. Jack pauses long enough for Anna to kiss her mother's forehead. Her mother mouths into her ear, "You should bang his brains out."

Anna laughs. She's too tired to bang anyone's brains out.

* * *

Maybe sex is like a dessert stomach. And the same way you can be totally full and still find room for ice cream, there's always room for wanting. Or maybe love makes its own energy.

Either way, this scene:

Jack spending the evening with Starr.

Taking care of her.

Carrying her.

Teasing her.

Unleashes something feral in Anna.

Anna's pulse gallops.

The part of her that wanted to collapse on the deck, lie flat in a starfish position, and stare at the sky loses to the part of her demanding to watch the man she has loved for the better part of a decade be that gentle with her mother.

For once in Anna's life, she's taking Starr's advice about a man.

Jack carries Starr to her tiny bedroom at the back of the house. His T-shirt stretches against his shoulders; his jeans sag low on his hips. With each step he is careful not to knock the framed photos off the hallway wall. He disappears through Starr's door and Anna listens.

"Your water cup is by the table and we're right outside if you need us."

Anna crosses the hallway while Jack has his back to her. He inches out of her mother's room quietly like he is afraid to wake a sleeping baby. When he turns, Anna takes up every ounce of his space. He gives a slight but delighted gasp before she pushes him against the wall and pins him with her hips.

"Hey." She grips both of his forearms and slips her cold fingers up over his elbows and inside the sleeves of his shirt.

"Hey," he says gently, dancing a little at her touch. A smile lifts the corners of his mouth. The electricity between them thrums like a drummer striking a cymbal.

Anna is no longer cold.

She takes him in. The shadow of a beard. The curve of his right eyebrow. The little divot missing from his earlobe from a dog bite. A single freckle shaped like Idaho.

She lets her body collapse fully against his and his arms come around her in a crushing hug. His fingers caress her back over her shirt. The breath she takes with her mouth against the fabric of his T-shirt is the safest moment of the day so far.

"Jack."

"Ann."

Jack's hair curls around the edge of his second-favorite ball cap. She's still wearing his first favorite. She removes both caps and tosses them toward the living room recliner. A photo of her from high school swings on its nail.

"You've been crying," Jack says, and his face scrunches with compassion. "And you're hurt." He examines the cut on her cheek.

"And you've been taking care of my mom."

"She wanted to hear Molly and see the stars."

"And you carried her."

He shrugs like this is the most normal action in the world.

She keeps going. "You gave me a job after I—"

"Yeah," he says, also like it cost him nothing.

She closes the distance between their faces, eyeing his lips, telegraphing her desire. She pauses inches away to ask, "Do you still—"

"Want you?" He finishes her question with a definitive answer. He slides his hands under her shirt and up the small of her back. The skin-to-skin contact makes her back arch and everything between her legs tingle. He places his lips on the dip in her neck and traces a breath all the way up to her ear. "Hell yeah," he whispers.

"Good." Anna calls on all her restraint, knowing she is moments away from the best makeup sex of her life, and pauses her cheek next to Jack's. Then she tilts her head ever so slightly until their temples meet. "I'm sorry I didn't listen. I stole so many years from us."

"We've got—" The words "a million more" are spoken into her mouth.

Their lips meet with forgiveness and passion and regret.

*　*　*

This is the place where you could learn exactly how Jack and Anna moved between sex and love and laughing and, oddly enough, an intense craving for tacos and beer.

But you won't.

Those moments belong to them.

All you get to know is they were awkward and beautiful.

Day Three

Day Three

CHAPTER 63

THE SEEDS OF VIOLENCE AREN'T grown in a single day.

So we return once more to the potential future. To a young man in Roseville, New Jersey, stretching sideways across his childhood bed.

Corey's chin falls over the edge of the mattress. His eyes are locked on his phone screen as music drills through his head. He flips over on his back and watches the fan blades spin. He was supposed to be at work an hour ago. He'll be fired. Again. He knows this is the case and inevitably considers his future. Does he have one? Should he have one?

Why is life so easy for some people and so hard for others? Is there a God up there calling the shots? A God who's watching him now and knows what he's considering?

He hopes not. And then he hopes so. That would mean there is one person who understands.

He tries to follow a singular panel on the fan in its ever-circulating route and grows dizzy. There are steps in the hallway that stop in front of his room. He wonders if his mother's pressing her ear to his door. He's not sure, but he thinks he hears her crying.

She won't come in.

She never does.

He understands why. She's just as disappointed as he is that he can't make something of himself. That he can't tamp down the anger he feels. It just seizes his brain and whispers terrible things. Things like, *You're not worth anything. You'll never be loved.* And other things too. Darker things like .. . *Payback's a bitch* and *There's a new gun in the garage.*

"Corey," his mother says from the hallway. "I thought you were supposed to be at work."

"Go away," he tells her and turns the music up until there is nothing but noise and the spinning fan overhead.

*   *   *

Good parents know when "Go away" means "Hug me." They barge through the door, through the noise, through the pain, and say, "I know you're hurting. I want to help." They keep coming back. Even when they're being pushed away.

Good parents also miss big moments, huge moments, with their kids. They're staring at their phone or wrapped up in their jobs or just ignorant about emotional intelligence. Sometimes they're scared to help because their own hurt is a lump in their throat. And they end up drowning in guilt for not being superhuman.

What's a good parent?

It's just so hard to know.

It's especially hard that day in Roseville, New Jersey.

But maybe, just maybe, we should root for this mom to be braver than she normally is.

CHAPTER 64

STARR IS LAUGHING IN HER bed, holding her hand over her own mouth to keep the sound from escaping. She is in the middle of a discovery.

The greatest pleasure isn't a man who knows how to treat her.

The greatest pleasure is knowing a man will treat her daughter right.

Jack and Anna are together again.

When you're a woman who believes she is dying, watching the ground underneath your daughter settle is the merriest of medicines.

Starr's cancer, while sudden and consuming, has a reprieve coming. The chemo cocktail that her very fine Hallmark doctor tries first works. Not quickly and not without pain, but she has more time than anyone understood that night.

Unfortunately, her daughter's relationship isn't so lucky.

The luck starts running out a little after midnight.

❊   ❊   ❊

The couple down the hall from Starr is so invested in each other they hear nothing else in the house. Not Topher's boots on the decking outside. Nor the squeak of Starr's bedroom door. They don't even hear him scoot the chair closer to her bed and rest his heavy boots against her bed frame.

He leans over her, leering, his long hair falling forward, almost touching her skin. She doesn't stir. He blows a steady breath on her eyelids. They don't twitch.

Next, he covers her mouth with his hand.

Starr's eyes rocket open then. Her pupils widen when she sees it's him. She closes her eyes and opens them again, as though she thinks he is a dream.

"Why's the *Juneau* in your barn?" He doesn't let her answer. He says, "Why's my brother always on your side? And why does a woman obsessed with security never move her hide-a-key?" He tsks and releases her mouth. "The only real question is, are you a bigger idiot or a bigger whore?"

Starr has three words she has used on him before. "Piss off, Topher."

He stands tall, his body ramrod straight. "Keep Anna on your side of the river and burn that barn to the ground after the Royale ends. Understand?"

Starr rolls over on her side defiantly, but it's clear he's gotten his message across.

Topher sees himself out and runs the blade of his knife down the length of Jack's truck.

CHAPTER 65

AS YOU WILL SEE, A great many things happened the night Gleb killed Lavinia.

Including Gleb Orlov starting a war.

As was typical, the war started with words.

       ✳   ✳   ✳

Gleb Orlov learned about fathers from his father. No warmth. No love. Position was *the* gift, his name the legacy. "You are an Orlov," his father boomed when Gleb begged to attend university. To play soccer on the national team. To be a boy. "You will be an Orlov."

Gleb's father's example never worked for Merkoul. As such, Gleb said very few things to Merkoul. It was Noah who saved the boy. "Bring him to me. His mother's mistake is not his fault. I'll raise him here and make use of him. I won't live forever. Someone has to stay here to wash the laundry," he said long ago. Gleb never questioned Noah. He brought the boy and they fell into a rhythm Gleb could keep. One week of the year he fathered the bastard for the sake of the business.

He did not understand . . . not then, not now . . . that for the boy, that one week was everything.

*　*　*

In Gleb's pocket is an Incan owl totem he bought from a man in Peru. He holds the statue now as a way to relax his fingers from the work they've put in on Lavinia's neck. When he was younger, he could squeeze a woman's neck like a chicken. And now, with aging, he has a nasty bruise in the palm of his hand from one attempt.

The owl is cool and soothing against the bruise. Gleb rather likes the totem for its faint yellow and green color and the delicate way the paint fades into the chiseled stone. He plans to keep it.

Murray's an adult. He doesn't need trinkets from other countries.

And if that's true, Murray doesn't need Gleb's fatherhood ruse either.

He's tired of crossing the Atlantic. His sciatica hurts after a single hour of flying. The money is good in Bent Tree and can be replicated elsewhere. Every country with division or fear wants automatic weapons, and that makes the entire map his storefront.

The clarity in Gleb's brain after an act of violence is almost worth killing someone else. The path forward emerges. He'll dump his portion of the Lodges on Murray as a "parting gift."

This will be Gleb's last trip to Kentucky.

That's too much to put in a phone call. He's not a monster. He'll tell the kid in person.

CHAPTER 66

GLEB DRIVES TO MURRAY'S HOUSE. He is barely through the door when he announces, "Lavinia is dead. Go tidy the scene. I'm not your father. Mail me a box of Buffalo Trace each year. My lodge is yours. This is goodbye for us." He throws himself onto the couch as if this speech has exhausted him.

After more than forty years of pining for fatherly affection, the phrase sticking in Murray's head isn't *"I'm not your father"* or even *"My lodge is yours."* It's *"Go tidy the scene."*

Go tidy the scene.

Go *tidy* the scene.

Go tidy *the scene.*

Doesn't that say everything about Murray and Gleb's relationship? One more time Gleb sends him away to do work he considers beneath him. Like Murray is his father's maid.

Correction. Gleb is the man he calls his father, not his actual father. As the implication sinks further into his understanding, Murray accesses indifference toward Gleb for the first time in his life.

And there he finds a dangerous freedom.

Gleb is unaware. He's too busy placing his deed to Orlov Lodge on the coffee table. "All yours, Merkoul. You will have the auction and I will leave you better than I found you. All is well with my soul."

Murray accepts Gleb's instructions while surreptitiously eyeing the fireplace poker.

Gleb bought him the iron fireplace set years earlier from a little shop in Scotland. Would one strike to the head kill Gleb or would Murray need to keep swinging? Gleb has a head like a melon. A big, fat watermelon. Oh, wouldn't that be satisfying.

However satisfying it might be, that situation is bloody and his latest fling recently purchased new gauzy curtains that hang behind the couch. Murray is already a bit nostalgic about them. He'd paused with his arms around her waist when the drill was still in her hand and said, "I like the yellow," and she had said, "I hate brown," because every bit of decor was some shade of brown.

Murray is incredibly tired. He funnels his growing rage into a plan while Gleb goes on and on about a stupid owl totem and then how to go about the auction without Lavinia. Murray can't help himself; he interrupts with, "When Lavinia turns up dead, your little auction is over."

"Merkoul, it is your little auction now. Tidy the scene. Then she will not turn up. She will be missing. Topher is a money man. He'll make his money and then he'll grieve. Go now before the morning and this will be fine." Then he flicks the ashes of his cigar on Murray's floor and says, "Goodbye, Merkoul." He spins the tiny owl figurine in his palm three times and drops it into the pocket of his pants.

"I will truly miss the bourbon," he says as his parting thought.

❊   ❊   ❊

Murray watches him go. The man who is not his father.

So many actions and energies have centered around making that asshole love him. All a waste. Gleb Orlov has no love for people.

Murray takes a paper towel from the kitchen holder and wipes up the cigar ash and then slides on his shoes. The plan is clear in his mind.

Go to Noah's, confirm Lavinia's death, and call the Collins boys.

Together, they'll figure out the auction.

Afterward, he will drive to the airstrip and make sure that when Gleb's plane takes off in the morning, it crashes instead of lands.

None of this is easy on Murray.

Murray isn't cut out for violence, unless it's against himself. A lesson he learned the hard way many years before. His semi-hands-off approach will be the final metaphor for Murray and Gleb's relationship. *You put me on a plane and sent me away. My turn. Enjoy your plane ride to hell.*

CHAPTER 67

FOSTER MADE IT ALL THE way to her in-laws' driveway before she dialed an old friend from her life prior to Gary Portage Jr. and Bent Tree.

The conversation proceeded as she predicted it would. Lots of cussing and screaming followed by her apology for not calling him sooner. When he finally quit yelling that she could have gotten herself killed—which she took as his love language—he sent a nearby team to quietly handle Lavinia's body. Then he drove to the Lodges and now has spent the past six hours questioning Foster in person.

Foster walks him through the crime scene at Noah's and tells him everything she knows about the auction.

"You were going to kill him yourself, weren't you?" he says when the last piece ties the auction to the Choir Girls. "For killing your mom."

"We'll never know," she says. "I called you instead." And then with the smallest of smiles, she says, "You can thank me later. You know this will be the biggest bust of your career."

She is right about the bust. Her colleague's trajectory in the agency changes that night. He was the right person to call, and he is precisely right about Foster's intentions for Gleb Orlov.

CHAPTER 68

MURRAY'S LIVE-IN GIRLFRIEND ARRIVES FIVE minutes after Gleb's departure.

Had she not, Murray would have been in the act of moving Lavinia's body when Foster's former agency arrived at Noah's.

Instead, Murray discovers two black fleet vans parked in the drive and keeps going.

Murray understands unofficial things because Bent Tree has many unofficial things. All you have to do to understand *unofficial* is visit the BeeGee for a cup of coffee and a biscuit between the hours of 6:00 and 8:00 a.m. You'll find a group of men gathered around a large table holding court over breakfast. Unofficially, they determine if the pastor stays another year, which businesses are granted permits, whether they champion the quarterback at the high school, how many officers will be added to the Sheriff's Department, when fishing season actually begins, whether someone's little Johnny or baby Suzie is a "good" or "bad" kid. Hell, they even control the boundaries of pizza delivery.

Unofficially, of course.

What is the difference between official and unofficial? Hardly anything in Bent Tree.

Murray's singular look at the two fleet vans parked at Noah's and the men dressed in all black moving between the vehicles and the cabin tells him a story.

They know.

They are some of the alphabet soup group. The FBI, CIA, ATF. So either this thing—the auction—that his father and the Collinses built got out of hand long enough ago that they are already here, or someone has tied the auction to the Choir Girl murders. Maybe even both.

Because of course they are connected.

Back before there were weapons for sale, they auctioned other high-end items. Like women. Like Starr Ryder and Jenni Lockwood. And plenty others.

*   *   *

Noah's cabin is on a one-way road with no outlets, so Murray drives all the way to the river and makes a show of checking the security cameras at the dock. That puts twenty minutes between his passes of Noah's cabin driveway.

He doesn't manage to time this trip to catch anything as interesting as the removal of the body or evidence bags, but he does happen to pass by exactly as a woman on the deck lifts her face to Noah's porch light.

Foster Portage.

A panicked laugh begins in Murray's stomach. By the time he reaches his own house, he opens the driver's door and retches.

That bitch played them all.

❊   ❊   ❊

Murray has a way out of this.

He need not set up dominos; they are already lined up and wobbling. All he has to do is make the first tap and they'll fall on their own. And he knows exactly the right tap.

He chooses Topher's number on his phone and hits Call.

The man answers with, "Hold on."

He listens as Topher exchanges words with a gas station clerk. "Two eighty-five," the woman says. Then a bell jingles and Murray hears Topher take a long slurp from a straw. Finally, "What?"

"This is a courtesy call."

"It's after midnight, Murray. Get to your point."

"Your mother's dead. My father killed her. He'll leave at five from the airstrip."

Murray hangs up. Topher's not a money man. He's a momma's boy. Oh, what a home movie this will be.

CHAPTER 69

JACK IS IN HER BED. The clock on her nightstand reads 2:01 a.m.

Anna has dozed off and on for the last hour. She wants to give herself over to sleep. Needs the rest. Today will be crazy one way or another. Either the Royale and auction will go on or Lavinia's death will be discovered and change everything.

Her mind jockeys between two very different scenes.

Lavinia's lifeless body.

The reality of Jack.

Jack spoons her. His mouth is nuzzled at the nape of her neck. He's naked. The heat of his core presses against her back, making it hard to breathe, much less sleep. She wears his T-shirt and a pair of athletic shorts that she grabbed on her way back from the bathroom. His hands are on her stomach, his fingers resting under the elastic band of the shorts.

Without understanding why, she starts to cry.

"Hey." Jack's voice is husky with sleep. "What can I do to help?"

The question only makes her cry harder. He woke up wanting to help her. She inches her body even closer to his.

"It's nothing." She doesn't like how dismissive that sounds and tries the truth instead. "I can't believe I got you both back."

"Me either," he whispers into her hair, not catching the mention of *both*.

She tells him about Foster. Jack listens without interrupting and doesn't speak until she asks, "How can I not remember either of you?"

"Because you were traumatized. Your brain shut that whole section of your life down." He kisses her hair. "And you were a kid. I'm two years older and I didn't remember you until I saw that photo in my grandmother's album. It's okay that you don't remember." His thumb makes slow and steady circles on the back of her hand. "It's probably some type of grace that you don't. That time in your life wasn't safe."

Anna's glad Jack can't see her face. Tears fall in such a rush she feels the dampness of the sheet under her left cheek. "I think maybe my mother was so full of love that when I look back, she's the blanket that covers everything."

"You're lucky, then."

"Tonight, at Noah's, Foster held my hand, and for a second, she was on the edge of my memory."

"That's good."

"I didn't tell her that we have the boat."

"Because of Starr?"

Anna's body shakes against Jack's. "I can't lose her. I'm so scared of losing her. I know I said I'd tell the police and I will, but . . . I don't know how to do this the right way."

"I shouldn't have to remind you, but I will. Starr Ryder is a strong,

tits-up woman. She's the kind of woman who will make cancer apologize for bothering her. She's pretty effing epic. And she made you. So
I'm pretty sure you'll figure out how to handle this in the right way."

"Yeah," she says, "just like you are."

"Well, thank you for finally agreeing I'm a strong, tits-up
wom—"

She swats him on the butt. "You're pretty effing epic, you idiot."
They start laughing and don't stop until Jack says, "Ann."

"Yeah?"

"Starr's not the only one who loves you deeply. Let me love you. I
know it's scary, but it's worth it."

* * *

Because Jack finds a way to speak directly into Anna's past, their past,
without chastisement or bitterness, the truth opens up.

Anna has been scared of security.

Luxor kids grow up fighting for everything. The fight means
they're alive, so when the fight isn't required, when love simply raises
its hand and says, "Present," they freak. They can't believe they deserve it. They push back and away. Which means they are always
fighting.

She didn't get Jack wrong all those years ago.

She got herself wrong.

* * *

Anna rolls over inside Jack's arms and presses a kiss on his chest.

They've had great sex in the past. They've already had great sex that evening. What they have next is transparency and vulnerability. They give wildly rather than waiting on the other to give. And isn't that when sex becomes love?

When she rolls off him, exhausted, all the happy chemicals bubbling in her brain, she says, "Saint Jack Augustine, tell me something good."

He pokes her in the rib and says, "I could show you something good again." When he sees she's considering a rally, he lifts his hands in defeat. "That's a joke. I'm exhausted. You wore me out." After threading his fingers through her hair, he says, "Something good? Let's see," and stares glassy-eyed at the window over her shoulder. "I don't know if this is good exactly, but I've wanted to tell you about it for a long time."

"Okay," she says.

"I've been doing this thing. For my son."

Jack explains an audio project he started the day he found out he was a father. How every day he records something for Beck. Short. Long. About nothing. About everything. Bits of life. So that if Jack ever finds him, he'll be able to show him how much he has been loved every day of his life.

Anna's sense of awe expands with every detail Jack shares.

"What did you tell him yesterday?"

His eyes move left and right as he tries to remember. "You know what? I didn't make one yet, so we'll fix that." Jack rolls away from her to the nightstand and grabs his phone. The light from the screen casts a pale blue ambience that makes them both squint. He scoots so his back rests against the headboard and Anna joins him.

"You want me to say something?" she asks, afraid she'll mess up.

"Yeah," he says. "I've told him all about you."

"You have?"

"Ann, he needs to know about love if I'm not there to teach him. And you're pretty much my only object lesson."

Anna's sigh is partially happy and partially sad. All this time she assumed she was the villain in Jack's story. If she'd been making audio files of the lessons she learned in the last five years, would she have spoken so kindly of him?

"You start and then tell me when to talk," she says as Jack's finger hovers over the Record button.

Jack kisses her cheek. "All you have to do is say something real."

Audio File #1728

JACK: Hey, Beck, it's the middle of the night here and I have an update. Anna, tell Beck hi.

ANNA: Uh, hi, Beck. It's nice to, uh, talk to you.

JACK: Needless to say, son, my universe got its own special sunrise today and I am basking in it big-time. We're very tired, but I didn't want the day to get away without checking in. All I can think to say is don't give up on what or who you love. You know me and how I can't help myself from sharing Saint Augustine. He once said, "Love is not breathlessness, it is not excitement, it is not the promulgation of promises of eternal passion. That is just being in love, which any of us can convince ourselves we are. Love itself is what is left over ..."

ANNA: "When being in love has burned away ..."

JACK: "And this is both an art and a fortunate accident." Son, find yourself a partner who will be there when being in love has burned away. Find yourself a partner who can finish your favorite quotes. And I guess maybe the most important part is not in the finding; that's a location service. You need it, but who you are after the finding ... that's the real business of love. Be humble. Be kind. Be confident.

ANNA: I'm going to interrupt now and tell you that your father lives by the advice he's sharing, Beck. He's remarkable.

JACK: Okay, okay. She's making me blush. We're off for the night. We love you.

CHAPTER 70

JACK WAITS TO UNTANGLE HIS body until Anna's breathing is loud and deep, almost a snore. It takes longer than he intends because he can't quit looking at her. Marveling. Being a them is about the best thing on the planet. By his count, he's been a them three times. With his granddad, with Murray, with Anna. The void left by Anna nearly killed him.

He feels good and alive as he inches off the bed and places his bare feet on the cold hardwood floor. After slipping into his boxers, he sinks onto the chair beside the window and searches for the moon. The globe is out of view, but the tips of the corn wave like a blanket in the wind. A piece of loose metal roofing flaps on the barn. And in the distance, above the tree line, is the glow of the Luxor Bridge. The lights along the cables and steel beams make a rainbow that connects Luxor and Bent Tree. The Ohio River is tucked beneath, invisible from here, but he feels the water snaking by the banks. He's spent so much time skimming over the surface in a boat, he knows every ripple by heart.

He's half tempted to take to the water and let it clear his head. If it weren't for Anna sleeping three feet away, he might have found his way to a boat.

Anna's story about Foster pushes him back in time.

Back to his own almost experience with the Choir Girls . . .

Jack and his grandfather skimmed over the Ohio and then slowly banked the boat toward Mayfield Creek. They motored past the dark murder scene, sending the smallest of wakes onto the beach.

Nine women were bound to wooden posts.

Jack imagines the effort that went into staging that scene. Unloading bodies. Cleaning the blood from their skin in the creek. Driving the posts into the slick silt and sand by moonlight. He listens to the thumping of a sledgehammer. He thinks of someone undressing and redressing the women so they all wear the same thing. The bindings. The lipstick. The way the women face the water.

A sight designed for boaters on the water, not hunters on the land.

Why would Gleb, if it was Gleb, go to that extreme?

Did it have to do with Texas?

Jack doesn't know.

He'd been right there with a front-row seat and hadn't seen a thing.

And now, roving mentally around the scene, patching together online stories, he's more convinced he saw the white cruiser that morning.

He recalls his grandfather's insistence that they were on the water alone that morning. That Jack had slept through the ride and perhaps dreamed the boat. As he looks back now, through adult eyes, he understands why his grandfather might have lied to him. He was probably scared to death. Nine women were dead. The last thing his grandfather would have wanted is someone thinking Jack saw something.

Whatever his reason, he made a believer of Jack. Murray was the only person Jack ever told about the white cruiser. And his grandfather tanned his hide so hard that Jack still has the scars.

After the police interview, his grandfather had brought him back to the dock at Warrior Landing. They'd headed straight for the kennels because they were dog men. No better way to wash your mind than with puppy breath.

Murray was there when they arrived, lying inside one of the kennels. One of the caramel-colored spaniels was the big spoon, the other the little. Murray's hair was wild from sleep. His clothes were covered in hay and dirt from the kennel floor. He had a tennis ball in each hand.

Jack holds that version of Murray in his head. He'd been . . . what? Fourteen? Fifteen? It wasn't too long after they met and Jack started spending time with Murray every day.

Jack remembers unlatching the kennel, licking his finger, and shoving it in Murray's ear to wake him. Murray had knocked him on his ass and laughed. Lexi and Tobin raised their heads to acknowledge the commotion, then lowered them again in sleep. Up until Jack graduated, Murray's pet name for him was Little Shit. He supposed, based on moments like that one, he'd earned the moniker.

"Guess what?" he said to Murray.

"What, Little Shit?" Murray asked.

"A bunch of people are dead. Grandpa and I talked to the cops about them." Jack spoke with a certain amount of pride. His understanding of death at the time was limited to one turtle, two goldfish, and an ill-fated trip to the taxidermist. No people. Not yet.

Murray sat up quickly, the color washed from his face, and said, "Wait. Who's dead?"

"I don't know. They were on the beach but I didn't see them."

"Then why did you talk to the police?"

"'Cause we were nearby and they wanted to know if we saw anything."

"And did you?"

Jack tried to lower his voice. "I don't guess so. Grandpa said we didn't even though there was a white boat coming out of the creek. I saw it."

He failed to maintain the whisper, the excitement too great, so Grandpa yelled out, "Jack! What did I say?"

In a heartbeat, Grandpa lifted Jack out of the kennel, carried him outside, and switched him with the lithe branch of forsythia. When Jack returned tear-streaked and with his rear aflame, Murray gave him a stick of gum and said, "Don't worry. I won't tell anyone about the cruiser."

Jack scooted his behind against the barn wall; his hip was touching Murray's. He measured his short little legs against Murray's. They came to the teenager's thighs. He asked, "Why're you in here? I thought you were with your dad this week."

"He's too busy for me."

"Oh," Jack had said, unsure of what might combat the hatred in Murray's voice, but then he put his small hand in Murray's and they stayed that way until Jack's grandpa came back to the kennel.

✶   ✶   ✶

Jack let his brain tour that old conversation. Let it whirl and jolt to various stopping points. Examining each until he landed on what he was searching for.

Gleb and Murray always spent the Royale together. On the night the Choir Girls died, Gleb had been *too busy*? The man was only in the States three to four days a year. A point lamented by every documentarian of the murders. Including the police notes. They all read that Murray was Gleb's alibi. And yet, on the morning of the murder,

Murray had been in the kennels. And if you happened to be his best friend, you knew he slept there.

Perhaps Murray's dad was too busy that morning because he was on Starr's cruiser murdering the Choir Girls. Murdering Jenni Lockwood. Spraying blood on the bed that hid Anna and Foster.

* * *

Everything points to Gleb. And Jack needs a way to prove it.

Earlier that evening, when he and Starr were on the deck, he had asked Starr point-blank, "Is Gleb Anna's father?"

Starr's answer shut Jack down. "He wished he was." Then an eye roll and, "It would have been so much easier if he was."

Jack pressed her for more details and Starr pretended to nap.

It was one thing to discover a discrepancy in the testimonies and another to understand why Gleb killed those women and staged them the way he did.

Jealousy? Rage? A cover-up?

While staring at the Luxor Bridge, Jack considers the interior of the boat and the display on the beach. Jack is one of the only people alive who is privy to both scenes because no one else knows the *Juneau* still exists.

The photos on every podcast website and documentary claimed the Mayfield Creek beach scene was one of the most pristine crime scenes ever. Its only rival: the Texas massacre. The killer washed the women's bodies. Added lipstick. Destroyed the footprints with a mulching rake.

But the cruiser is violent, unorganized, chaotic. Bloody.

The spaces feel like two different people.

The person who shot the women. The person who staged them.

Jack also has no idea how Texas fits into the equation except that Jenni Lockwood was from Texas and she and Starr traveled there together at one point. None of those documentaries knew that.

A horrible thought crosses Jack's mind. Could Starr have murdered the girls and Gleb covered up the crime? Wouldn't it make sense for her to have been on the boat that night? It was hers, after all.

That doesn't explain how Waylon knows. He might have found the boat much later and agreed to keep quiet. Between his love for Starr and his livelihood, he'd have a good reason. If the press found out one of the owners of the Lodges murdered the Choir Girls, the Royale certainly would have died, the loss costing everyone millions.

Or could it have been Waylon and Starr?

If Gleb was cheating on Starr with Jenni and Starr found out, could she have meant to confront Jenni and things went to shit? Did she panic and call Waylon? He was strong enough to drive the posts and hide the *Juneau* in the barn. He already admitted those were his boot prints in the blood.

Both scenarios explain why Foster and Anna are still alive.

Jack isn't about to suggest either theory to Anna. Not without proof.

He needs to go back to the barn and take a look at the boat with fresh eyes. Maybe identify something of Gleb's.

Jack slides back into bed with his plan in place. Later this morning he'll make a short pit stop in the barn without Anna.

CHAPTER 71

THERE ISN'T MUCH NIGHT LEFT for Foster's former team to get the proper go-ahead warrants and locate hundreds of assault weapons and multiple crates of British missiles ahead of the auction. Foster can't shake the feeling that she's losing the battle and the war all at the same time. "He'll flee," she warns on her way out the door. "Gleb doesn't have to be on sight to run things. He came to watch. To see how right he is. He'll take off the first moment he can."

"Foster, he won't slither away. Go home and get some sleep and let us do our jobs. We'll get him."

"You better," she threatens.

The night air is wickedly cold when Foster steps outside. Her shoulders are tight; her brain hurts. She looks to the stars overhead and sees only clouds. She has a thought: sometimes Gleb flies into the Lodges on a private plane. She almost goes back inside and tells her colleague.

We hold so many secret hopes. Sometimes those hopes sound like a wished-for vacation or a new job. Maybe a baby or a miracle cure. Other hopes are darker. More like Foster's in that moment: *I hope I get to handle this myself.*

Ten minutes later, she knows she'll get her chance.

Gleb's plane is on the runway.

Foster sprints across the field and hurls her body through the door of a small green outbuilding, one of those Amish-built barns that accompanies nearly all properties in Bent Tree. Thanks to the decaying boxes in the corner, the air smells of molded cardboard. Dead ladybugs crunch under her soles. Otherwise, the shed's empty.

Foster tilts her head right and left, listening to her spine crack. Her exhaustion is wicked.

When she was a soldier and then later an agent, a bold line of right and wrong plumbed her life. She agreed long ago to let justice combat evil.

But truth be told, justice isn't what she's after tonight. She doesn't want to stop Gleb, arrest him, or bring charges against him. No. She wants to watch Gleb Orlov die and then tie him to a post and leave him for the flies.

*　*　*

Anna answers on the third ring, her voice cloudy with sleep. "Hang on," she whispers. Foster pictures her scrubbing the sleep from the corners of her eyes, flipping on the lamp, padding toward the hallway to check on Starr. Ten seconds later, Anna says, "I'm in the kitchen now. How are you? Are you okay? I thought you were coming here and then you didn't show up."

Anna's tenderness softens Foster. Typically, no one asks how Foster is because the assumption is that badass rich bitches don't have bad days. Gary sometimes says her dick is bigger than his. That is her role, and she performs it with everyone. Everyone up until now.

Foster says, "Not great. Not safe. Not sure of anything."

"Where are you? Why didn't you come?"

"At the airstrip."

"You think Gleb will run?" Anna asks, following Foster's train of thought.

"Yeah."

"I can come."

Foster smiles at the offering. "No, there's an ATF team here," she lies.

Anna exhales loudly. "So you don't have to stop him yourself. That's good."

"Listen, Anna, I need you and Jack to stay in Luxor. Things at the Lodges will be bad today. I need to know you're okay."

"How did you know Jack is—"

"Yummy, remember?" Foster teases and then levels with Anna woman-to-woman. "If I'd had your night, I wouldn't have gone to bed alone, so I figured . . ."

Anna laughs and Foster knows she has guessed correctly. *Good for you*, Foster thinks. "I'll come to Luxor when I'm done here and we'll talk."

"Foster?"

"Yeah?"

"I think Gleb's my father."

Foster almost drops her phone. "What are you saying?"

"I don't know," Anna says.

"Don't ask me not to kill him. Please." Foster knows she's begging. And she knows she's said too much.

The line goes dead.

CHAPTER 72

THE SUN IS STILL BELOW the horizon. By the light above the kitchen sink, Anna scribbles a note to Jack on a napkin.

Foster called. Don't go to Bent Tree today. I'll be right back.

She texts Waylon next.

Mom needs you. Please come now.

That will be enough incentive to get Waylon over the bridge and away from the Lodges.

She pulls on a sweatshirt and wedges her feet into the mud boots by the door, knowing that if she goes back to her room to dress properly, Jack might wake up and talk her out of going to the airstrip.

And she's going.

The cold steals her breath when she opens the door. The temperature hovers around the freezing mark. A glimmering layer of frost coats the deck railing. Treading carefully over the slick surface, she questions the best route to Foster. Take Jack's truck? Take Jack's boat? There isn't a choice. The water's at least fifteen minutes faster and the sun is on the move.

Anna runs. The air stings her lungs. She doesn't slow. The lane to the creek is usually a ten-minute stroll. She's revving the boat's engine in less than three. The panic hits the moment the motor hums to life. It was one thing to face the fear with Jack and another to imagine herself on the open water alone at the helm. *You can do this.* She pushes back at biology and psychology, willing her body to do the thing that scares her so.

Foster might need saving.

Gleb might need saving.

If they do, Anna is hardly the right person for the job.

She goes anyway.

CHAPTER 73

FOR THE LAST FORTY YEARS, Gleb Orlov has employed a pilot named Renat to ferry him around the world. Renat's least favorite destination is Kentucky. Always when they are here, Gleb is more difficult. He has called Renat four times in the last hour.

"Is the plane fueled?"

"Remove Murray from the manifest."

"Any sign of trouble?"

"Fix me a Grey Goose screwdriver."

Renat, for his part, is dressed, fueled, and ready to fly when Gleb Orlov parks at the airstrip. He does not mention the woman hiding in the tiny barn nearby.

* * *

Topher has one eye closed. The other eye socket presses tightly against a scope. His finger lies on the trigger of the rifle his mother gave him for his thirtieth birthday. Today he shoots in her honor. Then he sells in her honor. Afterward, he'll decide whether or not to kill his brother too.

Around him, the reeds sway, providing the perfect cover. The only unnatural thing is a forty-four-ounce Slurpee cup from the gas station. His brother once said the only thing Topher feared was dehydration, and on this issue, Topher admits Waylon has a point.

Topher's plan is elegant.

He'll put a bullet through each of Gleb's calves, then his arms, then his gut, and lastly, he'll blow his head right off his shoulders. Six shots. Each timed as Gleb's body reacts to the previous wound.

Topher is a kid at the fair with a very sad heart and very good aim.

He never cared about money. Everything he's ever done is for his mother.

*   *   *

The sound of a car engine puts Foster on her feet.

She moves to the window and confirms Gleb is walking toward the plane.

She charges from the building, gun drawn, the grass crunching under her feet as she runs. "Stop right there," she commands.

The morning is completely quiet other than her voice, but he doesn't turn.

"Foster," Gleb says, still facing his plane's open door and steps. "Put down your gun."

Foster doesn't oblige. "It's over, Gleb. They know you murdered Lavinia. They know about the auction. Your missiles."

"But the real question is, do they know about Jenni Lockwood? Don't you want to know why she is dead? Am I not the only one who can tell you about your mother?" He is so smug. Foster tries not to react. Gleb continues and, as he does, turns to face Foster. "You look like her." He laughs from his belly. "You look precisely like her. You think I didn't know? I knew from the start. Why do you think I gave you a vehicle? So I'd know where you were at all times. Noah was supposed to con you, but he died. Now we're here and I have a plane to catch."

"Noah betrayed you," Foster said.

"You have proof?" He laughs again. "Of course not. We are Orlovs, not idiots."

"I have proof you killed Lavinia Collins."

Gleb retreats toward the plane. "Here is what will happen," he says. "You will let me leave and I will send you evidence of Lavinia's crimes. Maybe then you will learn about your mother's last moments. Maybe then you will find the weapons. If I die, the weapons still go out. The operation moves elsewhere to a place you will not find. If I die, you will always wonder."

"You're not in a position to—"

＊   ＊   ＊

Anna's path from Warrior Landing spits her out of the woods behind the airfield and its outbuilding. There isn't time to catch her breath. She hears Gleb goading Foster. Sees that Foster has Gleb at gunpoint. With every word Gleb says, Anna watches Foster's hackles rise and her nerves fray.

Anna steps from behind the building and yells Gleb's name. "Don't shoot," she yells, running hard toward Gleb.

"Anna, get out of here," Foster says.

Anna places her body between Foster and Gleb. "Not until I ask him a question. Then he's all yours," Anna says.

* * *

"You want to know if I'm—"

The rifle's report cuts Gleb off.

* * *

The situation spirals away from Topher. Anna Ryder is right in the middle of it all. He plans the shots. He counts down from three to slow his breathing and squeezes. The first hits the fuel tank of the plane. Another shatters the headlight of the plane. When he squeezes the trigger to take out Foster, Anna is already there. He pulls his aim just barely and hears both women hit the ground with a scream.

That leaves Gleb wide open.

Topher takes the shot.

* * *

Foster is disoriented, her ears ringing. Her cheek stings. She knows if she lifts her hand, it will come away red. She feels the blood rolling off her chin. The bullet skimmed her, buzzed by like a bee, taking skin on its route. One inch to the right and she'd be dead.

Another shot can still come.

Foster doesn't dare move.

Beside her, Anna's eyes are wide. She is bleeding too. Foster doesn't know whether the bullet grazed or landed. Either way, she is still alive. "Don't move," she whispers.

Based on the way Gleb fell, the shots came from the woods behind her. Her training instinct tells her he is dead. Anna wears his blood splatter on the back of her sweatshirt.

Very carefully, without moving her body, she scans the woods. The shooter will move eventually, and when they do, Foster will be ready.

* * *

Topher wiggles his phone out of his right cargo pocket and waits on Murray to pick up the call. When he does, Topher says, "This is a courtesy call. Your father's dead, you sick bastard." Then he hangs up and checks the scope. Nothing. They are all down.

Did he kill Anna? Or did he pull the shot in time?

He's lost in that thought, reaching for his Slurpee, when Foster's bullet pierces his hand and the Styrofoam. She puts another through his leg.

Topher can't run and he can't shoot. But he watches his daughter sit up and take a long, deep breath. Love is strange. Even when you don't want it, it finds you sometimes.

CHAPTER 74

WHILE THE BLOOD POOLS ON the airstrip, Waylon and Jack sit at Starr's kitchen table discussing a napkin and a text message.

Neither understands the meaning. Starr sleeps peacefully in her room and Anna is nowhere in sight. The truck is in the drive where Jack parked the night before. They determine she went for a walk to feed Molly.

The men are haggard, tired. They sip coffee and say little.

Their adrenaline isn't awake yet.

Foster called. Don't go to Bent Tree today. What does that mean? Why didn't Anna explain more? The Royale starts with the first official guest arrival and there is always someone at the main gate by 8:00 a.m. The sun slowly lights the world, pushing the kitchen spectrum from its golden lightbulb glow to daylight.

Both men seem agreeable to the idea of staying in Luxor for the day, although Jack is antsy.

✳   ✳   ✳

When the natural silence thickens and fills the room, Jack considers his middle-of-the-night theory. He takes the risk. "Who killed them, Waylon? The Choir Girls? Was it Gleb? Why were you there?"

Waylon yawns and stretches like he hasn't heard.

"Waylon, why were you there?"

Waylon is armed. Which makes Jack's straightforward tactic stupid, but sometimes the truth requires a brave question.

"Jack, you're a good kid and I like you, but I'm not answering that."

"Because you're involved?"

"No, because if that story finally comes out, you're not the one who should hear it first. Now, sit. I'll make breakfast while we wait."

Waylon pushes back from the table and heads to the fridge. Bacon in one hand, a carton of eggs in the other, he freezes. Jack follows Waylon's gaze to the entryway table. A huge Styrofoam cup from the gas station sits by the key bowl. Waylon whirls on Jack and points at the table. "Did you bring that with you?"

"Bring what?" he asks, unsure if they are staring at the same item.

"That cup from the gas station."

Jack shakes his head.

"Topher was here," Waylon says.

Waylon runs for Starr's bedroom. When he returns two minutes later, saying, "She's okay, but he was here," he pulls a handgun from an ankle holster and hands it to Jack. "I'm going. You stay here and keep them safe. I don't know what's going on, but if Topher was in this house, the shit's hitting the fan."

*   *   *

That is how Jack ends up with a gun.

Guns have a history of making men bolder than they should be.

CHAPTER 75

ALBERT TURRENT SITS ALONE. THE booth he occupies in the BeeGee is directly across from a table of men talking about the Royale. One man is counting Land Rovers that pass on Highway 60. Another counts Dodge Rams. They have a bet on the number of each vehicle. They are also discussing their wives and how they'd be made to attend the opening party at the Royale.

"I told her it was outside and she still wants to go," one man complains.

Another says, "Every year. We stand in thirty-degree weather and we don't even get to shoot something."

An elderly man among them snickers. "I mostly shoot blanks, but I know how to keep the ladies warm."

The other men cackle. Not a blushing cheek among them.

Albert doesn't like that type of humor. He doesn't like the way one of the men pats the lower back of the waitress when she delivers their refills. The woman says, "You're five inches away from a lawsuit, Bill," but he doesn't move his hand. He says, "Ah, shugga, you know you love me."

Albert is so engrossed that he doesn't register Leroy Elmes until the wiry undertaker drops into the opposite seat. The two met at the Royale years ago and bonded over a love of the Beatles. Leroy looks tired and punchy. His normally fluffy hair is oily and slicked against his head. "Go home," he says to Albert. "Auction's called off."

"How do you——?"

The undertaker interrupts, "Because I worked the body of Lavinia Collins last night. Feds called me in for a consultation when their regular guy wasn't available. Mark my words, there'll be a bust."

Albert doesn't know what to do first. Curse at the loss of the auction and the hundreds of miles he's driven or thank Leroy Elmes for saving his ass. "What a loss," he manages to say.

"I made some early trades. You interested?" Leroy asks.

"Always." It's nearly impossible for Albert to get automatic weapons in New Jersey. As a principal, he knows their danger and their value. But if someone comes for his school, they won't find a passive leader hiding under the desk in the front office. They'll find a war. "What are you selling?"

"An L85."

Albert whistles. British military assault rifles are impossible to purchase.

After they pay the check, the two men stroll to Leroy's car. No one notices the exchange of money or the movement of a gun case between their trunks.

They wouldn't have said anything if they had.

Five minutes later, Albert drives north. He's gotten more than he came for. He reaches for his phone and dials his wife. She will fight him for who gets to shoot it first. He can hear her now: "You wouldn't even know the auction existed if it weren't for me."

* * *

The men at the BeeGee stop counting Land Rovers and Dodge Rams that morning.

They count vehicles with sirens.

All of them headed toward the Lodges.

They will not have to take their wives anywhere that evening.

CHAPTER 76

WAYLON ARRIVES AT THE LODGES' gate and meets a blockade of
state police vehicles.

He doesn't dial anyone in his family to warn them. Instead, he
turns around and returns to the farm. He finds Jack in Starr's bedroom, guarding her with Waylon's gun. She hasn't even noticed.

Waylon takes her vitals and then scoops her into his arms. "Anna's
still not back?"

Jack shakes his head.

"We'll text her on the way to the hospital then."

CHAPTER 77

ALTHOUGH HER FORMER COLLEAGUE GETS the official credit, Foster Portage creates a legacy for herself that day.

The bust on the Royale auction is one of the most successful in ATF history. The weapons are accounted for. Years of purchasing documents are discovered in Molly's lean-to with hundreds of leads to track down. Waylon has evidence against his family. Every domino falls accordingly.

That is the story told by her agency.

Not the whole story.

Inside the former agent is a little girl.

That former agent wants fewer assault weapons in the wrong hands.

But the little girl wants justice for her mother.

She accomplishes one; the other is taken from her by Topher Collins.

None of the evidence they find ties Gleb Orlov to the Choir Girls.

✳ ✳ ✳

Directly after the shell ejects from her gun, Foster leaves Anna and runs directly to the location where Topher fell. The weapon needs to be cleared, the scene secured.

That part is easy.

Topher isn't trying to escape. He's crying over Lavinia's death.

✻ ✻ ✻

Topher finds out later he lost both of his parents on the same day.

He doesn't think it would have changed his choice had he known he was shooting his father. But he isn't certain. Love is sneaky in that way. It exists in advance of relationship. Like a mother growing a baby she has yet to meet. Like a child longing for a parent they've never had.

✻ ✻ ✻

The moment Foster disarms and restrains Topher, she lifts her phone and calls for help.

Across the field, Anna sits in the grass, her arms holding her knees. Blood makes a waterfall stain from her temple to her chin. She is white with shock. The top fold of her ear is missing. Foster wants to smack her for being so stupid. And hold on to her like a child.

She chooses the latter as soon as she confirms Gleb is dead. Topher's accuracy was clean and efficient. A kill shot to the head. There should have been one through Foster's too. "Thank you, God," she whispers and then goes to Anna.

Foster and Anna face each other and their foreheads touch. When

Anna shivers, Foster accepts a blanket from Renat. The old pilot goes and sits on the top step of the plane waiting to be interrogated. He is too old to run and too young to die.

"I told you not to come," Foster says with only the slightest chastisement in her tone. How could she add more? Anna is the reason she is alive. She acted faster than Foster, throwing them forward after the first shot.

Anna's breathing isn't normal. Her skin is colorless. Still, she asks, "Can you be at peace now that he's gone?"

"We'll see," Foster says. "Can you?"

"We'll see," Anna answers. "Is this over?"

"You're safe, but this won't be over for a very long time."

"You solved it," Anna tells her.

Did I? Foster thinks. At the time, there is no way to know if they'll find evidence linking Gleb Orlov to the Choir Girl murders. "I'm sorry," she says. "I know you need closure. If he was . . . your father."

"Starr can give me that, and I have a feeling she will now that he's dead," Anna answers. "I came here for you, not him. If you killed him, I'd lose us all over again. That's more of a loss than he could ever be. Even if he is my dad."

Foster squeezes Anna's hand and Anna squeezes back. Love is sneaky in this way too. It travels between two eyes meeting and the upturn of lips as they become tired smiles.

Had Anna's phone not buzzed with a text, Foster might have made a mistake that pushed Anna away. Because what she wants to do in that moment is take Anna's face in her hands and press a kiss against her lips. All her life she's been looking for Anna, thinking she'll find a sister of sorts.

But Anna is more. Much more.

Instead of a kiss, she examines Anna's crestfallen face and says, "What's wrong?"

"Waylon's taking Mom to the emergency room."

CHAPTER 78

MURRAY WATCHES GLEB DIE FROM his desktop computer. He feels nothing. Five security cameras cover the airstrip, and while there is no sound, there is a glorious show. Murray imagines turning the footage over to the police and a smile crosses his lips. Pippa wags her tail excitedly, feeling Murray's energy change.

Nothing ties Murray to the auction. Nothing ties him to the airfield.

He is innocent of this and has the evidence to prove it. Dozens of time-stamped cameras place him in this office, miles from the airfield. Murray puts his nose to Pippa's and her tongue curls up and licks his cheek. "For once," he tells the dog, "his dismissal helped us."

Murray will rebrand and rebuild. Stay on the right side of the law. Perhaps Jack will join him as a co-owner if he makes room for Anna to stay. He's harbored years of jealousy toward her. But he can put that away now. Gleb is dead.

That should make him sad, but it doesn't.

He opens a new window on the computer and logs into the Lodges' accounting software. He writes Anna Ryder a check for twenty-five thousand and transfers the money to her account. That will help them start over, clean and fresh.

Murray's most consuming thought as the agent knocks on his front door to inform him of Gleb's death: *Is it too soon to contact an interior designer for his office or should he wait until Monday?* He hates that dingy space with all its brown.

His next office will be yellow.

He has no idea Topher stored one box of missiles in his garage attic and that in three hours it will be found by a rookie agent.

CHAPTER 79

ANNA AND HER MOTHER OCCUPY two adjoining cubicles at Mercy Regional Emergency Room. The blue curtain dividers aren't drawn. Not even as the nurses come and go and hook Starr up to an IV and examine the damage done to Anna's ear.

Waylon and Jack stand next to their respective beds and oversee their care.

Anna breaks the news about Gleb's and Lavinia's deaths and Topher's arrest.

Waylon doesn't cry. He grips Starr's hand and says, "It's over. It's finally over."

Starr weeps.

* * *

Anna understands that she is about to hear her own story before her mother speaks.

Isn't it strange how you can be ready for the truth and not ready for the truth at the same time? That's life. We want what we can't handle because we also can't handle not knowing.

✳   ✳   ✳

The color in Starr's cheeks is brighter than it has been in days. The IV is working its magic. With energy comes the truth.

Starr begins, "I wanted to get out of Luxor. You know that. I met a group of women at the bar who had more money than I'd ever seen. When I asked what they did for a living, they introduced me to Noah Bright. 'There's an auction,' he said. And then he asked if I was a virgin and I lied and told him no. He said, 'That's too bad. You'd be worth more.' That was June. I met Gleb on the docks a few days later. We . . . well, we fell in love. By the time the Royale rolled around and it was time for the auction, I understood exactly who I'd fallen for. Another what my mother called a bad egg. But he'd already bought the *Juneau* for me and told me I belonged to him. I had no way out. I told Noah I would do the auction, hoping the money I made might be enough to get out of town. Gleb was so angry that I was up for bid, he let another man outbid him."

Waylon nods for her to continue. She puts her head under the thin white sheet and hides her face. Gently he tugs it down. "It's time, Starr."

"Topher," Starr says. "He's your father."

"And he knew about me?" Anna asks.

Waylon and Starr nod and Starr continues, "When Gleb found out I was pregnant, he told me if he ever saw me again, he'd kill me. And then Topher refused to help. He basically said the same thing. That if I told his parents he'd gotten a woman from Luxor pregnant, we'd be dead. I had nowhere to go but back across the river."

Waylon explains, "I didn't know about any of this until Topher got drunk one night and spilled his guts about the auction and Gleb and a woman from Luxor named Starr who claimed she had his kid. I had to try to make it right."

"You heard all this and went looking for Mom?" Anna says.

Waylon and Starr both nod and then Waylon whispers, "Best find of my life."

"So what happened with the *Juneau*?" Anna asks.

Starr says, "Initially I docked it. You were a baby. We barely had anything that Waylon didn't give us. I was working nights and exhausted. Then Waylon said Gleb wasn't around except during the Royale and the girls talked me into some Saturdays on the water. I'd either go out with them or rent it out for a little extra cash."

"The girls? You mean Jenni?"

"Yeah. She had a little girl. Eleanor. And was basically in the same situation as me."

"Foster."

Starr nods. "Jenni and I did everything together. With babies three months apart, we were each other's survival. You girls were inseparable from minute one. Jenni kept you both when I worked. I kept you both when she did. We even visited her parents in Texas once and you two cried because you had to sit in separate seats. You both loved the *Juneau*. The water."

"Mom, what happened on that boat? What happened to Foster and me?"

Starr starts to cry. "I don't know. I swear I don't. I was at work that night."

"That boat didn't hide itself in the barn."

Waylon speaks. "No, I did that. I wasn't supposed to, but I did. My mother called in the middle of the night and said she needed a big favor. I showed up and she handed me boat keys and said, 'Gleb

Orlov needs you to sink the boat docked at Warrior Landing.' I asked why. She told me to shut up and help my family. That Gleb Orlov would kill me, or all of us, if I didn't do exactly what he was asking. That was enough to send me to the dock. Mother didn't know that I knew who owned the *Juneau* or its owner's connection to our family. I didn't go down into the cabin at first. I drove out of the cove like an obedient son. But once I was in the open water, I killed the engine and went downstairs. There was blood everywhere. I've never been so scared in my life. I thought . . . I thought I'd lost you all. When I lifted that mattress and saw the two of you, I made a choice."

"You drove to our inlet and hid the boat," I conclude.

"Yeah. Your mother and I never agreed about this. About our silence. I thought it would keep you safe. She thought it kept you in danger."

"Is that why you broke up?" Anna asks.

"No," Starr and Waylon answer together. Eventually Anna will hear that story as well, and Starr will learn the truth and understand the love involved in Waylon's decision.

For now, Anna doesn't push them toward their story. She asks, "What about Foster? Why didn't you keep her here too?"

Starr fiddles with her IV, remembering. "We should have, but she was a firecracker, that kid. Whew! Talking about guns and blood and a little man who talked like . . ." She imitates Gleb's distinctive voice. "Eleanor remembered. There was no way we could keep her from spilling her guts."

"So." Waylon looks away from Anna before he speaks again. "I got in my truck and drove her to Alabama and left her on the steps of a church. I didn't know what else to do to keep everyone safe."

"And her father?" Anna asks.

Waylon and Starr look at each other with questions. Starr says, "Jenni never told me. I always assumed that meant it was Gleb. I think he raped her to punish me."

Anna is having an enormous moment. One she has waited her life to know. Instead of leaning in, she leans away from her mother and Waylon.

Guilt is a cockroach. The emotion crawls around and lives after atomic bombs go off. After the gunshots and survival. Guilt settles into Anna now, unwelcome and unwanted, but there all the same. She thinks about how much Foster wanted to have the truth told to her by someone who loves her. And how she has no parents left to give her that gift.

✻ ✻ ✻

Starr is wrong about Foster's father. Wrong about rape. Gleb did many disgusting, terrible things, but he never forced a woman to sleep with him. His pride would not allow it.

At that very moment, Foster's father is sitting in an Adirondack chair with a steaming mug of coffee, sharing a plate of croissants with his wife. Neither of them slept well the night before. And then the gunshots echoing across the fields woke them early. They are more anxious than they want to admit about Chester's decision to be a guide.

Lauris starts the conversation that will change their lives with a question she'd asked many times over their years together. "What else is bugging you, love?"

"I think, well, I think one of those girls who came over the other day might be my daughter."

Lauris folds her hand over Chester's forearm and relaxes. "Oh, I'm so glad you can see it too. The moment I saw her walk, I knew. The spitting image of you."

"Foster?" he asks.

"Foster," Lauris says with a triumphant nod.

A smile stretches Lauris's pretty lips into an arc that Chester can't resist kissing. "Jenni had a daughter." He tries out the words.

Lauris doesn't let the distance stand. "Jenni had a daughter with you, my love."

"What do I do?" he asked.

"First you prove she's yours, and then you prove you're hers."

"And how do I do that?"

Lauris knows this answer because her own father was literally her favorite person on earth. She says, "You love her more than anything else in the world." And because Lauris is a spectacular woman, who is delighted by the idea of a daughter who had not required the use of her uterus, she says, "Don't worry. I'll help."

CHAPTER 80

THE DOCTOR DISMISSES ANNA AFTER placing thirty-seven stitches in her ear. "You're going to have one hell of a headache," he says as he tears off a prescription for pain medicine.

Anna throws the script away and Jack shakes his head. "Do you always have to be such a hero?"

"I don't mess around with that shit," she says. "Too many people in Luxor are gone on that stuff."

"That's my girl," Starr says.

A different doctor gives orders for Starr to be monitored overnight. Her dehydration is severe enough that her kidneys need extra attention. Waylon agrees to stay and sends Anna and Jack home to rest. They are supposed to come back and relieve him at ten. He still hasn't spoken to his brother, and according to him, he doesn't plan to anytime soon.

In two years' time, Waylon will put away some of his anger and speak to Topher through the glass plate in prison. His consecutive terms are longer than his projected life expectancy. From behind that glass, Topher Collins tells Waylon where the body of the guide can be found.

He will never know that the gunshots that killed the guide were the same ones that spooked Molly and launched Noah Bright from his own deck with a powerful kick. Had the guide lived, perhaps the Royale would have gone on for another ten years.

Waylon will return to the prison many times in the course of their lives. The brothers will start over. Waylon will learn of Lavinia's many affairs with rich auction men and Topher's true paternity. Gleb. Which meant, on the day Anna lost the top part of her ear, she stood between her father and grandfather asking for answers that neither of them would give her.

Topher will spend most of the rest of his life wishing for his daughter.

* * *

The universe is getting ready to steal more than answers from Anna Ryder.

Jack drives Anna to the farm.

Neither is aware that this is the last time she'll lay across the bench of his truck with her head on his lap, him gently stroking her hair as they cross Luxor Bridge.

* * *

Most fights have several exit ramps. Jack misses the one that tells him this madness is over. Why? Probably because humans want tidy lives. Answers for everything. The satisfaction of complete understanding. Who can blame Jack for not being able to let go of his 3:00 a.m. questions? Or his need to walk through the boat one more time to see if he can find proof of Gleb's crimes for Anna and Foster? He wants that for Murray too.

Foster is at the house when they arrive, asleep on the deck lounger. First, Jack puts Anna in the shower and washes the blood off her body. Then while she dresses and crawls into bed, he wakes Foster and brings her to Anna. The two women tuck their bodies into semi-circles, with their backs touching, and sleep.

Jack goes to the barn.

CHAPTER 81

THIS TIME JACK TAKES LANTERNS and gloves. He opens the side door and lets the daylight fall on the hay, and then he goes to work. Throwing bales until he uncovers the cruiser's number and name along its fiberglass side. He stops, aware that if the boat isn't on a trailer, he might be making it unstable.

Coated in sweat and starting to itch, he lets himself rest on the stern, steeling himself to descend the steps.

Years before, in his twenties, Jack had a season of unwellness that led to self-administered B12 shots. He remembers the doctor explaining how to give a subcutaneous shot and how horrified he'd been. The needle was insignificant and yet, each time, before he plunged the needle through his own skin, he felt faint. But he'd learned to do something against his own instinct and he calls on that skill.

"You've already been in there," Jack tells himself. "You can do this."

The first step down is like the plunge of the needle. The courage is harder than the sting. His feet carry him into the belly of the boat.

The presence of lamps magnifies the horror. Dark splotches cover the white leather and surfaces. Then the thick, smeared trail through the middle of the floor and up the steps, where someone dragged the bodies.

Blood pools age. They transform, moving from red to black, from coagulation to a cracked black film. Had they been fresh, bright red, so obviously blood, Jack wouldn't have been able to stand there as long as he did.

He lets himself picture the room full. Three women at the bar. Four on the built-in couches. Two on the bed, drinks in their hands.

He pictures the galley door opening and someone descending. If they shot without coming fully inside, there would be bullet holes on the floor. These strays are on the walls. Whoever shot unloaded fast and likely from the place at the bottom of the steps.

According to the police report, the weapon used was a 9mm. Jack's grandfather taught him to target shoot on a Glock 17 and he guessed, based on the number of stray rounds, the killer used a similar weapon. In a frenzy like this, there wouldn't have been time to trade magazines.

Gleb must have left some evidence. Something other than bullet holes that said he was here.

Jack is scanning the kitchen when he sees it.

A tennis ball resting atop a drinking glass full of wine. Dark fingerprint smudges are left in its fuzz.

* * *

Jack dials. Not 911. He doesn't take the exit ramp. He steps into the fight.

"Hey," Murray says, too cheerfully. "I'm glad you called. There's something I want to run by you after things settle down around here."

"There's something I want to run by you too," Jack says, willing his voice not to shake.

And then Jack tells him he found the *Juneau* in Starr's barn.

Murray responds, his voice airy and in an upper register. "You're saying you see the *Juneau*? Are you sure?"

"I'm saying I'm on the *Juneau*. And, Murray, you left your tennis ball behind."

Game. Set. Match.

CHAPTER 82

MURRAY ORLOV STANDS IN HIS bathroom with the medicine cabinet open. There are enough pills if he wants to give up.

He's given up once before.

That night he had pills in one hand and his phone in the other.

He had wanted to call Jack and tell him what he'd done. More so, why he'd done it.

Jack was a boy with a chipped tooth and a stuffed elephant named Bear when they met. He was the first person to tell Murray he loved him, the first person to hold Murray's hand, the first person to make Murray feel worthy of being alive. The first person to spit swear they would always have each other. "No matter what."

Murray's thankfulness became something closer to love as they aged. When Jack was eighteen, nineteen, twenty, Murray hadn't been able to look at him without staring. He didn't know he was in love. He just knew Jack was the one person he couldn't lose.

Theresa's pregnancy threatened to take Jack away. So he removed Theresa instead.

And then there was Anna.

The madness he'd shoved down at fifteen—when he discovered his father wasn't coming to the Royale for him but for his sluts— returned. He got rid of them both and waited for Jack to return like a yo-yo. Easy-peasy. Murray scored five more years with Jack.

Jack would not come back from this.

* * *

Murray has one shot to keep his life.

He closes the medicine cabinet and speaks kindly to the police officers searching his property. "I'm going to get out of your way," he says.

"Don't go far," they say.

He won't. Just across the bridge and back.

There is a gun and a torch in his truck.

The time has come to burn the past to the ground. And Jack and Anna with it.

CHAPTER 83

BANG.

Anna rockets upright, her pulse instantly hitting a hundred before her eyes open.

Bang.

Cortisol and adrenaline kick her in the face. Blinking, she scans for the cause. Her bedroom solidifies as her brain wakes up. "What?" she says as she registers the extra person in the room and Foster's eyes widen with horror.

Murray Orlov has a gun to Foster's head.

"Up," he commands.

Foster gives her the slightest shake. *Don't do it*, she seems to be saying.

Murray fires the gun through the window.

Anna places her feet on the floor. "Where to?" she asks, even though she already knows.

CHAPTER 84

JACK DOESN'T HEAR THE GUNSHOTS. Or if he does, they fade into the background. They are crickets or bullfrogs or water bubbling over rocks. You don't hear them when they are always there.

He is on the boat, holding a tennis ball.

Should he have seen Murray's darkness? No, that isn't the question. He'd seen the darkness; he simply overestimated the power of his own light.

CHAPTER 85

FOSTER UNDERSTOOD DANGER LONG BEFORE she was deployed to the Middle East. But on those deployments, she came to understand the difference between violence and desperation.

Murray will kill her and Anna if they run.

What she doesn't know is why. Does he know she was at the airstrip? Does he suspect that she wanted Gleb to die?

Patience is her only weapon. She needs to move Murray from desperation back to violence. Let him believe there is still a way out of this.

Murray frog-marches them through the corn.

"Murray, you're smarter than this," Foster says as she reaches for Anna's hand. Squeezing her palm, Foster tries to telegraph her thoughts: *No sudden moves; bide our time. See what his plan is once we stop moving.* That gives them the best chance of escaping alive. She doesn't know where he is taking them. To the water? A boat? The barn? "You don't want to kill us. Your father was a criminal. He was going to die one way or another. But you don't have to."

"Oh, Mrs. Portage," he says cruelly. "I'm not going to kill you. The three of you are about to be in a tragic accident in an old barn." He taps his backpack triumphantly.

Foster hears the swish of liquid slapping the side of plastic. What does he have? Lamp oil? Kerosene?

"I mean, this county doesn't even have a volunteer fire department. Accidents like this happen in Luxor."

Foster can't see the way out yet.

At the barn door, Murray calls ahead, "Jack, Anna's here." The barrel of the pistol presses to her head. "Inside," he tells them.

Jack is nowhere to be seen.

"What's the point of this?" Foster says. "You have your father's entire business now. Why screw it up with a risk like this?"

"Ask Jack," Murray says. "Now go."

The gun pushes her toward a room at the front of the barn.

Molly brays from somewhere nearby.

Foster hears the donkey snorting but can't see her. Murray seems to take Molly's presence as a sign, urging the women toward the tack room where Molly stands in her bright pink coat. Molly's big nostrils huff as Murray appraises the small space. "Inside." He shoves the women against the animal and slams the door behind them.

"I do think the smoke will kill you before the flames," he says.

The heavy wooden crossbar lands in its cradle with a thud.

CHAPTER 86

THE OLD TACK ROOM IS no more than five by five. Other than Molly's overwhelming presence and a few scattered boards, the stall is empty. Its hickory walls are thick. Dirt dauber nests and cobwebs coat the boards that stretch all the way to the loft ceiling. They are sealed in a box with a donkey.

Anna and Foster examine every inch, top to bottom, searching for damaged wood. Nothing. Their prison is in pristine condition. Foster even climbs up the exposed crossbeams of the stud wall and says, "There's not even an inch of space where the walls meet the ceiling."

Anna guides her to the floor and they make a run at the door together. Their bodies bounce. Molly brays as the women land at her hooves. They try again. And again. Their shoulders bruise. Their mouths grow dry from screaming. They beat the wood with their fists.

The door doesn't rattle one bit.

*   *   *

On the other side of the wall, Murray scatters the fuel and lights the hay. The flames shoot up and begin to crawl and consume.

Jack lands on Murray's back, jumping from the top of the *Juneau*. They hit the ground with an *oof* and roll away from each other. They don't waste time circling; they charge. The flames rise, eating everything in their path.

You have seen two grown men fight on television, which means you can imagine the way they come at each other. How their muscles tense and the blood pours from their lips and noses. The sweat that coats their bodies and slings off their skin as they move.

Animalistic. No longer men.

You can hear the coughing.

Their lungs are already full of smoke.

Perhaps these men mean to say cruel things or argue the whys and hows. Their growls speak instead.

Flames catch on their clothes and then are extinguished as they slam each other into the ground, the *Juneau*'s hull, the walls of the barn. They will bring the place down on each other, one way or another.

* * *

Anna will not give up. She wills Jack to be strong. To come for her. To win.

He cannot come.

These women do not need a man. They need to think.

* * *

A whiff.

Then a gray cloud.

"Smoke," Anna says. It's rising around the door crack.

Outside the tack room, the hay crackles. A sweet, charred smell fills the air. Molly blows out a breath.

"This thing will go fast," Foster says. "All that hay."

They spin in circles, searching for any vulnerability they can exploit. There is nothing. They are two women and a donkey in an empty room. Anna leans her face into the grayish-brown hair at Molly's neck and breathes. Without realizing it, she starts apologizing to the animal. "I'm sorry, baby. I'm so sorry."

The tears come in a rush.

Foster's screams grow feral. She throws herself against the door, each time bouncing off into Molly. Molly's panic starts with a huff. Then a snort. She stomps her front foot and Anna tries to calm her. "Easy, girl. Easy."

And then Anna realizes she is saying the wrong thing.

"Foster, hand me that two-by-four by your foot."

The woman can't hear over her own screams.

"Foster, stop." Anna has to physically stop her. They are both coughing now. "Climb," she tells Foster and points at the framing boards Foster scrambled up earlier. Near the corner of the stall, they hoist themselves up and balance their toes on the crossbeams of the adjacent walls. Their knuckles whiten as they clutch the ceiling beam and widen their stances to a more stable position. They are roughly six feet off the stall floor and out of Molly's striking distance. When Anna thinks she is stable, she tests her footing. Not bad. But not great either. She needs to be stable enough to pound the piece of wood against the wall.

Foster reads her mind. "I'll counterbalance you," she says. "I'll face out, you face in, and I'll hold you so you can swing the board hard enough."

While Anna shifts out of the way, Foster puts her back against the corner and wedges her feet along the framework until she is fully tucked, braced, and balanced. "Okay, come on," she says and holds her hand out to Anna.

Anna works her way in front of Foster, placing her feet slightly wider. Foster slides her arms around Anna's lower waist and says, "Is that enough room?"

"We'll see," Anna says and rocks away from Foster and slams the two-by-four against the wall.

It sounds like a gunshot.

Molly's ears shoot up. She huffs.

Anna slams the board again. And again.

The frenzy hits Molly fast. Agitation raises her hackles. The fear makes her stomp both her front feet and then her back. Another slam of the wood and the beast leans forward and kicks her feet at the door.

"Again," Foster says.

Wood meets wood and the donkey bucks. Her hooves connect at the center of the door.

Something splinters.

Anna doesn't have to make the next strike. A gunshot fills the barn and that is all Molly needs to lose her mind. The door flies open.

✳   ✳   ✳

How do you win a fight?

That all depends on what counts as a win.

✳ ✳ ✳

The hickory burns and the roof trembles. The flames eat so much of the hay that the *Juneau* rocks until it lands on hay not yet aflame.

Jack can barely see through the smoke.

He can't catch his breath.

After dodging a jab from Murray, he stumbles away. That gives Murray time to reclaim the gun from where it had fallen.

"We're done," Murray says and lifts the gun.

"No!" Jack yells as Murray fires.

The shot hits Jack in the shoulder. He howls at the impact.

The door to the tack room bursts open. Molly charges out first. The distraction makes Murray turn his gun to the door. Toward Foster and Anna.

The world slows down for Jack.

Frame by frame, he watches Murray raise his arm to fire. He sees the *Juneau* swaying as the hay burns. He spots the narrow tower of hay that keeps it from keeling. Thinking only of Anna, Jack throws his body at the hay and brings the *Juneau* down.

CHAPTER 87

WHEN THE *JUNEAU* HITS, IT bounces and then settles. The hull is already aflame.

Thousands of pounds of wood and fiberglass land on Murray's legs.

Everyone screams.

Anna with fear. Foster with reaction. Jack with adrenaline.

But Murray screams for Jack.

And the boy made of light hears only his childhood friend.

Jack sprints to Murray's side and shoves at the cruiser with all his might. "I'm sorry. I'm sorry," he repeats, pressing his back against the plexiglass hull that ripples with heat. "Help me!" he screams to Anna and Foster.

Murray whimpers in pain. Tears are in his eyes as he looks at Jack and says, "You gotta go."

"No," Jack argues. "I'm not leaving you."

Is it fair that a terrible man hears the sweetest, truest words of his life right before he dies? That he is loved so purely by a man he only just tried to kill? No. Of course not. It's also not fair that a man lived forty years before being loved unconditionally by his family.

I told you at the start, Murray Orlov is a man to love and a man to hate. So hate him fully and then hear his final words. He looks past Jack to Anna and says, "New Jersey. She's in New Jersey."

And then the ceiling comes down.

* * *

The Catholic Church requires two miracles for sainthood. But what about one really good miracle? That should count for something, right? I can't tell you what happened in heaven when Jack Higgins sacrificed his life to hold the hand of Murray Orlov, but I think his hero, Saint Augustine, stood to his feet and clapped and said something profound.

Or maybe he quoted one of Jack's audio files and said, "Forgiveness doesn't need to make sense to everyone."

* * *

Anna and Foster are thrown to the ground.

Anna screams. Not the way she screamed for her own life. This scream comes from a different part of her soul. She knows Jack is gone. Knows that running toward the heap of wood and flames will yield nothing. But she does it anyway.

Had Foster not been there to carry Anna out of the barn, her story would have ended there.

CHAPTER 88

TWENTY MINUTES LATER, THE FIRE trucks from Bent Tree, from all of Rolland County and Western Kentucky and Southern Illinois, arrive on the Ryder farm. They scream to a stop right at the edge of the corn and find one woman screaming louder than every truck they brought. Another woman holds her so tightly she cracks a rib.

While the firemen work to extinguish the barn, an EMS worker named Emma Kate demands Foster and Anna be checked out at the hospital. Smoke inhalation. Open stitches. Shock. Broken hearts.

This is a pivotal moment for Emma Kate. She chose her profession because she grew up next door to the EMS building. Now, as she asks, "What's your name?" to the woman trying to catch her breath, she thinks, *I want to know where this ends, not where it starts.* When she clocks out that evening, she signs up for her first psychology class at the local college.

Her coworkers put out the fire.

There is hardly anything left except ash and water.

CHAPTER 89

THE NIGHT MURRAY KILLED JENNI Lockwood and the other eight women, he went directly to Gleb and confessed. "Your sluts are dead. They're all dead." He was just a boy who wanted to see the man in pain and instead ended up telling the story through choking sobs. Gleb was emotionless.

He quickly dismissed Murray. "I'll take care of this. Come on, Noah."

They fixed it, all right. They mimicked a crime committed in Texas and managed to leverage the violence as a power move against the Collins family. Lavinia had been restless, and there was nothing like slaughtering women for no reason to bring a partner in line. She never suspected Murray was the real villain, but Topher did.

On the night of the murders, Murray had gone back to the kennels, defeated.

Literally nothing he did mattered to his father.

But he still wasn't done trying.

CHAPTER 90

WHAT DOES IT MEAN TO survive your past?

That all depends on who loved you, who loves you, and who you let love you moving forward.

CHAPTER 91

LUCKILY FOR ANNA, HER WORLD is full of love. She is taken to a hospital, where her mother and Waylon are, and where she will hear the longer story of Foster spending a lifetime finding her.

Grief is giving yourself permission to be every irrational emotion at once until you can tell each one apart. Initially, they sit on top of you, but as you hold them, value them, they give you back your space.

And with those wonderful humans, Anna is allowed to cry. Allowed to curse. Allowed to rage.

Every tear she sheds is honored and understood.

No one asks her to get over Jack. Which is good, because she never will. No one placates her with anecdotes or pat phrases. No one fills up her silence with their own problems. No one questions when she laughs either. They let her be both sad and happy. Which is where many people fail.

They even let her fully feel her guilt.

Because of course she is cloaked in it.

And when the doctor asks, "Is there any chance you might be pregnant?" they silently hope she is. Because they momentarily think a baby will change the sadness.

She isn't. Not then. That comes three and a half years later, in a world she never imagined possible.

✻　✻　✻

A man and a woman stand in the hospital gift shop arguing over a tiger or a lion. The tiger is green with pink stripes. The lion is, well, lion colored. Both are equally soft.

"She's a tiger," Chester says. He knows this because he has listened to every episode of her podcast at least ten times and he can still picture the fiery way she'd laid those snapshots on his kitchen table and asked if he murdered Jenni.

"I'm not sure she'll love the pink," his wife says thoughtfully. "She's . . . a badass."

"We're getting both," Chester says.

Because what do you do when your only daughter is in the hospital?

You show up with gifts in your hands and words in your heart. Chester gives both freely. Even before the paternity test comes back, confirming he was right. Foster takes the news in a very un-Foster way. She takes a sledgehammer to the walls around her heart. She's always wanted a father.

And later, when Foster marries in his backyard, a minister will look directly at Chester and ask, "Who gives this woman in marriage?" and Chester will say the best five words of his life, "Her stepmother and I do."

CHAPTER 92

EVERY YEAR AFTER, THE NEW owners of the Lodges throw a party for the people of Bent Tree and Luxor at their home on Marsh Lake. There are no auctions. No guns. No under-the-table deals.

People cross the river and the creeks to attend. The men from the BeeGee sit at tables near the barkeeps from Luxor. The river workers from either side share plates and stories. The kids run up and down the banks fishing for crawdads. They have no idea their parents didn't always get along, because on that night, everyone does.

The food is excellent, the bourbon superb. Chester even pays for a massive fireworks show to capstone the event. For one night the sky stays bright and his hometown is known for more than limited bank accounts and murder documentaries.

Everyone loves this party except Molly the donkey and Gary the raccoon, who have become bosom friends. Obviously. Neither makes an appearance until daybreak on the morning after, when they arrive on the back deck for their daily supply of apples.

Sometimes Chester and Lauris's girls come home for the party. They all sit together in Adirondack chairs. Chester. Lauris. Waylon. Starr. Foster and Anna. Eventually, Foster and Anna's son, Higgins, has his own little chair, which he is never allowed to sit in because his grand-parents pass him around until he either throws up or falls asleep.

The girls don't go the first year. The one right after Jack died. They aren't together then. That took far more time, but in the end, it is Anna who asks Foster. Anna who makes the first brave move. Anna who proposes. But back when they were broken, grieving women, Chester sent them to art museums around the world. "Art will heal you," he said. He meant seeing it, and he was right, but Anna starts making art too. When she is on planes or sitting with her mother for treatment or next to Foster on the couch or watching the river from Chester's back porch, she draws. Turns out, she is better at art than at hosting detention at Luxor High School.

Her Etsy shop leads to a show; her show leads to a following; her following leads to worldwide recognition. Somehow a kid from Luxor, Illinois, one of the poorest cities on the US map, has pencil drawings in nearly every modern art museum in the world.

Including a temporary display at the Guggenheim.

The same fall of Anna's show, Corey William Turrent visits the Guggenheim on a senior field trip. Elementary school had been awful. Middle school far less violent but somehow worse. Corey is surviving high school but only with his head down and his life buried in video games. He hates his father and pushes his mother away. Mostly he thinks about death.

He stands in front of Anna Ryder's portrait and stares. The man depicted might have been his twin. Corey doesn't have the words to describe how the art affects him, only that it does. The man's kind eyes make him feel seen for the first time in his life. The museum attendant for the room remarks, "They say everyone has a doppel-gänger. I believe you've found yours."

Corey buys a postcard, which he tapes to the side of his home computer. When his mother sees it a week later, she breaks down and says, "I need to tell you something."

What follows is a confession.

"Albert's not your father. Your father was a man named Jack Higgins," she says. "And Jack Higgins is that man." She points to the postcard.

The relief Corey experiences is enormous. He doesn't like Albert. Never has. "Was?" Corey asks, the anger already rising. His real father is dead. He probably didn't love him either. And that's why Corey is stuck here.

Theresa's red hair falls around her face, the shame building, like it has so many times over the years. This time she doesn't shove it down. She says, "He made something for you. That artist, the famous one who drew that, brought it after Jack died. I kept it because I didn't know how to give it to you. But I think it's time."

Last Audio File

On the cloud is the final audio file Jack made for Beck. He made it sitting inside the *Juneau* waiting for Murray to come. It is the first one Corey hears.

Hey, Beck,

I've talked to you a lot about falling in love, but very little about friendship. Other than my family, my first friend was a man named Murray Orlov. We met when I was five and he was fourteen because we loved dogs. We were in the same space loving the same animals, and eventually we loved each other, because that's what happens when you realize someone around you is lonely.

You start to think, *He needs a friend. I can be that for him.*

And then you get to know him a little better and think, *He needs a father. I am not that, but I can figure out how to make sure that gap doesn't hurt as badly as it does right now.*

And then more time passes and you see his brokenness and you think, *There's nothing love can't fix.*

The truth is, I still believe love can fix anything.

But now I'm sure that it doesn't have to be *my* love that fixes everything and everyone.

I should have walked away from Murray Orlov. I should have seen his darkness. I hope when you see darkness you don't ask too much of yourself. I hope when you see darkness you trim your wick and know those who love the light will see you.

Today I entered a cabin cruiser called the *Juneau* looking for evidence that Murray's father killed the Choir Girls. What I found instead was a tennis ball covered in blood. Not evidence his father killed the women; evidence Murray killed them.

I just called him. He'll come.

I don't know what I hope. That he'll turn himself in? That he'll confess to the murder? Or that he'll tell me he's sorry? If he's sorry, I think I'll know that me loving him all this time meant something. All I've ever wanted is for my love to mean something.

Okay, my boy, I'll go for now.

I love you. Always. Always. Always. I love you.

CHAPTER 93

THERE IS ANGER IN COREY'S heart and guns available in his home.

But the children of Roseville Elementary will grow up to have their own stories because once upon a time, a man named Jack loved a boy he never met and took the time to tell him so.

*　*　*

We don't live to see all the ripples we make, but we must make them all the same.

Acknowledgments

MY DAD DIED IN JUNE 2023 and, to be honest, I feared that I didn't know how to write a book without his support and prayers. He was one of my favorite people on the planet and probably my biggest fan. So it is with such a grateful heart that I write this acknowledgment to and for all the people who kept my creative fire stoked and reduced my fears to bite-size chunks. God first and then all my family, friends, and industry champions.

Becky Monds, I can't do this without you. You give me courage and wisdom, and when I am slow . . . you calm me down and give me time. This book cost us all some bravery, and I want to thank you for always fighting for me. Amanda Bostic, you're right there with her. Hugging me. Hearing me. Loving me. Thank you.

To the entire Muse Team . . . WOW. What a creation process we have done together. We've reimagined my career, brainstormed this story, thought wisely through marketing, and collaborated at every step to bring my confidence and this narrative to a better place. Julie Breihan, Caitlin Halstead, Margaret Kercher, Colleen Lacey, Nekasha Pratt, Taylor Ward, everyone working behind the scenes, I can't thank you enough. KP, you're such a cool, wonderful voice in my life. I'm incredibly grateful for your sisterhood and for all the queso we've consumed.

Ruta Sepetys, David Arnold, and Jess Folk: you not only make my words better, you make me a better human. Thank you for being on this journey with me. I love you all and can't imagine writing books without you.

Greg Joles, you are one heck of a tour guide. I promise I didn't make you a murderer (even though you requested it). I am also happy to promise everyone in BC that *Tell Me Something Good* is a complete work of fiction. Nothing this devastating happened at your lodges, but I have a feeling the hunting is even better than I worded it.

Mom, Matt, and Julie, thank you for keeping the home fire always lit for me. I am always safe when I'm with you and I'm certainly well-fed. I'm raising a glass of bourbon to you all. Love you so much. We're figuring out how to do this without Dad, and I think he'd be proud (hahaha) of our attempts.

Ms. Ann, your table is where I find the best version of myself. Thank you for mentoring me. I love you so much. Louis T., you are the man with the best picnic on the planet, and I know you prayed and prayed over me as I created this. I love you to pieces. LB and Emily, the care and wisdom you show me creates space in my life to follow all my passions. Let's go to the office. Always. I love you. CC, you make me feel less lonely in the world. You're bedrock and very spiffy. I promise to shop more at J.Crew.

Carla, Christa, Leah, Katie, Matt, Laura and Jeremy (my gnomies), I would go crazy without you. The fact that we get to do life together is never lost on me. What a privilege. What a joy. I pray I am the friend to you that you always are to me. Go Fever! G'nome what I'm saying?

There are three other critical groups in my life: Broadway UMC, my Goonies, and the managers and staff of Warren County Public Library. Without your love and support, I couldn't do one job, much less two. I wish I could name each and every one of you here. Since I can't, please know I'm naming you in my heart.

Ginger, EK, and Christopher Willow, I like you, I love you, and I need you. I hope you see my love for you echoed in everything I attempt. You are the family I choose. Everyday. Forever and always.

Finally, to my readers, you will always be my better half.

Discussion Questions

1.   When Starr receives a cancer diagnosis, Anna rearranges her life to be a caregiver and breadwinner. Can you relate to Anna or Starr?

2.   Sometimes we cut people out of our lives. For good, bad, and unknown reasons. Have you ever needed a clean break from someone? If time has passed since the break, would you make the same choice again?

3.   Bent Tree is a rural town with so much natural beauty. Talk about a favorite place that makes you want to be outside more.

4.   Early childhood memories can sometimes get tucked into a hidden corner of the brain. Various people and places can bring those to the forefront. What is a healthy way to respond when an old memory interrupts your life?

5.   What compassions might you share with someone experiencing painful memories?

6. Jack Higgins makes audio recordings for his son whom he has never met. Share a special gift you received from a parent, caregiver, or mentor.

7. Gun violence is a hot topic around the world. What are some ways we can talk about this issue (or other hot topics) without creating division?

8. When you disagree with someone on a topic that deeply affects your life, how do you tend to respond? Do you agree or disagree with your own response? What do you wish you could change?

9. Is there anyone in your life you should give up on but can't? If so, why do you think this is true?

10. Have you ever been surprised by love?

11. Childhood friendships sometimes continue through adulthood. If someone knows your history, do they know you better than people you meet later in life? Why or why not?

12. All families keep things from each other, but Starr Ryder's keeping more than her share. Has a family secret ever impacted your life?

From the Publisher

GREAT BOOKS

ARE EVEN BETTER WHEN THEY'RE SHARED!

Help other readers find this one:

- Post a review at your favorite online bookseller

- Post a picture on a social media account and share why you enjoyed it

- Send a note to a friend who would also love it—or better yet, give them a copy

Thanks for reading!

LOOKING FOR MORE GREAT READS? LOOK NO FURTHER!

HARPER MUSE

*Illuminating minds
and captivating hearts
through story.*

Visit us online to learn more:
harpermuse.com

Or scan the below code and sign up to receive
email updates on new releases, giveaways,
book deals, and more:

@harpermusebooks

About the Author

Photo by Carla Lafontaine

COURT STEVENS grew up among rivers, cornfields, churches, and gossip in the small-town South. She is a former adjunct professor, youth minister, and Olympic torchbearer. These days she writes coming-of-truth fiction and is the director of Warren County Public Library in Kentucky. She has a pet whale named Herman, a band saw named Rex, and several novels with her name on the spine: *Faking Normal, The Lies About Truth*, the e-novella *The Blue-Haired Boy, Dress Codes for Small Towns, Four Three Two One, The June Boys, We Were Kings,* and *Last Girl Breathing.*

✳ ✳ ✳

courtstevens.com
Instagram: @quartland
Facebook: @CourtneyCStevens
Twitter: @quartland